CANCELLED

SONG FOR ATHENA

Recent Titles by Linda Sole from Severn House

THE TIES THAT BIND
THE BONDS THAT BREAK
THE HEARTS THAT HOLD

BRIDGET
FLAME CHILD

THE ROSE ARCH
A CORNISH ROSE
A ROSE IN WINTER

SONG FOR ATHENA

Linda Sole

This first world edition published in Great Britain 2003 by
SEVERN HOUSE PUBLISHERS LTD of
9–15 High Street, Sutton, Surrey SM1 1DF.
This first world edition published in the USA 2003 by
SEVERN HOUSE PUBLISHERS INC of
595 Madison Avenue, New York, N.Y. 10022.

British Library Cataloguing in Publication Data

Sole, Linda
    Song for Athena
    1.   Sisters - Fiction
    2.   Extortion - Fiction
    I.   Title
    823.9'14 [F]

    ISBN 0-7278-5654-5

Typeset by Palimpsest Book Production Ltd.,
Polmont, Stirlingshire, Scotland.
Printed and bound in Great Britain by
MPG Books Ltd., Bodmin, Cornwall.

Prologue

Is the reflection I see in the mirror really me – that woman with the white face and scared eyes? Or is all this a nightmare from which I shall soon wake?

How I wish it were! If only I could turn back the clock, return to that moment in time when all this started. Be safe again! Safe in my dull little world of boredom and routine.

What was that sound? It was like breaking glass. A cat knocking over a milk bottle . . . but no one has them anymore, they all use cartons from the supermarket. Besides, here in this cottage, I am too far away from my nearest neighbour, too isolated, to hear if the noise was coming from somewhere else. No, it has to be here!

I had thought no one knew about my little hideaway, but someone is trying to break in. Who knows I am here? No one except Sandy, and she wouldn't break in. Someone has followed me here . . . and the only person who would want to do that is the murderer.

My heart jerks with fear, and a crawling sensation begins at the nape of my neck. I am icy cold now. I can hear someone moving around downstairs, and I am afraid. Someone wants to kill me, and it is my own fault. I was warned not to get involved, to let sleeping dogs lie.

The past is the past, let it go.

Someone said that to me recently. I ignored it then, because I was so sure – so sure I had the upper hand. I knew that somewhere out there lurked the murderer I had been determined to find and punish, but now I was afraid he had come to find me . . .

1

One

I'm not sure why I picked him out of the crowd in St. James's Park that afternoon. It was warm, sultry, without a breath of air. Finally, after nearly three weeks of rain, summer had come to Britain and in London the temperature was soaring. I suppose it was the kind of day that makes the lonely feel even more isolated.

I had decided to eat sandwiches in the park, because I've always been a bit of a nature freak and I enjoy feeding the ducks and squirrels. That day, I needed to feel contact with something warm and living, and animals are so uncomplicated. They want food. I give it. No arguments, no excuses.

Human relationships are not that easy for me. Not since I threw Ben out – Ben of the blue eyes and golden torso, who taught me karate and made love to me when he had the time to spare, which hadn't been that often over the previous six months or so – due perhaps to the fact that his wife was five months pregnant. A wife I hadn't known existed until she turned up at my door one day and demanded the return of her husband.

After two months, I was missing Ben more than I'd expected. Maybe he wasn't worth crying over, but without his infrequent visits to anticipate, my life was fairly empty. Perhaps that was why the sight of lovers sitting on the grass in the sun, kissing, holding hands, or simply gazing longingly into each other's eyes, was so depressing. Even the antics of tiny brown teal diving for food failed to lift my spirits. I was restless, bored with my life as a secretary to the managing director of an import/export firm, and wishing something exciting would happen.

I was actually waiting for it, my senses heightened, as if somehow I knew life was about to change for me.

Then I saw him, standing a few feet away, just staring at me. He had that dangerous look about him, the look I'd learned to be wary of. A lean, powerful body strained beneath a well-cut business suit, his dark hair just brushing the collar, his eyes grey, the kind that seem to strip a woman naked in less than two seconds – eyes that continued to watch me intently as I gave the remainder of my lunch to the greedy ducks at the water's edge.

I was conscious of him watching me . . . his eyes on my legs. I've been told that I have sexy legs. That's not the reason I wear extremely short skirts: it's because I'm a fashion designer – at least I plan to be one day – and because I'm making a statement. As a woman I have every right to dress as I please and if men want to see that as being provocative that's their business. To go around covered from neck to ankle simply to avoid arousing the baser instincts of the opposite sex, would be giving in: admitting to a vulnerability that I refuse to accept.

At art school I joined a left-wing debating society with some friends because it was the thing to do, not out of any great desire to further the cause of women's lib or to burn mountains of bras – I seldom wear one, except when running – but inevitably some of the rhetoric rubbed off. Besides, I've reason enough to be careful around men of a certain kind. Ben wasn't my only bad experience.

Unfortunately, it's the dangerous kind I find attractive. If I can walk right over a man that's probably what I'll do – and keep on walking. So it's my own fault if I've been burned. I'm not arguing. One day I'll probably marry a good man and make his life hell – but not just yet.

I was walking now, following the path round the park, whiling away the time until I had to return to my stuffy office and the routine I had begun to find so tiresome. My thoughts were troubling me. Somewhere deep inside me, I knew it was time to make a change, but what kind of a change? Where did I go from here?

For some reason I glanced over my shoulder. He was still

staring; the man with the blowtorch eyes! Good heavens! Was he following me? A thrill of something like fear ran down my spine. Or was it excitement? If I was going to be stalked, I would certainly rather it was by someone who looked like him.

I noticed a group of policemen standing together in the park. They were in their shirtsleeves and had guns in holsters on their hips. Not something you often saw in an English park. I wondered what was going on – an alert of some kind perhaps? A down-and-out had wandered up to them and was offering to shake hands in a servile manner that made me think he must be drunk or on drugs; the police all reluctantly shook hands, for the sake of public relations.

I paused on the bridge to gaze at what I'd always thought of as the ice-cream palace of Whitehall, perhaps because I'd been licking a huge vanilla cone the first time Athena had brought me here. I'd been fourteen then, my beautiful sister nearly eight years older and on one of her rare visits to this country.

I don't know why she was in my mind that afternoon, but for some reason I kept thinking about her, wondering if she was all right – if she was happy with the changes she had recently made in her life.

Athena had been a successful model in America and spent most of her time there until about three months ago, when she'd suddenly given up her work and retired to a villa in Spain. I wondered if she was enjoying herself, or whether she found it strange after the exciting, fast-paced life she must have had in New York.

The man had walked past. He hadn't been following me after all! I laughed at myself and started walking again. What an imagination! It was probably because I was too introverted these days, spending too much time alone. I wasn't sure whether I was relieved or sorry . . . Then I saw him again.

He had taken off his jacket, holding it with one hand over his shoulder and watching the pelicans playing on their rock in the middle of the lake – the best place for them! They could be a nuisance and I'd once seen one of them attacking a woman's umbrella, which she had wielded in an effort to fend them off while eating her lunch.

The man turned from his contemplation of the birds as I approached, a slow smile spreading from his lips to his eyes. It was a rather nice smile and I found myself responding.

'They are amusing, aren't they?' he asked, his voice deep and sure, confident. 'Do you often spend your lunch hour here?'

'When it's warm,' I said, lingering despite all the screaming nerve ends that warned me to walk on by with my nose in the air. Every woman of sense knows that you don't pick up strangers in the park! Even if they are exceptionally attractive. 'It's good to get out of the office for a break for a while.'

'My exact sentiments,' he agreed. 'Look, I know how pushy this sounds – but do you have time for a drink? We could walk down to the river?'

'Do you often pick up strange women in the park?'

'You don't look that strange to me.'

I laughed. I couldn't help it – it was the way he said the words, making them a challenge. Most men would be afraid of approaching a woman like this these days in case they got sued for sexual harassment, but this one looked as if he might thrive on litigation! All my instincts told me I should keep on walking, but – what the hell! Life can become very boring if you always stick to safety, besides it was beginning to seem as if every man I knew was in some kind of a relationship.

I glanced at my watch: it was Gucci and rather nice, a present from Athena. 'I have to be back in twenty minutes . . .'

'Or they will send out a search party?' His fine, dark brows lifted and he fell into step beside me. 'We could grab a beer or something on the *Tattersall Castle* if you like? It's pleasant on the water when it's like this; you always get a slight breeze from the river.'

'Why not?' I glanced at him sideways. 'Are you here simply for the day, on business?'

'It sometimes feels like that,' he said with a rueful smile.

5

'I spend half my life flying from country to country in the pursuit of wealth – but London is my base. What about you?'

'I've lived here since my aunt died,' I told him. 'Aunt Margaret. She had a house in the country, which I sold and used as a deposit on my flat in . . . I need a base in London, you see, because when I set up my own business as a fashion designer I'll need to be here.'

Now why had I told him so much? He didn't need my life story, we were only having a drink.

'By the way, I'm Nick Ryan.' He looked amused, perhaps because I had stopped short of giving him my address. 'So, what do you do for a living now?'

'I'm Julia Stevens.'

We left the park and walked through Horse Guards Parade, where the tourists were stroking the noses of patient horses, taking a short cut down to the Victoria Embankment. He was right, there was a slight breeze off the river; it lifted a strand of my pale hair, blowing it into my eyes. I brushed it back impatiently, watching the flow of traffic on the river, hardly noticing the bronzed dolphins twined about intricate lamp standards or any other of the famous landmarks I'd found so fascinating when I first came to London.

'I'm a secretary for a firm of exporters,' I said, belatedly answering his question. 'It pays the mortgage but I don't like it very much. I'm saving hard to set up my own business – and that takes time.'

'You wouldn't rather work for someone else? Experience the trade as a trainee designer?'

'Not really. They take all your designs and put their own labels on them. A couple of my friends settled for that – but I want my own boutique where I can sell my own designs. I was thoroughly grounded in the basics at college, and can produce the finished garment. I have sold a few ideas free-lance, but when I go into business I shan't do that – so I have to have enough money to keep me going for a while before I start.'

'Sounds good to me.' His gaze flicked towards me as we walked on board the vessel moored by the embankment. 'What will you have? A beer or wine?'

'Just a coke, please,' I said. 'Shall we grab that table with the sunshade? It's the only one . . .'

He nodded agreement. I took possession of the table seconds before a party of Japanese tourists could, watching as Nick Ryan paid for our drinks from a wallet stuffed with credit cards and cash. That wasn't a surprise, because he had an air of success about him that breathed money – and something else. I wasn't sure what; it might have been power or ruthlessness.

I studied his profile from beneath my lashes, not wanting to make my interest too obvious. He really was good looking, so it followed that he was probably married; in my experience, it seemed all the best looking men were either married or gay these days.

'So what do you do . . . when you're not flying from one place to another?' I asked and sipped my ice cool coke. He took a business card from the top pocket of his jacket and handed it to me. I read aloud, '"Nick Ryan & Associates – Management Consultants". What exactly does that mean?'

'I tell other people how to make their businesses pay,' he said, a lazy smile crookening his mouth. 'I take an initial first look myself, send in a team of top accountants, then make my report. If I'm asked, I hang around and oversee the changes.'

'So you're one of those ruthless men who put everyone out of work, are you?'

'Something like that.' His eyes narrowed, reflecting either disappointment in my politically correct attitude or annoyance. 'You don't approve of making business efficient then? Think you can run it for the welfare of its employees, do you? Think that will work for you when you have your own clothing design firm?'

'That's different . . .' I saw the look in his eyes and felt foolish. 'I meant . . . I'm not likely to employ anyone at the start, or not many anyway. But I would like to think I was a fair employer, if and when I do have people working for me.'

'I doubt if anyone enjoys making their workforce redundant. In fact that's why they employ me, to do it for them,' he said. 'It's not my favourite part of the job, but sometimes it's the only way if the firm is to survive.'

'Yes, I suppose so,' I agreed reluctantly. 'Shall we talk about something else?'

'Have you been watching Wimbledon?'

'Oh yes,' I said. 'It was great – at least we had some British interest through to the semi-final, though I was disappointed it didn't carry on right through. I thought Tim could have won it this year. Are you a tennis fan?'

'I enjoy most sports, when I have the time . . .'

'Do you play or just watch?'

'I ski sometimes in the winter – and I used to play rugby years ago.'

'I run and keep fit,' I said. 'I belong to a club . . . it provides something to do.' I realized how revealing that was and, feeling suddenly uncomfortable, glanced at my watch. 'Sorry, there's not much time left – I ought to go.'

'I'd like to ask you to dinner this evening,' he said, frowning. 'I really don't make a habit of this, Julia. In fact I can't remember the last time I asked a stranger out for a drink.'

I raised my brows. 'You would like to ask me to dinner, but . . . your wife is expecting you home?'

'I'm divorced,' he said. 'No present attachments. My work makes it difficult. I'm flying to the States this evening for a couple of weeks. I won't ask for your phone number, because I think you might be uncomfortable giving it to a stranger – but if you decide I might be safe to know, you could ring me. You have my card.'

'Yes . . .' I hesitated, knowing he was waiting for me to laugh and give him my number, but felt somehow reluctant. 'Yes, I have your card. It was nice meeting you, Nick. Maybe I'll ring you one day.'

'I'd like that,' he said, and his smile made my stomach clench with something between nerves and desire. At that precise moment, I wasn't sure which was uppermost. 'I'm really not so very dangerous, Julia. I don't bite – well not on first dates – and I have good table manners.'

I laughed, but something still made me hold back my

8

number. Maybe I just wasn't ready to begin a new relationship.

'I must go,' I said. 'I'll think about getting in touch. And thanks again for the drink.'

'My pleasure.'

There was something almost wistful about the way he said those words. I knew he was watching me again as I walked away and the sensation was an odd mixture of apprehension and pleasure. It would be so easy to get involved with a man like Nick Ryan; I wasn't frightened of him in a conventional way. I didn't imagine he was going to rape or rob me, but somehow I sensed his impact on my life could be far reaching and I wasn't ready to let down my guard.

I wasn't the only one feeling restless that afternoon; most of the girls were yawning over their computers. Marion Jackson from accounts waved a lazy greeting as I left my office that evening.

'It has been so hot,' she complained. 'All I could think of was a sandy beach and iced drinks.'

'When are you going on holiday?'

'I'm not, that's the trouble. We're saving for a new car. That's what Mick wants and we can't manage both this year, not with our mortgage!'

'Shame,' I sympathized. 'Maybe you could persuade him into a weekend at the sea or something?'

'If I did the weather would change overnight!'

I laughed and we parted company. Marion disappeared into the yawning depths of the tube station, while I walked round the corner and caught my bus.

The streets were crowded with office workers on their way home, spilling over the pavements, crowding the coffee bars and restaurants with tables outside. Everyone seemed to be meeting friends, laughing and looking forward to the evening. Once again, I was aware of that odd feeling I'd had in the park, a kind of nostalgia and somehow being on the outside looking in. I was aware of needing something more, of a gap in my life.

My small but expensive flat was part of one of the once

grand terraced houses in Chalcot Square. I was lucky enough to own what had once been the basement, which meant I had the luxury of a garden.

After a deliciously cool shower, I poured myself an iced drink and was about to take it outside when the phone shrilled into action.

'Hi,' I said, picking up the receiver with a sinking heart. Ben had phoned several times recently at about this hour, always to ask me to get back together with him. Not that he had any intention of divorcing his wife: he didn't see why he couldn't have us both. 'Julia Stevens speaking . . .'

'Julia?' My sister's voice sounded odd and slightly muffled. 'Have you only just got in? I rang a few minutes ago.'

'Sorry. I didn't hear you, I must have been in the shower. I ought to have set the answering machine, then I would have rung you back. It's lovely to hear from you. How are you?'

'I've been better. In fact, if I tell the truth, I'm feeling lousy.'

'What's wrong – are you ill?'

'No, not so as you'd notice.' She gave a harsh laugh. 'Just sorry for myself. Bored, I suppose.'

'Join the club,' I said dryly. 'I almost melted in the office today. At least you can sit by that pool of yours and relax. The photos you sent were fantastic. You don't know how lucky you are.'

'Am I?' There was a note of bitterness in her voice, which made me realize she really was down. 'You couldn't come out for a couple of weeks, could you? I hate to ask, Julia. I know you have your own life to lead, but . . . I really do need you.'

Now I knew something was wrong. We had never been that close, even as children, because of the age gap, and Athena had left home to work in London when she was twenty, because of a row with Aunt Margaret. After my sister went to America, some months later, we'd kept in touch by letters and phone calls, but apart from a couple of brief holidays together we hadn't seen each other in years.

'You are ill,' I said. 'Or in trouble?'

'I'm lonely and depressed,' she said. 'I need someone to

10

talk to – someone I can trust. You're the only one I care for, Julia. The only one who really matters apart from . . . the only one I can talk to anyway.'

'Well, I'm not sure I can get leave immediately.'

'Please, Julia. I wouldn't ask if it wasn't important.'

I was startled. She sounded almost desperate. I did a quick rethink. She was my sister, and though I didn't know her very well I loved her. Besides, what did I have to lose? If my job folded, it wouldn't be the end of the world and I wasn't exactly in the middle of a red hot relationship.

'All right. I'll fix it at work tomorrow and catch the first flight I can get. Will that do?'

'You're wonderful,' she said and gave a gurgle of laughter, sounding much more like the Athena I remembered. 'It will be such fun, Julia. I promise you'll enjoy yourself. It's ages since we've been together. I'm really looking forward to seeing you, love. You won't change your mind, will you?'

I was suddenly looking forward to a break myself; it was probably just what I needed. 'No, I promise I'll come as soon as I can. I'll ring you as soon as I've booked my flight.'

'Great!' She sounded relieved, as if a weight had been lifted from her mind. 'So, tell me – how's the love life going?'

'It isn't. I told you in my last letter I'd thrown Ben out, didn't I?'

'He deserved it. You haven't found anyone else?'

'No, not really . . .'

'You don't sound too sure?' There was a teasing note in her voice now, and I could imagine the wicked gleam in her eyes. Athena's laughter had always been infectious and I couldn't help a little gurgle of laughter escaping as I remembered the way I'd let a stranger pick me up in the park.

'I've just met someone – but I'm not sure it's going any-where. On balance, it probably isn't. He's gorgeous but prob-ably dangerous to know. Besides, he's on his way to America for a couple of weeks.'

'Then I'm not spoiling anything for you, dragging you out here?'

11

'No, of course not. As a matter of fact, I could do with a holiday.'

'I'll pay all your expenses,' she promised. 'Bless you for understanding, Julia. Ring me soon.'

I was thoughtful as I replaced the receiver. Athena had sounded very depressed at first and I wondered what could be going on in her life to make her feel slightly desperate. I wouldn't have thought she was the sort to let things get her down – but then, I hardly knew her. Not really. It was difficult to remember her as she was before she'd left home. She was beautiful, I knew that, a little wild sometimes, very generous and impulsive – but what was she like, deep down, as a person?

She and Aunt Margaret had quarrelled over what my aunt termed 'bad company', which was anyone who didn't fit in with her old-fashioned ideas. Athena had resented her inter-ference, gradually finding it impossible to live under the same roof as our aunt; one night she had gone storming out of the house, never to return. Neither of us had heard from her for a couple of years, then she'd sent me a card and some money for my birthday.

'I'm living in New York,' her brief note had said. 'Working as a model and earning lots of money. I love you, Julia, and think about you. Think about me sometimes, love Athena.'

Over the years I'd received infrequent letters, cards and generous gifts of money. Once, she'd sent me a thousand dollars, which made my aunt turn up her nose in disgust.

'Far too much for a young girl!' she had said and made me save it.

Athena had sent me the train fare for that never-to-be-forgotten holiday in London; she'd given me the time of my life, buying me loads of clothes and taking me everywhere.

Afterwards, I'd begged her to let me move in with her.

'You don't know how awful it is living with Aunt Margaret,' I'd pleaded. 'I could come with you. Please say yes. I wouldn't be any trouble to you.'

'No, you wouldn't,' she'd said with a smile, 'but it can't happen, Julia. I'm too busy to look after you. One day per-haps . . .'

It was two years before she made another flying visit to London; this time we had only a couple of days before she had to leave. Once again I'd pleaded with her to let me into her life.

'It isn't as much fun as you think,' she'd told me then, a strange, pensive look in her eyes. There had been something odd in her manner then, something she seemed to be regretting. 'You're too young to leave home yet, love. When you are, I'll help you find a place of your own.'

As it happened, I didn't need Athena's help when the time came. My aunt died quite suddenly while I was away at art school, leaving everything she possessed to me. I'd written to Athena, but she hadn't come home for the funeral and she'd refused my offer to share the money with her.

'No, it's yours,' she'd told me on the phone. 'At least it means you'll be able to buy a place of your own now.'

There had been debts to settle and the capital hadn't been sufficient to buy the flat outright I wanted in London, but it was enough to get me started and I was managing well enough. I had some money saved towards the business I intended to start; it might be almost enough if the worst came to the worst and I did lose my job.

I was still thinking, worrying about what was really troubling my sister, when my best friend, Sandy Hale, phoned to make sure I was going to meet her at the health club that evening.

'You hadn't forgotten, had you?' she asked, an accusing tone to her voice. 'We arranged it last week.'

'No, of course I hadn't,' I lied. 'I'll be there, Sandy.'

'Good, because I want to talk. It's important, Julia.'

'I'll be there,' I promised again, abandoning my hopes of sitting out in the garden for a couple of hours. 'What's bugging you?'

'I'll tell you later,' she said and the phone crashed in my ear.

'It made me see red,' Sandy said, obviously furious over something that had happened at work. She was flame-haired, rather fierce and apt to lose her rag at times. 'They are going to make it the mainstay of their line this winter – and I'm not getting even a mention.'

Sandy was a friend from art school. She had been one of the brightest stars in our class and everyone expected her to land a terrific job with a top designer, but instead she had settled for working for a well-known high street chain.

'But you knew that when you took the job,' I pointed out. We were having a drink after our workout, which had been very strenuous and left me temporarily drained of energy. 'I don't blame you for feeling annoyed – but where do you go from here?'

'I wish I knew.' She looked at me speculatively, flicking back a wisp of hair from her eyes. Her fingers strayed to the heavy silver necklace she was wearing, twisting the locket nervously. 'Unless . . . I wondered if we might join forces, Julia? The more I think about your idea of setting up your own boutique to sell your own designs, the more I think it might work. Especially if there were two of us involved, to share the practical work and ideas.'

'A partnership, you mean?' I was silent as I thought about it. It made sense in a way, but I wasn't sure. We should have to pool our resources and our ideas, and even then money was bound to be tight for a start. Many a good friendship had foundered on the rocks that way. 'I haven't saved enough yet – what about you?'

'I've got a couple of thousand I could use,' she said, screwing up her mouth. 'But I would need most of that to live on until we got going . . . I wondered if I could start off working with you, putting in time and effort and buy in later?'

'I'm not sure that would work, Sandy. It would all have to be done properly at the start. We could probably have a work-for-shares arrangement . . . but that still leaves us short of capital.'

Her green eyes narrowed, glinting with suppressed emotion. 'You mean you would consider it if we could find the money?'

'Yes, I think so.' My doubts faded as I thought of the advantages. 'It could make things easier all round, and get us both started sooner. Yes, I like it. Why not?'

14

'Great!' She looked excited, eager. 'I think I might be able to borrow some money from my brother-in-law, that's if I can show him it's not all air dreaming. I'm not sure how much – but probably two or three thousand pounds.'

'It might be enough.' I sipped my drink thoughtfully. 'I'm going away for a couple of weeks, Sandy. If we both work out some figures – what we think we'll need for personal expenses, plus what it's going to take to set it all up – I know someone who might give us some advice for free. I could ring him when I get back from holiday.'

'I'll hang on where I am for the time being,' she said. 'My contract comes up for renewal next month, that's why I wanted to talk to you now – but I can think of some excuse for not signing it immediately.'

'Do that,' I said and grinned at her. 'I feel quite enthused. I've been feeling trapped, thinking I'd need another year or two at least but now . . . Oh, Sandy, it's what I need!'

'Stick it there, partner!' We laughed, shook hands and then hugged each other. 'Where are you going? You hadn't planned a holiday, had you?'

I was lost in thought as I walked home from the gym. Sandy's suggestion became more appealing as I thought about it. It would be a risk, of course. Neither of us had a great deal of money to play with – but, who cared! Sometimes in life you have to take risks. Besides, it would be such fun, the two of us working and planning the business together. The future suddenly seemed full of opportunities and interest. I hadn't felt this good about my life in ages.

Lost in concentration, I'm not sure when I first began to sense I was being followed. It wasn't particularly late, only just past ten, and the streets were still light, fairly lively, people passing by, standing at bus queues, coming out of the pubs. Yet something didn't feel right; it was a creeping sensation that started at the nape of my neck and trickled slowly down my spine.

I glanced over my shoulder. Nothing. But he had been there a moment or two ago. Why was I so sure it was a man? Oh, come on! It had to be, didn't it? There was always a story in the papers or on TV these days about some girl getting stalked, and more often than not it was someone she knew. Ben had been making a nuisance of himself, but I hadn't thought he was this bad.

'Hi, Julia.' A friendly voice called to me. Relieved, I saw one of my neighbours waving to me from outside a local restaurant. 'Been to your health club again?'

'Yes,' I said and smiled at him in relief. Philip lived next door. He was gay and had a steady relationship. Both he and his partner were great fun, neither of them remotely threatening as far as I was concerned. 'Where is Terry this evening?'

'He went home for a few days,' Philip said. 'His father is ill. Mind if I walk home with you?'

'I'd like that,' I said. 'I think I've been followed for a while now.'

'Where?' Philip looked round. 'Point him out, dear.'

'He stopped suddenly,' I replied. 'I sensed him but didn't actually see him. Maybe it was my imagination.'

'Quite possibly. I think I'm being followed all the time! Unfortunately, it's seldom true.'

He laughed and I laughed with him. Philip didn't make a point of flaunting his sexual preferences. He and Terry were discreet about what went on behind closed doors – and they were good neighbours. Philip had fixed things for me in the flat more than once, and I'd invited them both round for drinks occasionally – though not when Ben was around. He hated and despised Philip's set.

'I expect it was just my imagination,' I agreed. 'I'm going away for a while, but when I come back we must all get together for a party – in the garden if the weather is good.'

'Give me a ring,' he said. 'And don't worry about being followed, Julia. If you ever feel frightened you can call on us – Terry will frighten any stalker off. He's got such wonderful muscles!'

He pulled an expressive face, rolling his eyes suggestively to make me laugh.

'Thanks,' I said as we arrived at my door. 'But I'm sure it was just in my mind. I had an odd feeling at the nape of my neck – but when I looked back no one was there.'

We parted at the top of the steps that led to my front door. I ran down and let myself in. Philip stood at the top and waited until I had my door open. I smiled up at him and waved, grateful for his thoughtfulness. I supposed he must know what it felt like to feel threatened; he had been beaten up twice in the past because of his sexual preferences.

Once inside the flat, I double locked my door, then wondered at my own foolishness. I was usually pretty confident about handling myself and men who made a nuisance of themselves. It wasn't like me to have an attack of nerves. There was no reason for me to have felt threatened, and yet somehow I had.

Remembering the incident in the park earlier that day, I frowned. Nick Ryan had certainly followed me then . . . but I hadn't felt nervous of him. At least, I had but for very different reasons. Besides, he was on his way to America.

Despite my denials to Philip, I was fairly sure that someone had followed me for a while that evening. Whoever it was, had probably done it on impulse. I wasn't wearing one of my short skirts, and I didn't look that sexy in my shapeless tracksuit – but I supposed some men would follow any woman who was alone.

It was probably fortunate for me that Philip had been leaving the restaurant at that particular moment . . .

Two

The sun was glaringly bright, the heat seeming to meet me as I left the terminal building at Malaga and looked for a taxi. Athena had told me not to bother with hiring a car as she had two of her own.

'Besides,' she'd said when I'd rung to tell her what time I was arriving, 'my villa is a bit off the beaten track. You would probably get lost trying to find it.'

I'd hoped she might meet me at the airport, but she'd said she had an appointment she couldn't get out of and might be late.

'Come in a taxi,' she advised. 'I should be home by the time you arrive – and if I'm late Carla will look after you. You will like her, Julia, she's my housekeeper and a friend from way back.'

This wasn't my first trip to Spain. Sandy and I had gone on a package tour once with some other friends, but it was the first time for me on the Costa del Sol, the first time I would see my sister's home. On our previous holidays it had been just the two of us, but now I was about to meet some of Athena's friends, to discover a little about her life.

I gazed out of the taxi window with interest as I was whisked along the mountain road, which Athena had told me had been built to ease the traffic on the old coastal route. Some of the views were quite spectacular as you looked down on the resorts and the sparkling blue sea, though most of the apartment blocks looked much the same as any others along the coast.

When we started to climb away from the main road just a few kilometres outside Marbella, I realized the scenery was changing. Now the villas were much larger, set in lush, semitropical gardens and hidden away behind high walls and security gates.

My taxi stopped at last, outside a pair of impressive black wrought iron gates with the words *Villa Isabella* emblazoned in dusky gold. I got out, paid my fare and collected my bags from the boot of the car, then tried the gate. It was firmly locked, so I rang the bell.

'Yes – who is it please?' The voice sounded more American than Spanish. 'Speak into the intercom, please.'

'It's Julia Stevens,' I said as the machine crackled alarmingly. 'Athena's sister.'

'I'll press the buzzer. Please make sure the gates close after you. They sometimes need a little push.'

The heavy gates swung back unwillingly, revealing a paved courtyard set with large terracotta pots filled with trailing plants and bright crimson geraniums. Flowers seemed to spill out from every nook and cranny in a profusion of colour, filling the air with their perfume. I picked up my bags and walked through, jumping as the gates shut with a clanging sound behind me.

I glanced back uneasily. Despite the beauty of the gardens, I felt shut in, imprisoned somehow.

As I began to walk towards the house, a woman came from somewhere at the back. She was small and plump and had olive-toned skin, and was obviously Hispanic. I wasn't sure, but I could detect a slight reserve in her manner.

'Miss Stevens? I am Señora Estebe, but I am always called Carla.' She wiped her hands on the white apron she was wearing over a dark blue dress, and I saw that she did not wear a wedding ring. Perhaps she was a widow?

'I was preparing dinner. Forgive me. I am alone here this afternoon. Miguel went into Marbella to collect something.' She held out her hand for the largest case. 'Let me carry that. Your room is just through here. You have a pleasant view of the pool.'

'Isn't Athena back yet? She thought she would be . . .'

'Not yet. I'm sure she won't be long. If you want to change first, then I'll bring you some food.'

'Just a drink,' I said. 'I ate on the plane.'

19

'That food is not good for you.' She looked disapproving. 'But if you are not hungry, perhaps some freshly squeezed fruit juice?'

'Thank you.' I looked at her curiously. 'Did you come here with Athena from America?'

'Yes. I've worked for her for some years, but I was born in Spain.' Carla's mouth thinned as though warning me not to ask more questions. 'This is your room. I hope you will be comfortable here.'

I glanced round the room. It had cool grey marble floors, white lacquered furniture, pale peach curtains and bedcovers, and a large arrangement of exotic looking silk flowers in the corner.

'Thank you. I'm sure I shall. It is very attractive.'

'Your bathroom is through there . . .' She gestured towards a door. 'Excuse me. If you need me there is a phone. You have only to press the red button. I shall be in the kitchen.'

Not exactly a warm welcome, I thought, but not hostile either. I walked to the window and looked out at the pool, which glittered enticingly in the sun, its water a clear blue and inviting.

I was suddenly aware that I felt hot and sticky. Unlocking one of my cases, I took out a new bikini and laid it on the bed while I stripped off my clothes and watch. I'd seen some large white towels hanging in the ensuite bathroom so I grabbed one and took it with me.

There were several recliners and chairs placed on the grass near the pool. Throwing my towel on one, I ran to the edge of the pool and dived in. The water was shockingly cold at first, but after I'd swum a few lengths at top speed it seemed to warm up and I was feeling very refreshed as I hauled myself out and retrieved my towel.

It was only after I had dried my hair that I became aware I was being watched. I swung round and saw him: a tall, powerfully built man of perhaps thirty-five or so. Harsh-featured, his hair was a medium brown, thick, very short, his eyes a stony grey – and at this particular moment, I thought, angry.

'Who the hell are you – and how did you get here?' I demanded. 'I thought those gates were locked.'

20

'They were – Carla let me in,' he said, his eyes narrowing, hard. 'Sorry if I startled you. I'm Robert Lee, a friend of Athena's.'

'Oh . . .' I felt awkward, foolish for jumping to conclusions. He too had an American accent, but his tone was modulated, crisp and very precise, as though he came from the right side of the tracks. 'Sorry I yelled. You startled me. I wasn't expecting to see anyone.'

'Then I should apologize, Julia – you are Julia, aren't you? Athena has spoken of you often.'

'Has she?' I was still uncomfortable. There was something about him that made me uneasy, though I couldn't have said why; I just didn't take to him. 'Have you known Athena long?'

'For several years. I'm her . . . business adviser. She may have mentioned me?'

'No – not that I recall. She never talks about her work much.'

'No, I suppose she wouldn't, not to you.' His cool, assessing stare made me feel like a naive schoolgirl. 'You won't mind if I join you by the pool, will you? I was expecting Athena to be here – and I'm flying back to the States in the morning.'

'No, I don't mind if you stay here,' I said. 'Excuse me, I have to change.'

There was no way I was going to sit there with him. I didn't like Mr Lee, or the way he looked at me. Nor did I care for his assumption that my sister never told me much about her work, even though it happened to be true.

I wrapped the towel around myself and went back to my room, shutting the patio door and drawing the curtains before going to take a shower.

Ten minutes later I was feeling fresher, dressed in white shorts and a skinny top. As I opened my window I could hear raised voices coming from outside.

'I've told you . . .' – it was my sister's voice – 'I'm not coming back. I've had enough. It's over, Robert. We've both done well out of it, now it's time to finish while we're ahead. I'm starting a new life here.'

'Doing what? You'll die of boredom, Athena. Besides, I need you. It doesn't work without you and . . .'

I walked out on to the patio. He stopped speaking abruptly and scowled as he saw me. Athena swung round, startled, wondering what he was glaring at. She was just as beautiful as ever, though perhaps thinner than I remembered. She looked tired but the anxious look left her face as she saw me.

'Julia – darling!' she cried and came towards me, opening her arms in welcome. Her hug left me in no doubt that she was pleased to see me, and that she was upset about something. I imagined it must be Mr Lee's unexpected visit. 'It's so good to see you. I'm sorry I wasn't here when you arrived, but my meeting took longer than I'd hoped.'

'Athena. It's lovely to see you. I like your villa – and I've already been in the pool.'

We hugged and kissed again. She touched my cheek and then my hair. 'Such a pretty colour, like spun silk. Mine was always darker – and your eyes are azure, just like the sky.'

Athena had honey-coloured hair and her eyes were much greener than mine. She was wearing a fine white shirt over tight white jeans, and gold mules. She looked tanned, sexy and rich, not in the least in need of comfort from me.

'You've met Robert, haven't you? He's trying to get me to go back to America with him, but I shan't. I've retired, Robert. So you may as well accept it.' She threw a laughing, slightly malicious glance at him.

He scowled, clearly annoyed. 'You're being foolish, Athena – throwing away a fortune.'

'Money isn't everything,' she replied. 'I've invested wisely, Robert. Don't worry. I shan't want for anything.'

'Why won't you even consider my idea? I have the contract in my pocket . . .'

'And I'm saying no.' Her eyes flashed with sudden anger. 'Forget it! I've told you it's over and I meant it. *Now* I want to talk to my sister. Please leave, Robert.'

'You *will* regret this, Athena,' he said again.

'Shall I?' She raised her head, her eyes narrowed and suddenly icy cold. Her teasing manner had gone and she seemed angry. 'Don't threaten me. Remember I have claws, Robert. I don't want to use them on you – but I shall if you force me.'

'Damn you!' he cried. 'You think you're being clever – but you're walking a tightrope. It's a hard, cold world out there on your own. You would have done better to stick with me.'

'Perhaps.' There was a hint of triumph in her face, her head tilted, manner challenging. 'We shall never know, shall we? Please go now – and don't bother coming back.'

'You *will* regret this, Athena.'

He glared at her once more, then turned and stalked off, disappearing round the corner of the villa. For a moment there was silence, then Athena made an odd noise, which sounded as if it were somewhere between a sob of relief and a laugh.

'Well, that's that,' she said. 'I'm glad you were here, Julia. He can be difficult at times.'

'You seemed to be in control,' I said. 'What was all that about anyway?'

'He wants me to sign a big contract for a cosmetics firm. It would pay him a fat commission, so he isn't exactly ecstatic that I've turned it down, that's all. He just won't accept that my modelling career is over. It couldn't go on, but he can't see that.'

'Why?' I asked, curious now. 'What made you give it all up and come out here? You told me you were bored already. Why not go back to America?'

'Because I'm nearly thirty-two,' she replied with a wry smile. 'I've gone on for far too long as it is. Robert doesn't see it, but I'm starting to look old for the camera. I prefer to quit while I'm ahead.'

'You don't look old to me.'

'You haven't got a close-up lens,' she said and laughed. 'Besides, there are other reasons, personal things Robert doesn't know about. I want to make the break now, while I can. There are more important things . . .'

'As long as you're happy.' I gave her a long, hard look. 'You didn't sound happy when you rang the other night.'

'I was feeling low,' Athena said, her eyes shying away from mine. 'I'm prone to mood swings. I'm a creature of moods, I always have been.' She shrugged her shoulders, flicking her shoulder-length hair back from her face. 'They come and go. Besides, I wanted to see you. It's ages since we spent time together. I've always been so busy earning money I've had no time to enjoy life, now I'm going to enjoy spending my money. And I'd like you to share some of the fun with me.'

'I'm glad you asked me to come out,' I said, 'because I do need to talk to you. I'm thinking of going into business. You know the fashion industry, perhaps you could give me some advice.'

'But you're not ready yet – are you?'

'I may have to be . . .' I pulled a face. 'My boss told me he wouldn't keep me on if I insisted on taking this holiday at such short notice – so I quit.'

'Oh, Julia! I'm sorry.' Athena looked rueful. 'I'll help you out with money. It's all my fault.'

'As it happens, I'm not that bothered. A friend of mine wants us to join forces and open our own designer boutique. We'll sell our own exclusive lines for a start, then see what happens. I think it might work – if we can raise enough cap-ital.'

'If it's only a question of money?' She smiled, looking a bit like the cat who'd got the cream. 'I'll back you, Julia. Money is one thing I have plenty of, believe me.'

'If you really mean that, it would be a loan,' I said. 'We'll pay you back as soon as the business gets off the ground.'

'You're my sister,' she replied, giving me an odd look. 'The only relative I have. I've often wanted to do something for you. We can worry about paying the money back when, and if, I ever need it. We'll discuss details tomorrow, Julia. First we have to get changed. I'm taking you to a party this evening. I hope you've got something pretty to wear? If not, you can borrow something of mine.'

'You must be a size eight,' I said. 'I'm a ten. Don't worry, Athena. I came prepared for anything . . .'

The villa Athena took me to that evening was even larger and more exclusive than her own. There were three Mercedes cars and a Porsche already parked in the driveway. As we

24

walked towards the impressive wood panelled door, I could smell roasting meat mingling with the headier scents of jasmine and roses.

As we were shown inside the house by a smiling Spanish maid, I was immediately aware of the owner's wealth. The decor here was overpowering both for its richness and style: huge glass chandeliers threw their sparkle over elaborate black and gold tables, sumptuous black leather sofas, Persian rugs, glittering mirrors and paintings so thickly encrusted with oil paint that they looked almost like wood carvings. Everything shouted money, but I thought the overall effect oppressive, almost sinister. I was relieved when we walked through the open patio doors to the formal flower gardens, which were truly magnificent and filled with both colour and scent.

The pool was twice the size of Athena's, boasting a high diving board and underwater lights. Paved areas led to what looked like extensive wooded gardens and then down to a sandy cove I had glimpsed earlier.

Several long tables had been put up on the immaculate lawns, set with pristine white cloths and laden with a bewildering variety of salads, huge prawns, lobster, cold meats, fruit and bread; they beckoned temptingly. There were also three barbecues attended by men in white aprons and caps, who were serving roasted chicken, steaks and spare ribs sizzling hot from the grill. A waiter was circulating with trays of glasses filled with champagne, and another was serving drinks from a black marble bar.

At least twenty guests were drinking, talking or helping themselves to the food. Athena's gaze fixed on a man dressed completely in black; his silk shirt was opened at the neck, revealing a slash of smooth, tanned skin.

At first glance he was impressive, his pale, silvery blond hair catching one's attention. As he became aware of my sister, his eyes, which were an arresting, brilliant blue, narrowed with an oddly intense look. I sensed something at that moment. Wealth, power – a kind of menace? I wasn't sure, though the first two were obvious. On the third finger of his right hand, he wore a ring set with one huge white diamond that must have been worth a king's ransom. I realized this must be our host and the wealthy owner of the villa.

'Athena, darling,' he cried as we approached. He held his hands out to her and they kissed cheeks. 'I wasn't sure you would come.'

'Oh, Hans,' she said, pouting at him. 'How could I not come to your party? You would never have forgiven me. Besides, I wanted you to meet my sister Julia.' She turned to me with a smile. 'This is Hans Werner – one of my dearest friends.'

'Miss Stevens,' he said, inclining his head. My intuition was stronger now; I could definitely sense power in Hans Werner, but also something darker mixing in with the German correctness. An intriguing mixture. 'I am delighted to meet you at last. Athena has spoken of you to me many times.'

'Thank you, Herr Werner . . .' I stumbled over his name as his large hand crushed mine.

'Please call me Hans,' he said, a smile flickering over his mouth – a mouth I thought seemed slightly cruel, though it might just have been that his lips were thin. 'And perhaps it is permitted that I call you Julia? Since we are to be friends. We are to be friends, I hope?'

I was aware of steel beneath the charm. This was a man accustomed to having his own way. If he decided something would be so, then it would.

'Yes, of course,' I replied, blushing as his fine brows rose. 'That is – you may call me Julia, if you wish.'

'Stop mesmerizing her, Hans!' commanded my sister play-fully. She was excited, a light seeming to shine out of her. I sensed her mood was slightly reckless, as though she rode the crest of a wave. 'I shall not allow you to add Julia to your list of conquests.'

'You are unjust,' he reproached her, but his mouth had softened, was smiling. 'Your sister is safe with me. As you are well aware.'

Something seemed to pass between them – an under-standing? Were they having an affair? There was certainly an attraction there, an undercurrent of excitement.

26

'Please eat, drink, amuse yourselves as you will,' Hans urged. 'My house is yours.'

We moved on. We were offered champagne and accepted a glass each, sipping it as we wandered across the lawns. Athena seemed to know everyone. She introduced me to various people, but I sensed that none of them were important to her. She was marking time, anticipating something. She had come here this evening for one purpose – to meet Hans – his guests were merely a part of the scenery as far as my sister was concerned.

Why did I feel my nerve ends tingling? What was going on tonight?

Athena seemed to glow, her beauty almost incandescent. She was enjoying herself and yet the party itself meant nothing to her; she was nursing some secret knowledge that amused and pleased her. Every now and then I saw her eyes stray towards our host and I sensed her inner excitement – the adrenaline was pumping hard. Was she on the verge of having an affair with Hans? Or was there something more?

'Are you here for a holiday?'

My attention was drawn to the pretty young woman in a short, tight, pink silk dress who had just spoken. She smiled at me, flicking out her long dark hair.

'Yes. I'm staying with my sister for two weeks. I arrived today.'

'Your sister is Athena Andrews?' I nodded. 'Yes, I knew she was expecting you. Everyone knows everything out here. We are a very small community . . . I'm Jill – Jill Howard. We live in the apartments down the hill from here. Nothing grand like this!' She looked at me curiously. 'Everyone was excited when she came to live here. I mean, Athena was a successful model in America, wasn't she? I think I saw her photos in *Vogue* when we were out there – that was a few years back, of course. But she lived in New York, didn't she?'

'Yes.' I glanced at my sister. She was drifting away across the lawns towards Hans. 'Yes, until quite recently.'

'I haven't seen her in the magazines lately. I buy most of them, and you'd think I would have seen her. She is very beautiful, too beautiful to have retired, don't you think? You are pretty too, but you don't look much like her. I didn't catch your name?'

'Oh, sorry. It's Julia Stevens. Andrews is Athena's professional name. I think she did more catwalk shows than magazine work this last year or so.'

'Oh, I see. Are you a model, too?'

'No, I'm a secretary – or I was. I've just quit my job. I'm going into business for myself soon. Designing clothes . . .'

'How exciting,' Jill said. 'I'm afraid I just work as a receptionist at one of the complexes along the coast. Nothing exciting.'

'But it must be thrilling to live in Spain?'

'My husband likes the lifestyle; it's more relaxed than at home, more time for leisure. I get a bit bored with constant sunshine and long for a good old British fog sometimes.' She sighed and glanced across the lawn to where a man several years her senior was beckoning to her. 'Mark wants me. Will you excuse me, please?'

I nodded and smiled as she walked off. I was looking for Athena. Both she and Hans seemed to have disappeared, probably into the house, I thought. I walked slowly back towards the villa, feeling a little bit as if I'd been abandoned – although I knew it was ridiculous to think that. Then I saw them – they weren't in the house at all but coming out from a thick growth of shrubbery, their body language telling everything they were trying to hide. It was obvious to me that they had been kissing. Athena's face was flushed, eyes bright, hair slightly disturbed.

How odd! I wondered why she had made that desperate phone call. If she was having an affair why did she need me? I should have thought another woman in the house was the last thing she wanted at this precise moment.

She looked a little guilty as she came up to me.

'Poor Julia,' she said, a laugh in her voice. 'Did you think I had deserted you?'

'Not really. I just wondered where you were.'

'Oh, I went to look at some special roses Hans has had planted,' she said innocently, but her eyes betrayed her. 'Don't look like that, Julia. It isn't what you're thinking.'

'What should I be thinking?' I asked, teasing her. 'Not that you rather like the handsome Hans Werner, of course?'

'Yes, I do like him. We'll talk about this tomorrow,' she said. 'Let's have something to eat. Hans wants to go on to a nightclub later – and I'm starving.'

It was too late to talk when, in the early hours of the following morning, we finally got back to Athena's villa. It had been a long night and I was tired. Athena's friends seemed ready to drink and dance for ever, but I'd been up at the crack of dawn the previous day to catch my flight and could hardly keep my eyes open on the drive home.

'Poor Julia,' Athena said, teasing me as she saw I was dead on my feet. 'I can see you're not used to staying up half the night – but I couldn't miss Hans' party.'

'Is he special to you?'

'Oh yes.' A little smile played mischievously at the corners of her mouth. 'Very special. Good night, Julia dearest. It will soon be morning and then we'll talk about lots of things.'

I fell asleep very quickly and did not wake until almost noon. Catching sight of the time, I leapt out of bed and took a quick shower. When I emerged on to the patio wearing a white lace bikini, Carla was clearing some dishes from the tables by the pool.

'Good morning, Miss Stevens,' she said. 'May I bring you something?'

'Just coffee, please.'

'Nothing to eat?'

'Perhaps a yoghurt and a banana, if it's no trouble?'

'I shall bring you breakfast,' she said. 'You can decide what you want. Miss Andrews eats hardly enough to keep a bird alive. You don't want to follow her example.'

I smiled as she carried her tray into the house. Athena had obviously been up before me.

I sat on the edge of the pool, dangling my feet in the water and enjoying the warmth of the sun on my back when I suddenly noticed a man working at the far end of the garden. He was not wearing a shirt; his skin was tanned and shiny with sweat as he used a heavy hoe to break up the soil and root out the weeds. Every now and then he straightened up and wiped his forehead with a red handkerchief. He was quite young and looked very strong with bulging muscles in his arms and back, his body more that of a prize fighter than a gardener. When he turned to look at me, I saw that he was also very attractive. He smiled at me, revealing teeth that looked extra white against his tanned skin, then turned back to his work once more.

'That's Miguel,' my sister said as she came out of the villa wearing a black swimsuit covered by a filmy black and gold jacket. 'He is Carla's youngest brother. He worked as a security guard for a while in America, but when he lost his job I asked him to come and work for me. I feel safer with a strong man about the place – and Miguel is very tough, believe me.'

'Did he work for you in America?' I asked. 'Did you have a garden there? I always thought you had a tower block apartment in New York?'

'Yes, I did.' She put on her dark glasses and laid on a recliner. 'Miguel was my driver in New York. He sometimes drives me here – but he likes gardening. In fact, he does all the odd jobs around the villa. He is very useful to have about the place, believe me.'

I had an odd feeling that Miguel's real work was something very different. He looked as if he might be a bodyguard . . . but surely Athena didn't need protection? Not now anyway. She might have once, when she was a model and likely to be followed by all kinds of people, from genuine admirers to cranks – but surely not here in Spain?

'So,' Athena asked, stretching lazily, 'what do you want to do today, babe? Stay here and relax in the sun – or go sightseeing? It's too late for shopping; the shops would be closed before we could get into town – until this evening, that is. I prefer to shop in the evenings myself. It's cooler and there aren't so many tourists about.'

'I'm a tourist.'

'No, you're my sister,' she said and smiled. 'That's different, naturally.'

I laughed and pulled my legs out of the pool, and went to sit on a recliner near her.

'Tell me about Hans,' I said. 'How long have you known him?'

'We met a year or so back,' she said, 'at a friend's party. Then I didn't see him again until a couple of days ago . . .'

'You like him a lot, don't you?'

'Liking doesn't have much to do with it,' she said, lowering her glasses to give me a naughty look. 'Sometimes, if you're really, really lucky, a man comes along . . . a man who makes your body sing with pleasure just by looking at you in a certain way. He may be dangerous or he may belong to someone else, but you know that this experience is not to be missed, and so for one glorious moment you take whatever is on offer. Maybe if he was less dangerous, or easier to own, it wouldn't be so exciting.' She looked me in the eyes. 'Do you understand at all what I mean, Julia?'

'Yes, I think so. I always fall for the wrong ones.'

'This isn't love,' Athena said. 'It's too intense – too selfish for that. We are both of us selfish people. We both take what we want from life – but at the moment that happens to be each other.'

She laughed, shaking her hair back, her body arching sensuously as she basked in the sun like a lazy cat. I sensed a certain wildness in her, a need for excitement and amusement – and a restlessness. She was like a playful breeze that whipped along country lanes stirring up fallen leaves and carrying them with her. Her smile was infectious, and it would be easy to let yourself be carried away by her in this mood.

'Why on earth didn't you ring and tell me to cancel my trip? You can't want me in the way?'

'But I do want you here,' she said and reached across to press my hand. 'I've been looking forward to seeing you for ages. What is between Hans and me is something apart. Besides, making him wait is all part of the game.'

'It sounds rather risky to me,' I said. 'He looked dangerous – ruthless. I'm not sure I liked him, Athena. No, don't laugh. He would scare me to death!'

31

'That's what makes him so very attractive.' She laughed and shook her head at me. 'No, don't try to understand what drives me, Julia – you couldn't even get close. I sometimes wonder why I do the things I do, believe me.'

I felt a tingle of something at the nape of my neck. Something in her manner frightened me. She seemed so reckless and I sensed a deeper emotion hidden beneath the surface. Was it fear? Was all this talk of living for the moment a cover for feelings she was trying to hide?

Carla had brought out a tray piled high with different kinds of sweet rolls, jams, orange juice, a bowl of fresh fruit and a pot of steaming hot coffee with cream in a jug.

'I'll never eat a quarter of this,' I groaned as she went away. 'How do you manage to keep so thin, Athena?'

'I've never been able to put on weight,' my sister said. 'I must burn the calories up too fast, I suppose – it's the wicked life I lead.'

'I wish I knew the secret,' I said. 'If I ate this lot I should blow up like a balloon.'

'I doubt it.' Athena smiled. 'So, tell me about your friend and how much money you think you'll need . . .'

Three

If Athena's desperate phone call had conjured up pictures in my mind of her living a life of lonely exile, the next few days shattered that image. Even on the days when we were supposed to be having a quiet laze at home, there was a constant stream of visitors. I was amazed at how many friends she had acquired since her move to the Costa del Sol a few months previously, but, gradually, I began to realize that it was all froth and bubble. The kissing and smiles were meaningless, just a part of the glitzy, shallow lifestyle that existed in certain circles on the costas, where parties lasted until the early hours and breakfast was usually at noon. If these were Athena's only friends then I understood why she might feel low at times.

I suspected that she was closer to Carla and Miguel than anyone else. Several times I noticed her in close conversation with Miguel, and, when she went off alone on two separate occasions, he drove her to her appointment and brought her back.

The first time this happened I thought she was probably going to meet Hans and had stayed by the pool, but then she later told me he had returned to Germany on business.

'That was his farewell party the evening you arrived,' she explained. 'That's why I simply had to go.'

'Will he be away long?' I was puzzled. She seemed remarkably calm about it. 'Couldn't you have gone with him?'

Athena laughed, an odd, secretive look in her eyes. 'To his home? Oh no, that wouldn't work. He will return to his villa in a few weeks. I can wait. I have a great deal of patience when I really want something.'

Once again I was aware of that inner excitement I had noticed when she spoke to Hans at the party.

The next time my sister announced she was leaving me to amuse myself for the day, I asked her where she was going.

'It's just business,' she said vaguely. 'You would be bored waiting around for ages. It's much better that you stay here and sunbathe or swim.'

She obviously didn't want to tell me what her business was, and she didn't want me with her. I decided to go into Marbella for the day. I wanted to spend some time looking at what was available in the fashion boutiques of one of Spain's most exclusive resorts.

I'd noticed that when it came to clothes, Spanish designers had their own very distinctive style. I liked the neat, waist-hugging jackets with very short skirts which had their roots in the traditional costume of the matador and were perhaps at their best in Don Miguel, a very expensive shop with clothes to die for. But there were lots of interesting boutiques with their own particular look, and these gave me some ideas to think about. Much of what they sold was probably too elaborate – the Spanish love bold embroidery and bright colours – but, as I wandered round the narrow, winding streets towards the Orange Square, a theme began to evolve in my head, something I thought might translate very well into English style.

When the shops began to close for their long midday break, I found a restaurant on the sea front and ordered a salad and a coke. It was easy to pass the time there, watching the yachts going in and out of the marina and crowds of holiday makers strolling in the sunshine along the pink marble promenade, past waving palms and olive trees.

It was almost three o'clock when I arrived back at the villa. Unusually, the gate was wide open so I drove straight in and parked the small car Athena had given me permission to use whenever I chose.

There was a car I didn't recognize parked outside the villa, but no sign of anyone as I let myself into the house and went straight to my bedroom, dumping various packages on the bed. I stripped off hastily, changed into a bikini and made for the pool.

The water was gloriously warm after the initial shock, and

I swam several lengths before getting out and drying myself. Still no sign of anyone – and yet I could hear voices from somewhere in the garden.

Was that Athena? I heard a woman's cry and alarm bells triggered. It sounded as if she were frightened or angry. Abandoning my towel, I ran towards the sound, round the side of the villa towards the rose gardens. Then I saw them. She was with a man and they seemed to be struggling; he had hold of her wrists and she was trying to defend herself – or it looked that way to me.

'Leave her alone, you bastard!' I yelled and swooped on a small but heavy hoe Miguel had left lying on the flower beds. 'If you hurt her you'll be sorry!'

I had the hoe gripped in my right hand and must have looked as if I meant to use it as a weapon as I charged towards them like an avenging fury. My wild appearance had a startling effect. They stopped struggling; Athena turned towards me in alarm and cried out to me to stop – and the man let go of her.

'No, Julia,' my sister said hastily as I walked closer, a purposeful air in my manner. 'It isn't what it looks like. He isn't hurting me. Put that thing down and don't be silly.'

I was hardly listening, for as the man let her go and turned to stare at me I recognized him. It was the man from the park, the man I had met only a few days earlier – Nick Ryan!

'What the hell?' he said as recognition became mutual. 'What on earth are you doing here?'

'You were supposed to be in America,' I said accusingly. I was still angry, and suspicious. 'Why are you here – and why were you attacking my sister?'

'Your sister?' He looked stunned. 'I had no idea . . .'

'Do you two know each other?' Athena rubbed at her wrists, then glared at him. 'She's right, you were hurting me, Nick. I know it was my own fault, so don't look like that.' She gave me a reassuring look. 'It was just a little disagreement that got out of hand, babe. Nick and I are old friends. We go way back, don't we, darling?' She flashed him a brilliant but warning smile. 'He wouldn't really hurt me – would you?'

'There have been times when I could cheerfully have broken your beautiful neck, Athena,' he replied, still seeming stunned by seeing Julia, but a slight smile was beginning to light up his eyes. 'If I had wanted to hurt you, you would have known it by now, believe me.'

He was angry, but trying to hide it. I wondered what it was that neither of them were prepared to tell me.

'His bark is far worse than his bite,' Athena said, recovered now from whatever had caused her alarm in the first place. 'Do put that stupid thing down, Julia. Nick isn't going to hurt anyone.'

I laid the hoe down on the earth, feeling slightly foolish. It had been an instinctive reaction, and I wasn't sure what I would have done if Athena had really been in danger.

'So – how long have you two known each other?' she said as I continued to glare at Nick. 'You didn't tell me about that, Julia.'

'We've only met once,' I said, and the look I gave him was meant to convey it would be the last. 'I thought you were flying to America for two weeks?'

'I was there for a few days, then I came here.' His eyes narrowed to menacing slits, and I wasn't sure whom he wanted to attack next – me or my sister. 'Believe me, I certainly had no idea you were Athena's sister.'

What was that supposed to mean? That if he had known, he would never have asked me to have a drink the day we met in the park? Did he have something to hide?

Athena was clearly more at ease than Nick Ryan. She was smiling, evidently amused, watching us with interest. Whatever they had been arguing about clearly bothered him more than her.

'Shall we have a drink by the pool?' she asked with an air of innocence. 'I need to think about what you said, Nick. Can you give me a few days?'

'You can take as long as you like providing the answer is yes,' he said, as the look of steel returned to his eyes. 'You know where you can reach me, don't you?'

'Surely you're not going?' she said, arching her fine pencilled brows. Her manner challenged and mocked him. 'Why

don't you take us out for dinner this evening? I'm sure Julia
would like to go to another nightclub, wouldn't you, babe?'

'Not particularly,' I replied. 'Besides, I don't think Mr
Ryan wants to oblige.' I raised my eyes to his, daring him
to disagree.

'I don't see why not,' he said, surprising me. 'I won't stay
for that drink, Athena. I do have other business here, believe
it or not. Pick you both up at eight?'

'Lovely,' she said and smiled sweetly, a glint of triumph
in her eyes. 'You haven't forgotten how to be nice after all,
Nick darling. I was beginning to think you had turned into
a surly brute.'

The look he gave her could have killed at nine paces, but
she merely laughed and slipped her arm through mine, leading
me back to the pool and ignoring him as he walked away.

'Tell me, Julia, did you enjoy your day?' she asked. 'Did
you buy anything nice?'

'An embroidered tea shirt and some matching mules,' I
said, trying to wrench my mind away from the subject of
Nick Ryan and back to clothes. 'Oh, and a pair of jeans. I
was mostly just window shopping.'

'Thinking about your boutique, I expect.' She looked at
me sideways. 'I've arranged for ten thousand pounds to be
paid into your account in London. If that isn't enough, you
can have some more next month. A lot of my money is tied
up . . . but I'm expecting some more funds soon.'

'Ten thousand . . .' I gasped, forgetting Nick Ryan as the
shock hit me. 'That's an awful lot of money, Athena. Are
you sure you can afford to let me have it?'

She shrugged, a little smile of satisfaction in her eyes. 'It's
not very much really, Julia. I always meant to give you a
nice present, but as I said, most of my money is tied up in
watertight investments – until I get what's owed to me.'

'What's owed?' I was surprised. 'Does someone owe you
money?'

'Some people owe me money,' she said, her eyes glittering. 'They don't like the idea of paying . . . but they will
eventually.'

'Why don't you take them to court? Sue them for the money?'

37

Athena's laughter rang out. Her eyes were brilliant, and wickedly alive, full of secrets.

'No, I don't think so, Julia. You've no idea how difficult that would be. I have my own ways of getting people to pay what they owe, believe me.'

'Well, as long as giving me that ten thousand doesn't leave you short,' I said. 'You know your own business best.'

'Oh yes,' she said, an odd, defiant expression in her eyes. 'I know exactly what I'm doing. I was young and foolish once and certain people took advantage of that . . . but I'm wiser now and I shan't be cheated again. You can be quite certain of that.'

A chill went down my spine. There was something here I felt was unpleasant, something that frightened me, though I didn't know why it should. I wanted to beg her to be careful, but I held back, sensing that she wouldn't listen. I still didn't know my sister very well, but I had come to realize there was a reckless streak in her – a tiny demon in her head that drove her to do things that others might fear.

Nick Ryan picked us up as arranged at eight o'clock that evening. He was driving a very new and expensive Mercedes, which smelt of leather inside and was as fast on the road as it was sleek to look at.

Athena insisted on sitting in the back, forcing me to take the seat beside him. I was very conscious of the power of the car, the speed at which he drove along the motorway – and the underlying fury of the man himself.

Why was he angry? What had Athena done to him? Or was it me who had aroused this simmering fury?

However, his manner as we ate at the exclusive restaurant on the harbour in Puerto Banus could not have been more charming. He was attentive, generous in ordering the best of everything, including a very rare and fine champagne (which I noticed he hardly touched himself) and, when a party of Athena's friends attached themselves to us towards the end of our meal, agreeable to suggestions for going on to a popular nightclub.

'Why not?' he asked when Athena looked to him for approval. 'The night is young and I have plenty of time . . .'

I was not sure why that statement sent chills down my spine, but it did. I sensed something going on beneath the surface – something that perhaps worried my sister, even though she was not prepared to let it show.

What hold did he have over her? I wondered. Was he blackmailing her in some way? Did he know something about her that she was ashamed of, or frightened of revealing?

The nightclub was softly lit, smoky and pulsating with the beat of hypnotic music. Outside the night air was sultry, still reflecting the heat of the day. Nick found a table by an open window, where there was a welcome breath of air, then signalled to a waiter to bring us drinks. One of the men in the new party had asked Athena to dance and several of the others had followed them on to the dance floor in the adjoining room. Suddenly, I was alone with Nick.

'Do you want to dance?' he asked. 'If you do we'll wait for something slower.'

'All right,' I said, looking at him hard. 'How long have you known my sister?'

'Eleven . . . twelve years, I suppose.'

'Before she went to America then?'

'Yes . . . before that.' He was frowning. 'Hasn't she told you about me?'

I shook my head, eyes narrowing as I saw what I thought was guilt in his face. 'What is there to tell?'

'You must ask her,' he said. 'I don't tell tales out of school.'

'Oh . . .'

'Don't jump to conclusions,' he advised and looked at me through cold eyes. 'You didn't say you were coming out here when we talked that day in the park.'

'I didn't know. Athena rang up in a mood of depression and I caught the first available flight.'

'Do you usually do everything she asks?'

'No . . . she doesn't usually ask. We've hardly seen each other for years. Not after she was twenty really. She didn't come to visit us at the house after she left home in a hurry – though she did have me to stay with her for a couple of holidays. She came back to London on a flying visit once.'

He nodded, looking at me thoughtfully. 'Do you have any idea why she left?'

'She quarrelled with my aunt – something about getting into bad company, I think.'

He was silent, a brooding expression in his eyes. 'So you don't really know her very well?'

'She writes and phones now and then. We've had a couple of holidays together but no . . .' I realized that even now my sister had revealed very little of her private thoughts to me. 'No, I don't suppose I do know her . . . not well.'

'That figures.' He sipped his mineral water. 'So, when are you going home?'

'At the end of the week . . . at least that's when my flight is booked. Athena was talking about me staying on longer, but I don't think I shall. Sandy is expecting me back.'

'Sandy?' His brows rose. 'The man in your life?'

'Just a female friend – and soon my business partner. We're hoping to open a boutique sooner than I'd thought.' I hesitated, then took the plunge. 'I was going to ring you. I thought you might give me some advice on how to set up a business . . . the practical stuff.'

'Can you afford my rates?' He wasn't smiling, his manner intent, challenging. 'Or did you expect me to do it for free?'

'I suppose I was hoping you would.'

Surprising me, he laughed. 'At least you're honest, Julia, that's something. A lot of people I meet in a social way offer to pay, hoping I'll turn down the offer and do it out of friendship.'

'And do you?'

'No. I charge them the same as anyone else.'

'Well, it's what you do for a living. I suppose you could do it for nothing all the time if you liked.'

'Ring me,' he said. 'If you've got a business plan I'll look at it and give you my opinion for what it's worth – but don't show me rubbish. I can't put up with fools playing at business. You're either in it to make money or you might as well give up before you start.'

'We'll work it out properly first,' I promised. 'And thanks.'

'If it's the only way I'm going to get you to give me your

phone number . . .' He smiled with his eyes this time, seeming to shake off the mood that had clung to him all evening. 'They're playing my kind of music now – shall we?'

I stood up and gave him my hand. The music had changed from a jungle beat to something soft and dreamy. As Nick drew me close, I shut my eyes and leaned my head against his shoulder, breathing in the mixture of expensive after-shave and his own particular body musk, which was even more intoxicating. He was a very exciting man to be with and dancing with him had an all too predictable effect on me.

His breath was warm and sweet against my face. I liked the feeling of being in his arms and knew that he was enjoying the contact, too. From that first moment in the park, when our eyes met, I had been aware of something . . . something pulling us together. It would be very easy to become involved with this man.

When the music changed suddenly, back to a wild, pul-sating beat that shook the room, I was disappointed. Nick released me, lifting his brows as if to ask if I wanted to go on dancing. I shook my head and we turned together, threading our way back through the tables.

'Where is Athena?' I asked of one of the other women who had just returned from the powder room. 'She isn't dancing. Is she in the cloakroom?'

'Oh, didn't she tell you?' one of the men said. 'She had a headache and decided to go home. She seemed to think you would follow when you were ready, said she didn't want to spoil your evening.'

'A headache . . . was it bad?' I looked at Nick, anxious without knowing why. 'Would you mind if we left? I think she must be ill if she went off like that without a word to me.'

'Do you?' He seemed to doubt it. 'In my experience Athena usually does exactly what she wants – and she knew I would take you home.'

I gave him an angry look as we went outside to his car. The port was crowded with expensive yachts, their lights twinkling like tiny jewels out on the dark water; the harbour itself packed edge to edge with Ferrari and Mercedes sports cars. I felt somehow out of my depth in this world of opulence and riches, and my uneasiness made me strike out.

'You have no right to say such things,' I said. 'She wouldn't have left like that unless she had a good reason.'

'Oh yes, I'm sure she had a reason. It just might not be the one you imagine, that's all.'

'Why do you hate her?' I snapped. 'What has she done to you?'

'What makes you think I hate her?' he asked mildly. 'Athena is a selfish woman, Julia. If you ever learn to know her you will understand that – but she has a lot of charm and I don't hate her. She makes me angry at times, and there are others who may feel less than friendly towards her, but she can be generous to her friends.'

His attitude towards my sister made me annoyed with him. I maintained a distance between us as he drove me home. Athena was not selfish, at least, I'd never found her so – and I didn't like Nick finding fault with her so easily.

The gates opened when his car approached. Carla must have been waiting for us. Nick stopped outside them, leaving the Mercedes' engine running. I looked at him before getting out.

'Don't you want to come in?'

'No, I don't think so,' he replied. 'I've decided to fly back home in the morning. Tell Athena – and remind her I'll be in touch soon.'

'All right . . .' I hesitated, uncertain now. 'You won't mind if I ring you when I get back?'

'I'll be disappointed if you don't,' he said, smiling in a way that made my stomach clench suddenly with desire. 'I'm sorry if I spoke out of turn, Julia. I don't dislike Athena – I just accept her for who and what she is, that's all.'

'I – I love her,' I croaked. 'I may not know her well, but I do love her.'

'Why shouldn't you?' He smiled again. 'Good night, Julia. I'll look forward to that call . . .'

The gates shut behind me with a hollow clang. I stood just inside them, watching the tail lights of Nick's car disappear down the hill, then sighed and walked towards the house.

It was all a bit of a mystery the history that Nick and Athena seemed to share. It was a very strange coincidence that he and Athena were old friends and that I had met him in the park. However, Athena had lived a full and busy life in New York, and Nick Ryan obviously spent a lot of time there . . . so why did it seem ominous to me? Why did I find the idea that they had been involved in the past so worrying?

I entered the house to be greeted by an anxious-looking Carla.

'Is Miss Andrews not with you?'

'No . . .' I stared at her. 'I thought she was coming home. I was told she had a headache . . .'

'She is so reckless,' Carla muttered. I sensed that she was really upset. 'Always she does this . . . risking so much . . .'

'What do you mean?' I felt a thrill of fear. 'Where is she, Carla? Where do you think she has gone?'

'How should I know? She comes and goes as she pleases.' A shuttered look had come over her face, as if she realized she had said too much. 'She will come back when she is ready. It is not for us to question her.'

'Where is Miguel?' I asked. 'Is he here? Do you think he ought to go back to Puerto Banus and look for her?'

She seemed to hesitate, then shook her head. 'It would make her angry. You do not know her temper. She would not like it if she thought we were spying on her. Go to bed, Miss Stevens – and forget what I said. Please?'

'Yes . . . of course,' I agreed. 'Good night, Carla. I was told she had come home – but perhaps she went on somewhere else with another friend? She seems to have so many of them.'

'Yes, yes, she will be with a friend,' Carla said. 'Excuse me now. I must make sure that everything is locked up for the night.'

I was thoughtful as I went to my own room and undressed. Why was Carla so worried about my sister? I'd had a feeling for some days that things were not entirely as they seemed, that beneath the endless round of pleasure and parties there was something my sister wasn't sharing with me. I sensed something was wrong, but it wasn't easy to put my finger on exactly what was making me uneasy.

I'd been here for over a week now, and I still knew no more about my sister's past than I had before I came. She talked about friends she knew, places she had seen – but told me nothing about her own life. She must have had several relationships in the past, but she never spoke of a man by name . . . never mentioned having lived with someone . . . or having loved someone.

In her brief letters to me, she had sometimes said she was having a relationship, that she was happy or bored, but when I thought about it there was never a name . . . never many details.

The only man she had ever spoken of by name was Hans Werner – and she'd said that wasn't love.

As I undressed, my thoughts veered away from Athena to her surprise visitor. Nick Ryan was as much a mystery as my sister – and I had an odd feeling that if I solved the puzzle of one, I would reveal the other.

'Athena!' I cried as I went out on to the patio the next morning and saw her relaxing with a cup of fragrant, black coffee in one of the basket chairs. 'When did you get back? I was worried when I got home last night and found you weren't here.'

'Sorry, Julia,' she said. 'I left a message for you.'

'They told me you had a headache. Where did you get to?'

'I heard that Hans was back,' she said, 'so I called him and he asked me to come over. I took a taxi . . .' She smiled, naughtily. 'He brought me home half an hour ago. Are you shocked because I spent the night with him?'

'No, of course not. But you might have told me. Carla was quite worried about you.'

'Carla always worries,' she said dismissively. 'Sometimes I must have my private life. I did not tell you because I didn't want to. I'm sorry if that offends you, but it is the way I am.'

Was this the selfishness Nick had accused her of showing

sometimes? She did have the right to privacy, of course, but I *had* been worried for a while.

'Nick brought me home,' I said, changing the subject. 'He says he is flying back to London this morning, and will be in touch soon. He asked me to remind you – he said it as if it was important.'

Athena yawned and nodded. 'Nick knows what he has to do,' she said carelessly. 'It is not important. He is not on my list of priorities. I don't know why he is bothered.'

'What do you mean? Is he one of the people you said owed you something?'

'Nick?' She laughed to herself as if what I had said was very funny. 'He might have something to say to that. No, no, Julia. It's just something he wants, that I may have somewhere. Forget it. I have no quarrel with Nick, which he ought to have known if he'd thought about it instead of flying off the handle. That little argument you saw was my fault. Really, you mustn't blame him.' She gave me a direct look. 'I think you rather like Nick, don't you?'

'I might. I'm not sure how I feel about him yet. We don't know each other well enough.'

'Then I should advise you to be very careful,' she said. 'I'm not telling you how to run your life, Julia – I'm the last person to do that! – but men like that are for life or not at all, believe me.'

'Were you . . . ?' I hesitated, thinking she might resent the intrusion into her past. 'I mean did you and he . . .'

'Have an affair?' Her fine brows arched mockingly. 'We had a relationship years ago, but we didn't sleep together if that's bothering you. It was heading that way but . . . something happened.' She shook her head as I questioned with my eyes. 'No, that is something I'm not going to tell you. He might one day, but that's up to him.'

I accepted this in silence, then: 'Have you ever been in love, Athena? I mean really in love – not just sex.'

'The lie down and let him walk all over you bit?' She pulled a wry face. 'Yes – once. Believe me, that was enough. He did walk all over me. If it wasn't for . . .' For a moment there was such bitterness and anger in her face that I was shocked, then it disappeared as if it had never been. 'Well, that's all over now. I've done very nicely for myself so I shouldn't complain.'

'But you don't love Hans?'

'No,' she said. 'I don't love him, but I might marry him. He's a millionaire, you know – probably a billionaire if the truth were told. Yes, I might marry him, Julia. I haven't quite decided what to do about Hans just yet . . .'

Four

The sound of an alarm bell going off in the house woke me that night. As I jumped out of bed, I could see the floodlights were on outside, and, in the few seconds it took me to pull on my bathrobe, I heard three sharp, cracking noises like a gun firing. I was about to go out on to the patio when my bedroom door opened and Athena rushed in.

'Don't!' she cried. 'Stay inside, Julia. Miguel will deal with it.'

'What's going on? I thought I heard shots?'

'Miguel probably fired his starter pistol as a warning. We've had an intruder, but whoever it was will have gone by now.'

'Starter pistol?' It had sounded more powerful to me. My nerves jangled as I fired a volley of questions at her. 'Did he get into the house, Athena? Have you rung the police? You're not hurt, are you?'

'No, of course not.' She smiled, but couldn't hide the fact that she had been scared, if only for a moment. 'There's no need for the police. A lot of villas and apartments have been burgled recently, but there isn't much the police can do. It's a fact of life, Julia. I expect whoever it was, was more frightened than we were when all the lights and alarms started going off.'

'I didn't even know you had them,' I said, feeling bewildered and wondering why she had so much security. 'I could have wandered outside and set them off without realizing.'

'They aren't always switched on,' she said, frowning. 'I had them installed for Carla's sake, she's always so nervous. Personally, I think they cause too much trouble.'

'I agree with Carla. You obviously need them. You might have been attacked, Athena.'

47

She shrugged carelessly. 'If it happens, it happens,' she said. 'Nothing is for ever. I'm going to have a cup of tea in the kitchen – what about you?'

'Yes, please. I shan't settle after this anyway.'

'Don't worry,' she said. 'Whoever it was, Miguel will make sure he has gone.'

I followed her into the kitchen. Carla was pouring boiling water into a pot. Dressed in a bright pink bathrobe and slippers, she looked upset and more vulnerable than her daytime self.

'I was going to bring you a tray,' she said to Athena. 'And you, Miss Stevens.'

'We'll have it here with you, Carla.' Athena went to put a comforting arm round her shoulders. 'Don't upset yourself. It's all right. It was just someone who hopped over the wall in the hope of finding something worth taking. Nothing to worry about.'

'That's what you say,' Carla muttered gruffly. 'After what happened the last time . . .'

'Has it happened before?' I looked at my sister anxiously.

'Not here.' Athena directed a meaningful glance at her housekeeper. 'The apartment in New York was ransacked – and a janitor was injured. It wasn't just my apartment that time, Julia. The security at the building was breached and several people were burgled. Understandably, it made Carla nervous.'

'Is that why you decided to come out here?'

'It might have been one of the reasons.'

'Oh, Athena! And now it has happened again.'

'It's not the same,' she said and looked annoyed, as if we were making too much fuss. 'This was a bit scary because it woke us up suddenly, but it's not serious.'

The outer door opened and Miguel came in. He was wearing only a pair of dark coloured shorts and leather mules on his feet. In his hand was a wicked-looking gun that was most certainly not a starter pistol.

'It was gypsies,' he said. 'Two of them. They came over the wall and the lights caught them. They were trying to get out again – I made it easier for them.' He grinned as he laid his gun down. 'They won't be coming back in a hurry, believe me.'

'There you are!' Athena threw a triumphant look at Carla. 'I told you that was all it was. They probably thought the villa was empty and unprotected, the way so many of them are half the time.'

Carla looked unconvinced, but I was relieved.

'I wondered why you had those heavy security gates,' I said, 'but now I understand. Especially if there are a lot of break-ins going on.'

'Oh yes,' Athena said carelessly. 'It's quite a problem on the costas. Usually it's just the gypsies taking advantage of foreigners, who leave their holiday homes unprotected.' She finished drinking her tea, yawned lazily and smiled, apparently taking the whole thing in her stride. 'I think I'll go back to bed. Don't forget that Miguel is driving us both to Granada tomorrow, Julia. Touring the Alhambra is quite strenuous and if you don't get some rest you'll be dead on your feet.'

'Yes, all right,' I said and kissed her cheek. 'Good night again – or is it good morning?'

I was thoughtful as I went back to my bedroom. Why was Carla so nervous? The villa was well protected and Miguel obviously acted as a bodyguard to my sister – but why did she need one? What was it that no one was telling me?

The rest of my stay at Athena's villa passed without incident. My sister had decided to devote herself to me and we went everywhere, to all the places she laughingly dismissed as being meant for the tourists, including a dolphin safari off Gibraltar and the crocodile park in the Guadalhorce Valley. We also went to a gala night at the casino of the Fortuna nightclub, where I watched my sister gamble the equivalent of several hundred pounds.

'Don't look so worried,' she said as she saw the expression on my face. 'This is peanuts. Besides, I can control my gambling. I know just how far I can go, believe me.'

Her eyes held a strange glitter, and I sensed she wasn't only talking about the euro she had hazarded at the tables.

I smiled and shook my head at her. It was her money, she was entitled to spend it as she pleased – and she had spent generously on me, buying me shoes, bags and a gold chain set with coral beads.

I tried to stop her, but she said I was a spoilsport and she was only doing what she had wanted to do for years. I thanked her, hugged her, and told her how much it meant to me to be with her.

'I love you, Julia,' she said, looking serious for once. 'You and . . . well, there are one or two others I care about, but you most of all.'

Before I knew it she was seeing me off at the airport.

'I'm so glad you came over,' she said, hugging me. 'We shan't leave it so long in future. You can spend your holidays with me, Julia – and I'll visit you in London sometimes.'

'Yes, you must,' I said and hugged her again. 'I know we haven't been close in the past but I want us to be from now on, Athena. If you're worried or upset, ring me. I do love you.'

'I love you, too.'

'Thanks for helping Sandy and me with the business. It's a loan to both of us, which means we'll be on an equal footing. And we will pay you back one day, I promise.'

'Don't worry about it. There's plenty more where that came from. Believe me, money is the least of my worries.'

She hesitated, as if on the verge of telling me something, then we heard a flight announcement.

'That's your flight, Julia.'

'I'd better go through. I'll be in touch.'

'Ring me sometime,' she said. 'And be happy, babe.'

'I shall . . .' I waved as I walked through departures. 'Take care of yourself – and good luck with Hans.'

Just before I went through into the departure lounge I turned to look once more. Athena was still in the building, standing there alone. I had a sudden odd feeling, as if she were in some kind of danger, and I almost turned back – then she caught sight of me, smiled and waved. I dismissed my silly fears and went through.

Athena would be all right. She had Carla and Miguel . . . and she was enjoying herself having a wild fling with Hans. She was an independent woman, not a vulnerable girl, and she would not thank me for interfering in her life. There was no reason for me to worry about her, none at all.

My telephone was ringing when I got into my flat after paying off the taxi. I dumped my cases and bags on the floor and snatched it up, breathing hard.

'Hello . . .' I said. 'Julia Stevens speaking . . .'

There was an odd crackling sound and then the line went dead on me. I stared at it in annoyance before replacing the receiver. It sounded as if it might have been someone trying to get through on a mobile and that meant it could have been anyone – most of my friends had them these days, so no help there – though I didn't think it could have been Sandy. She'd had one for a while, but gave it up because she thought it too expensive.

I went into the kitchen to make coffee, and just as I was about to pour myself a cup the phone rang again. I snatched it up.

'Hello . . .'

'Hi – so you're home then.' The man's voice sent tingles down my spine. 'I've been ringing you for days, then one of your neighbours told me you were coming back today.'

'Ben . . .' I sighed. 'Why do you bother? We've been through this so many times. You know my answer.'

'I miss you, Julia. Can't we just have a drink together? I'm not asking for anything more. Just an hour of your time.'

'What's the point? It's over. You're married – and you can't tell me it isn't a proper marriage. Not when Sheila is having your child.'

'You hate me for that, don't you?'

'No, I don't hate you, Ben. I just don't want to go out with you again. Not now – not ever. You lied to me, over and over again. Honestly, I don't think you're worth the effort.'

'Bitch!'

I stared at the phone as it went dead, then hung up. It was

the first time Ben had ever spoken to me like that; he usually tried persuasion. If anything had been needed to harden my resolve then his reaction was it.

When the phone rang again a few minutes later I almost didn't answer it. If it was Ben, he was going to hear something he wouldn't like.

'Yes – who is it?'

'Shall I hang up and ring again?'

I laughed as I heard Sandy's voice.

'Ben was just on the phone. He called me a bitch because I wouldn't go for a drink with him.'

'I wish I'd been there,' she said, a grim note in her voice. 'So – how did things go with your sister?'

'Great. I had a wonderful holiday,' I said. 'She has lent us ten thousand pounds, Sandy. Isn't that wonderful?'

'Terrific!' she cried, the excitement rising in her voice. 'I've managed to scrape up a couple of thousand extra and, with what you've already got saved, it should be enough to get us started at least. I've been having some costings done while you were away, Julia. If we can come up with a good business plan we might be able to get further backing, if we need it.'

'Athena says she'll let us have more later on,' I said, 'but I really think we have more than enough to give us a good start. I've been looking round some of the boutiques in Marbella, and I noticed that a lot of the designs are only produced in two or three popular sizes. We'll be trying to attract young women, so we can start with the smaller sizes and increase the range as we go – and we can always have a made-to-measure service for larger customers. That way we'll have a greater turnover of stock, because we'll know if something works or not – and we shan't be stuck with rails of stock that doesn't move.'

'What we need is a reliable team to make our stuff up,' Sandy said, 'and I think I've found them. They're a brother and sister and they've just started their own small business, too. They do have some regular work for one of the big chains, but they like the idea of working for exclusive designers like us. If we make a success of it, they could come over to us full-time.'

'You have been busy,' I said and laughed. 'And all I've been doing is sunning myself.'

'You got us the money,' Sandy said. 'I told Bernard and Susie we might go down this weekend – they've got a cottage in Cambridgeshire and they've invited us to Sunday lunch. I've already seen the quality of their work, and it's good, but you'll want to check it out before we sign any agreements.'

'Have you seen any premises that look right for us?'

'Not yet – but I've got details of two that might suit us. I thought we would take a look tomorrow. If we can find what we want, we could open up with a fresh look for autumn – what do you think?'

'The sooner the better,' I said. 'One thing I did do while I was away, was to work on a few ideas for jackets and skirts. It's a range that can be mixed and matched, and includes both long jackets and short, all in toning shades. I'll show you tomorrow.'

'Sounds good to me,' she said. 'I would come over now, but I have a date tonight.'

'Someone new?'

'Yes, as a matter of fact.' She sounded a little shy. 'I'll tell you about it tomorrow. I have to go now.'

'Bye then . . .' I sighed as I replaced the receiver. After spending the last two weeks with Athena, I was going to find this evening rather long. 'See you tomorrow.'

I hung up then finished my coffee and headed for the shower. I was about to step under it when the phone rang again.

'Is that you, Julia?'

'Yes – who is this please?'

'It's Nick Ryan. I thought you might be home. How do you feel about dinner this evening?'

'Oh . . .' I caught my breath, my heart going on a dizzy spiral of conflicting emotions. For a moment I couldn't answer, then realized it was exactly what I wanted. I'd tried to put Nick out of my mind these past few days, but the thought of him had lingered. 'Yes, I'd like that. Where shall we meet?'

'I'll pick you up at eight. OK?'

'Do you know where to come?'

I heard his laughter at the other end. 'You are in the phone book, you know. See you later . . .'

My heart was beating very fast as I replaced the receiver. Yes, I was in the book, but so were several other J. Stevens. Nick must have rung them all to be sure which was my number – and I was almost certain he was ringing from a mobile. Had he tried to ring me earlier?

I was thoughtful as I headed for the shower. It had been in my mind to ring his business number in the morning, but he had got there first. Which must mean that he wanted to see me . . .

I was wearing a simple black suit I had designed and made myself when I opened the door to Nick at five to eight that evening. He took a good look and smiled approvingly.

'And I'm early,' he said. 'You look stunning in that, Julia. Is it your own design?'

'Yes. How did you guess?'

'Just a hunch. It looks like a one-off, not something you could buy in a high street store.'

'This is the kind of thing I want to specialize in,' I said, inviting him in. 'Smart, exciting clothes the young, modern woman can wear right through the day and into evening if she likes. But I want them to look different, because so many shops sell things that look the same as their rivals.' I paused to look at him. 'Would you like a drink or shall we go straightaway?'

'I don't drink much,' Nick said. 'Just the occasional beer on a hot day – or a sip of wine with dinner. You may have noticed?'

'Yes, I have,' I said. 'Is there a reason?'

'Yes, but not one that need bother you. I don't have an addiction.'

'I didn't imagine you did. I think you have most things under control, don't you, Nick?' I picked up my bag and glanced round. Everything was off that ought to be. 'I'm ready . . .'

'Let's go then. I've a table reserved at Langans – all right with you?'

'Fine.' I smiled as he took my key and locked the door behind us. 'Yes, make sure it's double locked. I'm thinking of increasing my security after what happened at the villa the other night.' He raised his brows at me as we walked into the lift. 'Some gypsies came over the wall and set off the alarms in the middle of the night. They ran off when Miguel fired into the air, but it makes you think.'

'I doubt if you need the same security as your sister.'

'What makes you say that? Do you know something I don't?'

'Why do you ask that?'

'It's just a feeling . . .' I looked at him. 'You would tell me if you knew, wouldn't you?'

'Your sister may have made enemies in the past,' he said. 'She worked in that kind of a world. It was glamorous on the outside no doubt, but underneath there must have been a lot more going on – drugs and various other unsavoury activities. I imagine that is why she employs a bodyguard, don't you?'

'I suppose there must have been. You hear about it all the time,' I agreed. 'I've never thought about that side of it. Athena told me once she hated drugs and would never touch them. She never talked much about her work. I know she was a model. I've seen some pictures of her in designer clothes posing for the camera.'

'Did she send them to you?'

'Yes. A couple of times. Why?'

'No reason.' He frowned. 'I shouldn't worry about Athena too much if I were you. I imagine she has all the angles covered.'

'You don't like her much, do you?'

'I don't dislike her,' he said, opening the door for me to go outside. 'I've no illusions concerning Athena. I've learned not to expect anything from her, that's all. I know you don't like me saying it, Julia, but she is selfish.'

'Not with me. She lent me ten thousand pounds to start my business – and doesn't care when she gets it back. She says I only need to ask and I can have more.'

'Athena cares about you,' he said. 'Maybe that's her saving

grace.' He saw my face, realized he was getting in too deep and frowned. 'Why don't we make a pact not to talk about her? I'm far more interested in you.'

'Are you?'

He was hailing a taxi. When it drew into the kerb, he spoke to the driver, then opened the door, following me inside.

'Why don't we let things take their own course?' he said and smiled. 'We don't have to let the past spoil things for us, Julia. Neither of us were born yesterday. Let's see what the future brings, shall we?'

I nodded, then sat back, watching the lights of London flash by. Nick was right, we both had a past, but that didn't mean we couldn't have a future together – did it?

I wasn't sure. I sneaked a look at his profile. He was certainly good to look at, and I already knew there was a strong physical attraction between us. That dance in the nightclub in Puerto Banus had told me that, if I hadn't already sensed it. But was I ready for another affair?

Maybe I wouldn't have chosen to get involved just yet, but there isn't always a choice. I sensed it was now or never as far as Nick was concerned – so maybe I would just let things drift and see how they worked out.

Three hours later, Nick unlocked my door for me and stood back for me to go inside, holding the key out to me as I hesitated.

'Are you coming in?' I asked, catching my breath as I gazed up into his eyes. The look I saw there told me exactly what to expect if he accepted my invitation.

'Do you want me to?' he asked, huskily. 'Are you sure? I don't want to rush you, Julia.'

'I'm not sure of anything,' I replied honestly, 'but I do want you to stay – if you want to?'

'You know the answer to that one.' He walked in, closed the door behind him and reached out for me, drawing me into his arms and bending his head to take possession of my lips. And possession was the right word; Nick wasn't the new man, who could be led around on a chain, but I had always known that – it was what made him both exciting and dangerous. 'I've been wanting to do this ever since I first saw you in the park.'

Desire from him surged through me in a white hot flame. I no longer cared what was right or wrong, or that I might regret this afterwards, all I knew was that this feeling would not be stilled. I clung to him, my body moulding to his as though I might melt right into him.

'Oh . . .' I whispered. 'I knew it would be like this . . . Nick . . .'

I'm not sure how we managed to get to the bedroom. Our things were scattered in a trail on the floor as we hastily helped each other to undress, buttons flying in our sudden haste. We couldn't wait, either of us. It had never been this way for me before, a pulsating eagerness that had me panting with longing to taste and touch every last piece of his body.

'You're so beautiful,' I breathed as my hands explored his chest, my fingers moving in the sprinkling of crisp dark hair. 'I've never, ever wanted anyone this much before.'

His mouth covered mine as he scooped me up and carried me the last few inches to the bed; he was kissing me . . . my lips, my eyelids, my throat, making me arch and gasp with pleasure. His mouth moved down my flat navel to the moist hair between my thighs, tasting, invading the secret places of my femininity, his flicking tongue sending me wild with longing until he lowered his hard, firm body to mine and, with one sudden thrust, drove the length of his huge, throbbing penis inside me.

I gave a cry of pleasure, arching to meet him as he began to move with a slow, sensual rhythm that set me bucking and moaning beneath him.

'That's so good . . .' I cried. 'Oh, so good . . .'

'You're lovely,' he murmured. 'As sweet and warm as I expected. Give yourself to me completely, Julia, come with me, darling . . .'

'Ohhh . . .' I moaned frantically as the spasms shook my body again and again, making me curl my legs over his back as we climaxed as one. This had never happened to me like this before, not these multiple orgasms that made me scream out his name. 'Nick . . . Ohhh . . . NICK!'

'Julia . . .' He buried his head in my breasts as we subsided into a panting heap. 'You lovely, lovely woman.'

I curled into him as he rolled over on his side, taking me with him, holding me pressed against him as if we could never again find where the one ended and the other began. We lay like that for a long time, then at last he released me and lay on his back, staring up at the ceiling.

'A cigarette would be good now,' he said, 'but I don't any more.'

'I never have. Aunt Margaret did and they killed her at forty-five.' I turned my face to look at him. 'Coffee . . . or ice cream?'

'Ice cream?' His brows went up and I could see the amusement in his eyes – a warm, teasing laughter that made me want to join in. 'So now I'm discovering your vices. That's a bit decadent, isn't it?'

'I'm thirsty and ice cream is cool on the throat – so what is it to be?'

'Coffee for me,' he said. 'But I'll get it – if you point me in the right direction.'

'I'll show you – and I think I'll have some ice cream.' I got out of bed, was about to reach for a dressing robe and changed my mind. It was too late for modesty now. 'The kitchen is through here – and ground coffee is in the jar marked sugar, because I never use sugar.'

'Sounds about right,' he said, grinning as I dived into the fridge and brought out a tub of special luxury ice cream. 'And what is in the jar marked coffee, may one ask?'

'Instant coffee – the other is fresh.'

He nodded and reached for the filter machine, filling it with water from a bottle in the fridge, then scooping in the rich roasted beans I'd bought earlier.

'Smells good – this about right?'

'Yes . . .' I spooned some of the ice cream into my mouth, then offered him the next spoonful. He tasted it and smiled. 'Sure you don't want some?'

'No thanks.' He was watching as I leaned against the door. 'Are you going to take a shower? If not, I would like to while the coffee is brewing.'

'Are you not staying the night?'

'Not this time,' he said, and kissed me on the shoulder. 'I'm expecting some calls later – and I have some reports to finish.'

'Calls at this hour?' He nodded. 'Oh, I suppose there's a time difference in New York.'

He wrinkled his brow. 'There are a lot of different time zones, Julia. Another evening, I'll have my calls routed here, but a couple of them are important; I can't leave them to the answering machine – so I have to go.'

'OK. I understand.'

I went into the bedroom, slipping on my robe as he headed for the shower. When he came out to the kitchen fully dressed, I had the coffee waiting.

'Sugar or cream?'

'Neither, thanks.' He took the mug I offered and drank a few sips, nodding appreciatively. 'Not bad. I'll give you the name of the brand I prefer for future reference. That's if you're going to invite me back again?'

'Of course – if you want to come?'

'Oh yes, I want to come – just the way we did earlier,' he said and grinned wickedly. 'I'll be in touch, Julia. I must go now.'

'Don't you want to ring for a taxi?'

'I'll pick one up, I expect,' he said. 'It's not much past midnight.'

He leaned towards me. I caught the fresh tang of shower gel as his lips touched mine briefly.

'Be seeing you,' he said. 'Take care of yourself, Julia.'

I watched as the door closed behind him, then headed for the bathroom myself. Stepping under the shower I was aware of a feeling of anti-climax. It had been so good with Nick in bed – but now I felt bereft, deserted. I wanted him here with me. I wanted to talk . . . to share the silly things, like making breakfast together and reading the papers in bed.

Besides, making love with Nick once wasn't enough. It had been a glorious experience, but I discovered as I returned to bed to inhale the scent of his body on my pillows, I already wanted him again. Closing my eyes, I could almost feel him beside me, inside me.

I groaned as the desire welled up in me. Being with Nick was addictive. Just as I'd suspected from the first, which meant that the parting when it came was going to hurt like hell. Breaking up with Ben had hurt my pride as much as anything; I knew it was going to be different this time. I already knew that Nick meant more to me than any other man I had ever known.

The knowledge scared me a little. But it was too late now. I had let Nick into my life and nothing was ever going to be the same again.

Five

Sandy looked at me in despair as we came out of the third property we had viewed that morning.

'It was so tiny!' she said. 'And they want six months rent in advance – that's half our capital gone before we start.'

'We might have to wait for a while,' I said, frowning. 'Or I might be able to take out a second mortgage on my flat.'

Oh, Julia.' She sighed deeply. 'This is getting a bit frightening. Maybe we need to think again?'

'Let's not give up yet,' I said. 'We'll find something we can afford. Come on, let's go and have a coffee.'

'All right – but I don't see us getting a place with rents as high as those we've seen this morning.'

'Maybe we're looking in the wrong places. People like us do start their own businesses, Sandy, if only in a small way. Don't worry. We'll find something.'

'I'd hoped it would be settled before we went down to see Bernard and Susie this weekend.'

'We're going ahead with our plans,' I said. 'We might not be able to sell our clothes in the way we'd planned. We might have to start out in one of those small units in a converted warehouse, similar to those we looked at earlier, but I'm not giving in now. Even if I have to ask Athena for more money.'

'You're tough,' Sandy said and grinned. 'Did you have a chance to show anyone the business plan yet?'

'No . . .' I was waiting for Nick to ring but I didn't want to tell Sandy about my personal involvement with him. 'I'll probably leave it until we get back on Sunday. I'll be more certain of the facts by then.'

'I'm sure you're going to like Bernard,' Sandy said, looking a little self-conscious. 'Susie too, of course.'

'It's the quality of their work that counts,' I replied. Sandy had confessed that Bernard was the new man in her life. I wasn't sure it was a good idea to mix business and romance, but if the brother and sister could supply what we needed, which was good cutting and finishing, I wouldn't make an unnecessary fuss over Sandy's private arrangements. 'We're going to be selling an up-market product. We can't afford to be let down on quality.'

'We can always do a bit of hand finishing ourselves if we have to,' she said. 'It isn't as though we can afford to employ our own cutters and machinists yet.'

'No, but that doesn't mean we have to accept less than the best work available, Sandy.'

'They *are* good. I promise you they are.'

'Then everything will work out,' I said. 'Come on – I'm dying for a coffee.'

I wasn't going to be going out that evening, even if I hadn't wanted to stay by the phone . . . if I hadn't been waiting for Nick to ring.

It wasn't one of my nights for my health club, and I had a lot of work to do anyway. I'd already converted some of my ideas into patterns, and I was going to make up a few items from what I thought of as my 'Spanish' collection. It wouldn't be practical for Sandy or I to try making everything ourselves; we were going to be far too busy running the business and designing our future ranges once we had the boutique open, but a few samples would give the firm we were thinking of using an idea of the standards we expected from them.

At college, I'd studied every angle of the fashion business, from the first tentative sketches of a garment right through to the wearable article. Once the business was up and running, we would employ specialists in pattern making and cutting, but I was good at these things myself and felt I would always want to be closely involved. The secret of a perfect fit was getting these basics right.

I'd liked the embroidered jackets I'd seen in Marbella, but thought them a bit too fancy for English taste. Just one piece of embroidery, perhaps on the cuffs or maybe the pockets, would look classy without going over the top.

I was trying out some fancy stitching on a sample of material when the telephone shrilled. My heart jumped and then started to race wildly. It had to be Nick. Waiting for him to get in touch was agony. He had promised to ring soon.

I snatched up the receiver. 'Hi – Julia speaking.'

'Julia Stevens?'

It was a man's voice, but one I didn't recognize. It had an odd, muffled sound that made me uneasy.

'Yes. Who is this please?'

'Just shut up and listen. Tell your sister to back off or she will regret it.'

My heart caught with fright. 'Who are you? What are you talking about?'

'Shut your mouth, bitch. She'll know who it is. Just give her the message.'

The phone went dead suddenly. For a moment, I was too stunned to move. I felt sick and my hand trembled as I replaced the receiver. The threat in his voice had been almost physical. I took a deep breath and snatched up the phone again, then keyed in 1471, listening to the operator's voice.

'You were called today at eighteen twenty. The number has not been recognized.'

So whoever had rung me had withheld their number. Why would they do that? What was the point, unless they wanted to make sure I could not trace them?

Who had rung me to get to Athena? Who knew she was my sister? My closest friends, of course, but it wasn't one of them. Someone I had met in Spain? The voice had sounded odd – perhaps disguised by a handkerchief over the mouthpiece? But why ring me? Why not speak to Athena herself?

Was my sister in danger? What had she done to make someone that angry? Because he had been very angry, whoever he was. I'd sensed something was going on beneath the surface of her life when I stayed with her, and I believed her capable of reckless behaviour. Was she mixed up in something dangerous? Was that why Carla was so nervous?

63

I dialled Athena's number in Spain. It rang for several minutes before being answered.

'Yes. Miss Andrews' residence. Who is calling, please?'

'It's Julia. May I speak to Athena, please?'

'Oh, Miss Stevens,' Carla said. 'I'm sorry. She isn't in this evening. Shall I ask her to call you back in the morning?'

'Yes . . .' I hesitated. 'I'm leaving here at ten tomorrow. I'll be away the whole day. If I miss her, I'll ring again tomorrow evening. You will tell her it is important, please?'

'Very well, Miss Stevens.'

'Oh, Carla . . .' I caught her before she put the phone down. 'She's all right, isn't she? You haven't had any more trouble at the villa – no one trying to break in?'

There was a pause before she answered, then: 'Miss Andrews is very well. She will be sorry to have missed you. I'll tell her you rang, Miss Stevens.'

'Yes, thank you. Please ask her to ring if she can. It is important.'

I was uneasy as I replaced the receiver. Surely the call I'd had earlier wasn't a hoax? No one would do that – would they? Why should they? Like a lot of other young women who lived alone, I'd had unpleasant calls before, but this was different. I was disturbed by the threat I'd heard in the man's voice. It had frightened me, and I wished I could have spoken to my sister immediately.

Why had I been warned? Did whoever it was believe that I could influence Athena?

It was a mystery. I felt anxious about my sister, but there was nothing more I could do for the moment. Carla would only be upset if I told her about the warning. Perhaps I would ring Athena again in the morning before I left for Cambridgeshire.

The incident had unsettled me. I looked at the jacket I had been working on without interest. Athena was more important. If she was in some kind of trouble . . .

Where might she be? Perhaps at Hans Werner's villa? I could at least try to contact her there.

I reached for the telephone, dialled directory enquiries and asked for an overseas number. It took a while, but eventually

I was given what I needed. I dialled immediately. It rang for some time and then cut off, as international lines have a habit of doing. No one at home. Was Hans out or away again?

Perhaps Athena was somewhere else with him? It was no good, I would just have to try again later. I rang three times, the last at nearly midnight, then I gave up. He might not even be in Spain.

In the morning I rang Athena's number again. Her answerphone cut in, asking me to leave a message.

'If you're there, Athena, please ring me straight back. I'm leaving in ten minutes and this is important.'

I was frustrated as I hung up. There was nothing more I could do. Maybe I would try ringing her again when we got down to Cambridge.

It was fine and warm when we arrived at Bernard and Susie's cottage, which was a short distance from the city centre. They both came to the door to greet us when the taxi drew up, inviting us to take a walk round their garden before we had lunch.

'We have a view of the river at the back,' Bernard said. 'It's especially nice in the summer. Susie likes to work outside sometimes. She's the one who takes care of the accounts and general business. I oversee the factory – in particular the cutting.'

He was a tall, thin man with fair hair and a weak chin. Not the kind of man who would appeal to me in a sexual way, but his manner was pleasant enough – and I liked his sister at once. She was petite, darker than him and energetic. The real power behind the throne.

'We've brought several samples of a job we're processing at the moment,' she told me. 'It's a high street chain but decent stuff, not the cheap end of the market. Bernard wouldn't be interested in that. Sandy said you wanted a quality product but this is our regular work. We would put our best people on anything you sent us, of course. It's what we really want to do, but we've had to take what we can get. We had thought of employing our own designers and starting up a range of our own – but if this works out it could be good for all of us.'

'I've brought something to show you,' I said, relaxing a little. I wasn't a hundred per cent sure about Bernard, but I liked Susie. 'It's the first of a range of separates I'm thinking of running as our main line this season – in two weights for autumn and winter. That's if we can get things up and running in time.'

Sandy and Bernard had wandered down to the edge of the river. A rowing boat with crew and cox was speeding by on the brownish water.

'It's the Cambridge college crew – or one of them,' Susie said. 'See the man on the bike on the other bank? He's coaching them. They're up and down the river all day long at the weekends.'

Sandy and Bernard were deep in conversation.

'We're having a problem finding the right premises,' I said. 'We've looked at several but they're either completely wrong for us – or too expensive.'

'Yes, I know what it's like when you're just starting out.' She looked sympathetic. 'We had the same problem. That's why we sited the factory down here.'

'I thought you worked in London?'

'I have a showroom and office there. It's very small, hardly room to swing the proverbial cat. Bernard works down here – the factory itself is near a place called Cottenham. We have a huge converted barn.'

'Do you have a problem finding the right workers?'

'We brought three skilled men with us, but it's easy to find machinists in the area. Cambridge and the surrounding district is thriving because of the Science Park. People are happy to move into the area.' She looked at me speculatively. 'You wouldn't consider opening up here for a start? I know of a shop in King's Street that might suit you. It isn't huge, but big enough for what you need.'

'In Cambridge?' Susie nodded. 'I don't think so. I'm sure we need to be in London for the kind of venture we're thinking of. It is a specialist boutique. Quite unique and unusual.'

'Cambridge is less than an hour on the train,' Susie said. 'I don't know whether you plan to design for other shops too – or just your own boutique?'

'I suppose we might like to franchise eventually,' I said, 'but that's a long way down the road. Ideally, I would like to set up a chain of our own shops in time.'

'Well, why not start here and branch out to other provincial towns before you open in London?'

'What's that?' Sandy asked, joining us. 'Open a shop here?' She looked excited at the idea. 'It might work, Julia. We could probably afford the rent on a decent shop here.'

'I was telling Julia about a shop in King's Street,' Susie said. 'There are several shops selling designer clothes there already – which bring in the right customers to the street. I think they are quite successful.'

'Oh, Julia,' Sandy cried. 'I like it. Let's stay over tonight and take a look at it in the morning.'

'Cambridge may be thriving,' I warned cautiously, 'but it isn't London.'

'I've been thinking,' she said. 'We might try selling some of our stuff by catalogue . . . send them out through the post or in magazines or something. Just leaflets at first, then build up to something more . . .'

'Designer clothes by post?' I stared at her. 'You might have an idea there. It would certainly increase our chances of getting known. And we could do the larger sizes on special order.'

'It wouldn't matter that we aren't in a fashionable London street,' she said. 'We could have our base in Cambridge – which would be handy for checking on the way our things were being made. And one of us could visit the factory every few days.'

'Yes . . .' I hesitated. 'But what about when the shop is open? One of us has to keep an eye on it. I'm not ready to leave London, at least until I sell my flat – if I do.'

And that might depend on how my relationship with Nick developed, though of course I didn't mention this to Sandy. I wasn't sure yet where Nick and I were going, not sure enough to talk about it with my friend.

'I can give a month's notice on mine,' Sandy said, looking excited. 'All I have to do is to find somewhere to stay here.'

'I think there may be a flat over the shop,' Susie said. 'Don't bank on it, Sandy, but I think I'm right.'

Her eyes lit up and she grabbed my arm. 'It's perfect, Julia. Please say you will consider it? You can work from London, and I'll see to this end of things.'

'Let's have a look at the samples,' I said, smiling at her enthusiasm – which I suspected had something to do with the fact that she would be living within easy reach of the cottage and Bernard. 'And then we'll take it from there . . .'

It was an interesting day. Susie showed me the garments her brother's employees had been working on; the quality was acceptable, but I felt we would need slightly better finishing.

'I'd like to talk to you about the patterns,' I said to Bernard after we'd eaten lunch on the lawn overlooking the river. 'I'll probably make them up myself at first, but then I might ask you to take on a specialist. We would talk about the costing when it came to it.'

'I've been thinking of doing that myself,' he said. 'Did Susie tell you we were considering starting up with a designer of our own?'

'Yes. Are you sure you don't want to do that? Only I'd rather not start with you if you think you might.'

'If you give me your business, I shan't think about it,' he said, 'but I'll put out a few feelers for a good pattern maker. I shall do the cutting myself. The chain store stuff is done on the machines, of course, but I know you'll want hand cutting on certain things.'

'Yes, I shall.' Bernard seemed to know what he was doing. I had warmed to him during the day. 'So what do you say to trying a couple of the designs I've shown you? If we're both happy with the result, I think we can sign a contract next week.'

He smiled and offered his hand. 'That's what I wanted to hear, Julia. I'm sure you will like the premises in Cambridge. And I have a friend in the printing trade you can talk to about those leaflets.'

I had tried telephoning Athena from the cottage three times during the day, but the answerphone was still on. It worried me a little, but there was nothing I could do. Hans was still not in either – or at least he wasn't answering his phone.

68

Oh Athena, where are you? Why don't you pick up your phone?

Bernard and Susie had invited us to stay over at the cottage, though Susie had to go back to town that evening.

'Bernard isn't much good at getting breakfast,' she said with a smile for her brother, 'but you're both welcome to stay here.'

'I'd like to stay,' Sandy said. 'What about you, Julia?'

'I don't want to cramp your style,' I said. 'I think I'll go into Cambridge with Susie and check out a hotel for future reference – and it means I'll be able to have a walk round the town before it gets busy, see what I think of the shop before we do anything more.'

'You're not having second thoughts, are you?'

'No, I think it might do for a start,' I said. 'Stop looking so worried, Sandy. I'll make an appointment to see the shop and ring you when I have a meeting set up. You can catch a bus into town and meet me.'

Susie dropped me outside a small hotel in central Cambridge; it overlooked a fairly quiet street, and from my bedroom window I had a view of pleasant gardens and a different part of the river.

I rang Athena's villa again before I went to bed. There was no reply. After some hesitation I rang the mobile number on Nick's business card; a voice told me that the line was temporarily unavailable.

'Switch your damn phone on, Nick,' I muttered. 'Why haven't you rung me?'

He might have left a message on my answering machine at home by now; I wasn't home to find out.

I went to bed feeling frustrated and on edge. If I could have talked to Nick he might have come up with some ideas about how I could reach my sister, and I had a growing sense of urgency – a feeling that she was in terrible trouble.

'So that's that,' I said to Sandy as we came out of the solicitor's office the next afternoon. 'We've burned our boats – there's no going back now.'

'I don't want to. Do you?'

'No, I don't,' I said and hugged her arm. 'I'm beginning to feel excited. It isn't quite what I had in mind – but I think your idea of selling by mail order might work – at least as a way of getting known.'

'I'm sure it's going to,' she said. 'I'm going to give notice at my flat tomorrow, and then I think I'll move down straight-away. I'll be here to oversee the shopfitting – and I can come up to town once a week, or you can come down to me. If we really work at it, we might be open within a month.'

'That's pretty ambitious. You'd better bring your designs round this evening,' I said. 'We ought to start deciding which ones we're going to lead with, and then I can make a start on the patterns.'

'I'll go home and fetch my portfolio,' she agreed. 'I can't wait for it to happen, Julia.'

'Nor can I,' I said and smiled at her. 'It's going to mean a lot of hard work for both of us – but it's exciting.'

We shared a taxi as far as my flat, then Sandy took it on alone. Her excitement at signing the lease on the shop had temporarily driven my worries about Athena out of my mind, but they returned as I ran down the steps to my front door.

As I went in I saw the green light on the answering machine was flashing madly, which meant there was more than one call. I pressed play and waited.

'I know you're there, Julia.' Ben sounded odd. 'Look, I don't blame you for not wanting to speak to me after what I said. I'm sorry. I want to see you. Please? I'll ring you again.'

'Oh, Ben,' I sighed in frustration. 'Aren't you ever going to give up?'

'If you're there pick up the phone, Julia.' My spine tin-gled as I heard Athena's voice. 'I have to talk to you. Damn! You've already left, haven't you? . . .' I heard a noise like a strangled sob. 'I wanted to explain but I can't risk it – not on this damned thing. Listen, Julia. I'm in trouble. I think . . . I'm almost sure, someone is going to try and kill me. Don't panic, babe. Miguel will protect me . . . but just in case, I want to tell you two things. The first is that I love you. You'll never know how much – or how much I regret things didn't turn out differently. You wanted to come and live with me. It wasn't possible – but I wish it had been. I've wasted a lot of years and done a lot of things I regret, but the worst is not having spent enough time with you. The second thing is, that I've sent you something. Keep it for me somewhere safe – like in a bank. If nothing happens, I'll pick it up soon. If not . . . well, you'll know what to do when the time comes. Take care of yourself, babe, and ring me as soon as you come in!'

'Oh, Athena!' I gasped and stopped the messages, my heart in my mouth. Why had I stayed in Cambridge overnight? Why hadn't I been here when my sister needed me? I dialled her number with shaking hands. 'Athena . . . Athena . . .' I was almost crying, in a panic. 'Let her be there . . . let her be all right . . .'

I heard someone pick up the phone at the other end and relief surged through me.

'Athena? I've just got in . . .'

'Miss Stevens . . . is that you?' Carla asked. 'Oh, Miss Stevens – I've been trying to reach you all day. It's Miss Andrews . . .'

She sounded so strange, as if she had a cold. 'What's wrong, Carla? Where is my sister? She's all right, isn't she?'

'Oh, Miss Stevens . . .' I heard her sob and I knew it wasn't a cold. She had been crying. 'She . . . they took her to the hospital this morning but it was too late. She was dead before they got there.'

Fingers of ice crept down my spine. I clutched at a table for support. I couldn't be hearing this. It wasn't happening . . . it couldn't be happening. Athena dead? It wasn't true. Oh God, I didn't want it to be true. Please don't let it be true. Not Athena. Not my sister . . . it mustn't be true.

'Are you there, Miss Stevens? I'm sorry . . . it must be a shock. Are you all right?'

'What happened?' I asked, sounding calmer than I felt. I had to hang on to my nerves or I would start screaming, and if I started I might not be able to stop. 'Was it an accident?'

'She was alone at the villa last night,' Carla said. 'Miguel had an accident in the car . . . the brakes failed. I stayed at the hospital with him all night.'

71

'Miguel? My God! Is he all right?'

'He was lucky; they say it is just a broken leg and some bruises . . .' Carla caught back a sob. 'I'm so sorry, Miss Stevens. I shouldn't have left her alone like that – but she made me. She promised to set the alarms but she forgot, like she always did if I wasn't there to look after her. It's my fault . . . my fault . . .'

She was crying now. I could hear her sobbing at the other end of the phone. She was obviously in a terrible state.

'Please, Carla,' I said. 'Try to calm down. I know you loved her – but I need to know. How did she die? Exactly what happened? Was it an accident or . . . what?'

'The villa has been ransacked,' Carla said and blew her nose. 'The police say it was intruders. They must have thought the place was empty and when she woke up and disturbed them, they . . . hit her on the back of the head. I found her this morning when I came back . . .' She took a deep sobbing breath. 'If I'd come back sooner, she might not have died. It's my fault, Miss Stevens. I wasn't here when she needed me. I should never have left her alone all night.'

'No, it isn't your fault, Carla. You know it isn't – just as you know it wasn't burglars who killed her.'

There was silence for a moment, then: 'I don't understand you. The police said it was . . .'

I was suddenly sure in my own mind. 'But we know different, don't we, Carla? What happened to the brakes on Miguel's car? Did someone tamper with them? Was it deliberate so that both you and he would be out of the way?'

'Why should anyone do that?' I could hear the fear in her voice.

'I don't know. I was hoping you could tell me, Carla. What I do know is that Athena was frightened. Something happened recently . . . something that made her believe her life was in danger.'

'What makes you say that?'

'Because she left a message on my answerphone. And someone told me to warn her to back off – whatever that means. What does it mean, Carla? What was Athena mixed up in? Why should someone want to murder her?'

'I don't know, truly I do not know . . . anything,' Carla sounded nervous. 'She never told me much, but she always took risks. I knew she would go too far one day.'

'What do you mean?'

'When will you come out?'

'I'll catch the Iberia flight tomorrow.'

'I'll tell you what I know then,' she said. 'Miss Andrews told me about her will. She left almost everything to you. You will have to arrange for . . . I'm sorry, I can't. Forgive me.' She was sobbing again as she put down the phone.

I stared at it for a moment, then the tears started to roll down my cheeks.

'Oh, Athena,' I whispered. 'What did you do? What did you do that drove someone to murder?'

Six

The doorbell was ringing insistently. I lifted my head from the cushions on the sofa, coming out of a stormy bout of weeping as I realized it must be Sandy. I wiped my face with the heel of my hand, then I headed for the door.

'Sandy . . .' I gasped as I saw Nick, gave a wail of despair and flung myself at him. 'Oh, Nick! Nick, I'm so glad you're here. It's awful! I can't bear it. I can't . . .'

He held me for a moment as I was caught by another sudden burst of harsh sobbing, then tipped a finger under my chin so that I looked up at him.

'What's all this? Something I did – or didn't do?'

'No, of course not.' I took a deep breath to try and steady myself. 'I've just been told. Athena . . . she was murdered last night. At least, I think it happened last night. Carla found her this morning but it was too late. Oh, my God, Nick. I can't bear it. I can't bear it. My sister has been murdered!' I opened my mouth to scream as the horror swept over me.

'Stop it!' He gave me a little shake to stop me falling into hysterics, but his face registered both shock and horror. 'What are you talking about? How do you know she's dead and it was murder?'

'Carla told me an intruder hit her on the back of the head, and the villa was ransacked. What else could it be?'

'I don't know . . . if she was killed in a struggle . . . maybe an accident.'

'That's still murder,' I said harshly. The anger was beginning to come through now. 'Besides, I don't believe it was a burglar. I think someone went there intending to kill her. I think it was planned.'

'You had better come and sit down,' Nick said. 'Tell me everything you know about this, Julia.'

I felt in my pocket for a tissue and blew my nose. 'I'm sorry to cry all over you. I'll make some coffee.'

'I'll make it,' he said, then frowned as my doorbell rang. 'Expecting someone?'

'Sandy was bringing some of her designs over. We were going to start planning our autumn range.'

'You can't cope with that now,' he said. 'Tell her what happened, and say you'll ring her another day. I'll put that coffee on.'

I agreed meekly. Nick had taken charge and that was what I needed for the moment. In my present state, I wasn't fit to make any decisions.

Sandy was too shocked to protest. She offered to come in and stay with me, but when I told her Nick was with me, she nodded and smiled understandingly.

'As long as you're not alone,' she said. 'I don't know what to say, Julia. Sorry doesn't seem enough – but if I can do anything to help. Anything at all . . .'

'Yes, I know,' I said and gave her a quick hug. 'I'm sorry to postpone our meeting. I know you wanted to get on with things.'

'It doesn't matter,' she said. 'Don't give it a thought, Julia. I can start things going, and you'll feel better in a week or two, when you've got over the shock. We don't have to be open by a certain date, it's up to us.' She swore and looked ashamed. 'Oh, hell, I sound so selfish, even to be thinking of the business at a time like this.'

'It isn't your fault.'

'I *am* very sorry, Julia.'

'Yes, of course. I know,' I swallowed hard. I didn't want to talk about any of this, but it was important to her. 'I'm flying to Spain tomorrow, but Bernard has those preliminary patterns to make us a few samples. You can discuss details with him, can't you? I'm not sure when I'll be back.'

'Don't worry,' she said again. 'I can cope for the time being. I'll go and let you relax. I'm sorry, Julia. Really, dreadfully sorry.' There were tears in her eyes by this time. 'It hasn't sunk in yet. Heaven knows how you must feel . . .'

'I can't . . .'

'No, of course not. Sorry. I'll go.'

Nick brought the coffee through as I closed the door behind her. He smiled and patted the sofa beside him.

'Come and sit down,' he said. 'Drink this and then you can tell me why you think someone deliberately set out to kill your sister.'

I took the mug from him and sipped. It was very sweet and milky, quite horrible. I supposed he thought I needed something for the shock, so I drank it.

'That's better.' He gave a nod of approval. 'Your colour is coming back. You looked dreadful when I got here. Not that it's surprising. Being given that sort of news would knock anyone sideways. It's worse than if she'd had an accident in her car.'

'Miguel was hurt in a car crash yesterday. The brakes failed. He's in hospital with a broken leg and bruising. Carla was with him all night; that's why she didn't find Athena until the morning – until it was too late. If she had been there . . .'

'And you think that's the way it was planned?' Nick's eyes narrowed. 'You think someone made sure Carla and Miguel were out of the way first?'

'Yes, I do. Athena knew someone might try to kill her.'

'She told you that – when?'

'It must have been on Sunday. She left a message on my answerphone. I've been in Cambridge for two days. She . . .' I took a shuddering breath. 'She wanted to tell me something important but she was afraid to say it on tape, so she just told me . . .' I choked and could not continue.

'That message was waiting for you when you got in?' Nick gave me a long hard look and I nodded. 'So what happened then?'

'I rang Spain immediately. Carla answered. She said Athena died in the hospital this morning.'

'That was pretty rough on you.' He looked grim. 'No wonder you were in a state when I got here. You shouldn't have had to face this alone.'

'It was such a shock. I just started crying and I couldn't stop.' I blew my nose hard, not wanting to cry again. I needed a clear head to think about this, because it was so frightening. 'She's my sister, Nick, my only family. We hadn't always been close but that was changing. Athena told me she regretted all the wasted years. She wanted us to be together much more in the future. And now it's too late.' I gulped back my tears. 'If I knew who killed her . . .'

'What could you do?' Nick frowned. 'The police will find whoever it was, Julia. He will be punished.'

'You mean he'll go to prison for a few years?' Anger flashed through me like a quarry blast, a low, white heat, banishing my desire to weep. 'That isn't enough. I'd like to kill him. He took my sister's life. He ought to die for it.'

'That's a knee jerk reaction, natural but not sensible,' he said. 'I doubt you would carry it through, Julia. I can't see you as an executioner.'

'I'm not so sure. If he were here now I would shoot him.'

'With what? Do you have a gun?'

'Of course not.' I smiled ruefully. 'Oh, all right. I know it's just silly talk, but I want revenge, Nick. I'm angry. What right had he to take her life?'

'Look, I think you're letting this get to you too much.' There was concern in Nick's face, concern for me, and I knew his next words were meant to comfort me. 'I expect whoever it was, was frightened. It was probably an instinctive reaction to being caught. It was just unlucky she walked in on him.'

'You're suggesting it was a casual intruder, aren't you?'

Nick frowned, seeming to hesitate before he answered. 'I don't know who killed Athena, Julia, but I think it the most likely explanation – unless you know why someone might want to kill her? Did she give you any reason for her fears?'

He was clearly trying to set my mind at rest, but something in me wouldn't let go.

'No. No, she didn't,' I admitted. 'But she must have had a reason.'

I was thoughtful as I finished my coffee. Now the first shock was over, I was starting to see things more clearly. I had an ache inside me that wasn't going to go away for a long time, but anger had replaced the tears. Instead of feeling weak and miserable I was burning with a desire for revenge. I was certain my sister's murder had been a cold-blooded killing – and I wanted to know who had killed her and why.

'Would you like me to come with you tomorrow?' Nick asked, surprising me. 'I have some business meetings in the morning but I could cancel.'

'Do you mean it? Would you really do that for me?'

'Yes – if you need me?' Nick's fingers trailed down my cheek, sending a little shiver of desire through me. 'I think you know you're rather special to me – but I don't see you as a clinging vine. If you need me I'll come. If not, I'll be waiting here when you get back.'

'I needed you this evening,' I said, 'but I think I can cope in Spain. Carla will help me and Athena had lots of friends.' I gazed up at him. 'But I would be grateful if you would stay with me tonight. I don't want to be alone, Nick. Not tonight.'

'I came prepared to stay.' He leaned towards me, his mouth sweet and gentle on mine. 'I even brought my own toothbrush.'

'Then you intend making this a regular thing?'

'I think so, don't you?'

'Oh yes . . .' I gave a shaky, choking laugh as he reached out for me. 'Love me, Nick. Please make me forget. I'm hurting and I'm frightened. Help me. Just for tonight . . .'

'It's all right,' he whispered. 'It's all right, my love. You're safe with me. I promise, you're safe with me.'

Nick was standing by the telephone when I came out of the bathroom the next morning.

'I've booked your flight,' he told me. 'You pick up your ticket at the check-in desk.'

He seemed to hesitate.

'Something on your mind?'

'I tried to play back Athena's message while you were in the shower, but it isn't there.'

'Not there? It has to be. I stopped the messages . . .'

78

'You must have erased the tape,' he said and frowned. 'You were in shock, Julia. You pressed the wrong button. It's easily done. I've done it myself before now. It's a pity, though. The police might have been interested in hearing it.'

'How could I have erased it? I'm sure I just pressed the pause button. It should still be there.'

'The tape is blank – no messages at all.'

My hair had fallen into my eyes. I pushed it back, feeling irritated with myself. How could I have done something so stupid? And yet Nick was right, it was easy enough to do. When I thought about it, I realized I had done it a couple of times in the past.

'I was in such a panic when I heard what Athena was saying, that I must have done it, not concentrating. I feel so upset. I wanted to listen to it again, to make sure I hadn't missed anything.'

Tears stung behind my eyes. Most of it had been such a personal, loving message – the last time I would ever hear Athena's voice.

'Perhaps it's just as well. You've got to try and get over this, Julia. Mourn your sister, that's right and natural – but don't dwell on the manner of her death. Don't let it eat at you, make you bitter.'

I felt a flicker of annoyance. Why was he so insistent that I should forget? Athena had been murdered. It hurt like hell but it also made me angry. I'd spoken of shooting her killer, but I knew that was beyond me. I couldn't go out and shoot someone in cold blood, but I wanted revenge. I wanted to hit back somehow. And I wanted the truth.

'What's going on in that head of yours?' Nick reached out to touch my cheek. 'Are you sure you can cope? I'll be in London for a couple of days if you need me.'

'I tried phoning you Sunday evening,' I said. 'Your mobile was switched off.'

'It was the battery,' he replied, an odd flicker in his eyes. 'Something was the matter with it. I replaced the whole phone yesterday so it won't happen again.'

'Call me this evening. Please?'

'Are you staying at the villa?' He frowned as I nodded. 'Is that a good idea? You might feel better at a hotel.'

'Carla will set the alarms. Besides, I don't think the intruder will come back, do you? He either found what he wanted – or he knows it isn't there by now.'

'What do you mean?'

'I'm not sure. It's just a feeling that he wanted something she had, that's all.'

Nick frowned. 'I would feel better if you went to a hotel, Julia. Even if it is safe, there's no need for you to go through the trauma of staying there.'

'Perhaps I will, I'll see how I feel when I get there.' I moved closer to him, lifting my face for his farewell kiss. 'Thank you for being here, Nick. I'm not sure I could have got through last night without you.'

'I could still cancel and come with you?'

'No. You have work to do here. It's only a matter of filling in a few forms. I shall have . . . I'm going to bring her home if they will let me.'

'If you have any trouble I'll come out.'

'Thank you. It helps a lot, knowing you're around.'

He kissed me again, a long, lingering, possessive kiss that left me wanting more. As the door closed behind him, I sighed. Why had I refused his offer to fly out to Spain with me? Nick would have taken care of everything – but that wasn't what I wanted. This was all I could do for my sister and I wanted to do it myself.

Was it only a few weeks ago that I'd come to the villa for the first time? It was all so different now. I had arrived in brilliant sunshine then, now it was night. The heavy gates were wide open and a police car was parked under the flood-lights in the driveway. I paid my taxi fare, and carried the one small bag I'd brought with me up to the front door.

It opened as I approached and Carla came out accompa-nied by two burly policemen. One of them frowned as he saw me and spoke to Carla in Spanish, and she answered in the same language, using my name.

'He asked who you were,' Carla explained. 'They have

finished here but someone will be back to take a statement from you in the morning.'

'*Buenos noches, Señorita Stevens.*' The officer touched his cap. 'We are sorry for your sister's death.'

'Thank you.'

I turned to Carla as they got into the car and backed out of the driveway.

'Have they been here long?

'Two days,' she replied heavily. 'Yesterday there were six of them here. They have been all over the grounds and the villa. I wasn't allowed to touch anything until this evening. The inside of the house is still in a mess. I'm sorry.' She looked wretchedly tired, drained and unhappy. 'I feel I've let you down.'

'It isn't your fault.'

'You could go to a hotel. I can call a taxi if you wish?'

'Are you staying here?'

'Yes. Until . . . everything is settled.'

'Then I'll stay,' I said. I followed her into the entrance hall. I could see some vases were missing and there were still pieces of broken glass in a corner. 'How is Miguel?'

'In pain with his leg – but his anger is worse than the pain. He blames himself for what happened to her. If he had checked the car first, he might have discovered the fault. If he hadn't had the accident, he would have been here to protect her.'

'How could he have known the brakes would fail? It isn't his fault, Carla. And it's not yours either. You mustn't keep blaming yourself. We can't know what really happened – not until the police discover who was responsible.'

'Your room was not touched,' she said. 'That was strange, don't you think?'

'Yes – unless the intruder had found what he wanted.'

'He took her room apart.' Carla's voice shook, but there was anger as well as grief now. 'If I were you, Miss Stevens, I should not go in there. Not until I have a chance to clean it.'

The sitting room had been tidied, but cushions from the sofa had been ripped with a knife blade. Pictures and orna-ments were missing, seemingly smashed as the intruder searched, and afterwards taken away by Carla – or the police?

'What was he looking for, Carla?'

She hesitated, then sighed. 'The key to her safety deposit box, I expect.'

'What had she got to hide? It must have been something important if he killed her for it.'

'I don't know,' Carla said, her eyes avoiding mine. 'Miss Andrews . . . she was reckless. She used to laugh at me when I told her to be careful. I think she made enemies. She thought she was in control, that she held all the cards in the game.'

'What are you saying?' A horrible suspicion had begun to creep into my mind. 'Athena wasn't . . . she wasn't black-mailing someone, was she?'

I remembered the look of excitement in her eyes, the way she had spoken of there being lots more money to come.

'I don't know,' Carla said. 'I think perhaps she was angry. She told me that certain people had hurt her – and that they would be made to pay. "Carla," she told me. "I know so many secrets. I could make a lot of people pay for what I know – but only those who deserve it will suffer." That's what she said to me, Miss Stevens. I begged her to be careful. She didn't need money. She had all she would ever want – but it was the excitement, you see. And the game. She liked playing games.'

Carla's words shocked me, though they shouldn't have done. I had suspected something for a while; little things Athena had said and the look in her eyes had made me think she might be doing something not quite lawful, something dangerous.

'Your sister is a bad lot,' Aunt Margaret had told me after she ran away all those years ago. 'One of these days she'll end up in prison – if not worse.'

And now that prediction had come true. Athena's reckless nature had led her to a violent death.

'But blackmail,' I said, as a chill trickled down my spine. 'That's so horrible. I can't believe she would do that, Carla. Why would she?'

Carla shrugged. 'Miss Andrews was a law unto herself. She went through the bad times, Miss Stevens. She wouldn't talk about them – and they were before I started to work for her so I can't tell you anything – but I know she had suffered. There were nights when she couldn't sleep . . . she told me the demons haunted her, but I never knew what she meant.'

'Thank you for telling me this much,' I said. 'I'm just beginning to realize I never knew her at all. Not the real Athena.'

'She loved you, miss, that I do know. Always talking about you she was, planning how it was going to be in the future.'

'I loved her,' I said. 'And I'm going to find out who killed her, Carla. I don't care how long it takes or what it costs me. I have to know. I have to know the truth.'

'Be careful, Miss Stevens. Whoever killed her is evil. If he has killed once, he could do it again. The past is the past, let it go.'

'I can't,' I said. 'I have to know who killed Athena and why.'

I managed to sleep for a few hours despite the thoughts chasing themselves round in my head like puppies after their own tails. I was up and dressed before Carla; I wanted to see Athena's room for myself.

I hadn't been able to face it the night before but now I wanted to see just what damage had been done.

Carla hadn't touched it. I suspected she hadn't been able to bring herself to move anything after the police finally gave permission, and I could understand why. I had never seen such wanton damage. Nothing had been left in one piece.

The mattress and pillows had been slashed to pieces. Her clothes had been pulled from the wardrobe, some of them ripped apart as if the intruder had become frustrated and taken his anger out on her things. Her bottles and jars of cosmetics and perfumes had been smashed. A small leather jewellery box had been pulled apart, the semi-precious trinkets scattered heedlessly on the floor.

There was nothing of any significant value here, but the chains were gold and I found a pair of diamond earrings on her dressing table. A burglar would certainly have taken them. I wondered where Athena kept her best stuff. I knew she did have a couple of really valuable bits, because I'd seen her wear them. Had they been in the box – or were they hidden in a safe? Had the intruder found that safe?

Everything had been tossed out of the drawers: her underwear, scarves, stockings. Several handbags lay on the floor and her shoes had been thrown about as if whoever it was had thought he might find what he sought hidden there.

'Oh, Athena,' I whispered, a sob in my throat. 'Who did this? Who hated you enough to do this?'

'You shouldn't have come,' Carla's voice came from behind me. I turned to face her, seeing the grief she could not hide. 'You should have let me make it right again. She would not want you to see this.'

'It's all right,' I said. 'I'm glad I've seen it. It makes me more determined to find him, Carla. He's going to pay for this, believe me. If it's the last thing I ever do, I shall make him pay for what he did to her.'

'No, no!' she cried, looking upset. 'You must not try to find this evil creature, Miss Stevens. He will kill you just as he killed her.' She could no longer control her tears. 'It is too late for her. Let it go now. She would not want you to risk your life for nothing.'

'He has to pay,' I said. The determination was settling into a hard core inside me now. 'Don't worry, I'm not going to do anything silly. I just want to make sure the police put him away for a long, long time.'

'You have your breakfast now,' she said. 'I will bring it out to the pool – then I will clear up this mess.'

'Is there a safe?' I asked. 'Did Athena have a safe to put her jewellery in?'

'It is in the wardrobe, under the tiles,' Carla said. 'The police asked the same thing but I did not tell them – it was not touched. You cannot find it unless you know where to look.'

'Show me, please.'

She went to the wardrobe, lifted a pile of fashion magazines and then slid out a loose tile. The floor safe was cemented in and still locked, apparently undiscovered by both the intruder and the police.

'It needs a key,' I said. 'Do you know where she kept it?'

'No. I have never asked,' Carla said. 'I would have thought in a handbag or her box . . .' She looked at the leather jewel case that had been ripped apart. 'Perhaps he took the key.'

'I don't know if we could open it without one,' I said. 'When you clear all this up you may find it.'

'I think it was just some cash and her best jewels,' Carla said. 'She told me once that I worried for nothing, that she didn't keep anything important here. "I wouldn't be that stupid," she said. I think most things are in her safety deposit box in London. Her will is there. She told me about it – just in case. Those were her words: "just in case".'

'If it's just money and jewellery, it can wait,' I said. 'It's the key to the safety deposit box we need, Carla. Do you know where the box is – in a bank or is it some kind of left luggage thing at a station?'

'It is a bank,' Carla said, wrinkling her forehead. 'I am sure it was in London – but that's all I know.'

'Well, perhaps her solicitor will know,' I said. 'He is bound to get in touch with one of us.'

'I can tell you the name of her Spanish lawyer,' Carla said at once. 'He came here to the house once. He has an office in Marbella. I can give you the telephone number later.'

'Good. I'll make an appointment to see him. Perhaps she left something there that will give us a clue where to begin looking.'

'I think he just dealt with her Spanish property,' Carla said. 'I will look for a key when I clear up. And now I shall bring your breakfast to you by the pool.'

'Yes, all right.' I sighed as I looked round the devastated room. 'If the keys were here I think they must already have been found.'

The interview with the police was easier than it might have been because Carla spoke fluent Spanish. Even so it took a couple of hours before everything was written down to their satisfaction.

'When can I take my sister home?'

Carla repeated the question in Spanish. She shook her head as she listened to their answer, then looked at me.

'You will have to get several forms signed by various officials before they will release the body. You should see her solicitor tomorrow and he will start the process. You must be prepared for it to take some time. Her . . . her body will be preserved in the meantime.' Carla's face contorted with grief. 'They must be satisfied that what happened here was the result of a break-in – that no one else was involved.'

'Yes, of course.'

My heart sank. I'd hoped it could all be finished in one trip, but it sounded as though it could drag on for a long time.

'Can't I see the lawyer today?'

'The office will be closed from one o'clock until four. You might get an appointment this evening – if he will see you.'

'I'll ring him now. I want to start the process as soon as possible.'

'I'll telephone for you,' Carla said. 'But I do not think this is something you can hurry. In Spain everything happens in its own time.'

Athena's lawyer confirmed my fears. He would begin the process of having her body released, but he feared it might take some weeks.

'If it had been an accident I could have made the arrangements within a few hours,' he said, 'but this is more complicated. There will have to be the autopsy, of course – and sometimes it takes a while to arrange these things. I am sorry, Miss Stevens. I do understand your feelings, but I'm afraid the authorities will not release her to you until they have completed their inquiries.'

'How long will that take?'

He shrugged. 'I'm afraid I cannot tell you that. I will do my best to speed things up but . . .'

'Should I stay in Spain or go home?'

'You have given your statement to the police?'

'Yes. I was in England. They can check my whereabouts with various people.'

'I'm sure you are not under suspicion,' he said and smiled. 'My advice would be to go home and leave things to me. I shall contact you immediately I have news. If you wish, I could arrange things this end. There would be no need for you to return – unless you wish to dispose of the property? I made your sister's Spanish will for her when she bought the villa. It is left entirely to you.'

'I'm not sure what I want to do. I haven't thought about that side of things yet.'

'No, of course not. There is no hurry, Miss Stevens. But if you were to give me power of attorney I could do everything for you. I shall need it to carry out your instructions in regard to Miss Andrews' body . . .'

'When could we do that?'

He consulted his diary. 'I have an hour free tomorrow morning. I can make an appointment with the notary – you will need to sign in front of him. Would eleven thirty be convenient for you?'

'Yes, thank you. In the meantime, if there is any way of hurrying things . . . ?'

'I shall do my best,' he promised. 'I am only sorry that this terrible thing has happened. Miss Andrews was a charming person.'

'And she left nothing here for me – a letter or package?'

'Nothing. I am sorry. Perhaps with her English lawyers?'

'Yes – if only I knew who they were.' I shook hands. 'You have been very kind, Señor Sanchez. Thank you for your help.'

'My pleasure. I shall expect you tomorrow.'

I was thoughtful as I drove back to the villa in the car I had rented. I was wary of using Athena's second car in case that had been tampered with too. It had been naive of me to think I could arrange everything myself in a matter of days. If Nick had been here he might have done better. I was already missing him and wishing he was with me.

When I drew into the front of the villa I saw that a large Mercedes was already parked there and my heart skipped a beat. Was Nick here? Had he flown out to be with me despite my assertions that I could manage?

When I walked into the house I heard voices. Carla was talking to someone – a man. That wasn't Nick's voice, but I had heard it before. I was prepared before I saw him standing with Carla in the lounge. He turned as he heard my shoes on the marble floor, his expression one of extreme shock.

'Julia,' he said. 'I came as soon as I heard the news. It is terrible. I cannot believe she is dead. We were together only three days ago – before I returned to Germany.'

'Herr Werner . . .' I said. A prickling sensation had started at the nape of my neck. 'It was good of you to come.'

'I was very fond of Athena.' He frowned as he sensed my reserve. 'But I thought we agreed we were to be friends? You have not forgotten, Julia?'

'No, I haven't forgotten.' I forced a smile. 'You must forgive me, Hans. I've just been to see Athena's lawyer. He says it may be weeks before the Spanish authorities will let me take her home.'

'That is nonsense,' he said, frowning. 'She was attacked by an intruder and the blow to her head killed her. Allow me to help you in this, Julia. I shall have her body flown to London in my private plane no later than this weekend.'

I felt the sting of tears behind my eyes. 'I should be very grateful if you could do that,' I said. 'I think once the funeral is over I shall feel better.'

'You have my word,' he said and smiled at me. 'Please, you must trust me, Julia. I was a good friend of your sister's. If things had been different we might have married, but . . .' He shrugged his shoulders.

I remembered Athena's smile when she told me she might marry him. She had been confident of getting her own way, whatever she decided; she had believed the choice was hers.

'What do you mean? If things had been different?'

'I have a wife,' he said. 'It is no longer a marriage. We do not live together but I could never divorce her. Your sister understood that.'

'Yes, I see,' I said. 'Of course.'

The tingle had begun at the nape of my neck again. Had Athena known about his wife? If she had, why had she been so confident of having her way? I did not think Hans Werner was a man who would easily change his mind.

Unless Athena had some means of changing it for him?

Seven

I paused for a moment, knowing I could not afford to alienate Hans. It was feasible that a man with his money and power might be able to cut through the red tape which would normally prevent me taking my sister's body home before all the long, official process had been duly carried out.

'I'm sure Athena was happy with things the way they were,' I said, avoiding his penetrating stare. 'She . . . She told me that you meant a great deal to her, Hans.'

'As she did to me.' He inclined his head, his tone of voice flat, unreadable. 'I believe I have no need to tell you that I shall count it a privilege to do everything in my power to be of service to you, Julia. If you need money, a reliable lawyer?'

'Thank you, I can manage. But if you could arrange to fly Athena home . . .' I swallowed a sob as the grief threatened to overwhelm me once more. 'I'm sorry. This is all so difficult for me.'

'I understand completely,' he said. 'Forgive me for intruding on you at this time, but I felt I had to come.'

'It was very kind of you.'

It was kind of him, but why did I suspect there had been another reason for this visit? Or was it just that my nerves were on edge and I was looking for threats that weren't there?

'I shall leave you now, but tomorrow we shall see Athena's lawyer together and take care of all this nonsense. What happened here is quite clear and it is ridiculous that you should not be allowed to take your sister home. Now tell me, what have you done so far?'

I explained what arrangements I had already made and it was agreed that he should collect me and take me into Marbella the next morning.

'I'm going to fly home almost at once afterwards,' I said. 'There is no point in my staying on here – and there are things I need to do at home.'

'Of course, of course,' he said, and bowed punctiliously over my hand. 'You may safely leave everything this end to me, Julia.'

I thought he looked pleased to learn that I was going home and it made me wonder. I had a feeling Hans did not want me to stay in Spain – why? And why had he made a point of telling me he was married?

I believed that I might discover the truth about a lot of things if I could only find the key to Athena's safety deposit box – but where could I look that hadn't already been thoroughly searched?

Carla had thought it odd my room hadn't been touched. She had seemed to make a point of it. When she'd first told me, I'd assumed that the intruder had already found what he was looking for, but after Hans left, I decided to search my own room.

Carla believed Athena had been asleep when the murderer broke in, and I had no reason to doubt her, but since she had not been at the villa herself, she was only guessing. Perhaps, if Nick's theory was right, my sister had returned to the villa to find the intruder already ransacking her house. If there had been a struggle, as Nick suggested, and she was killed . . . then whoever it was might have run off in a panic, leaving one room still untouched.

I stripped the covers from the bed, examining the mattress and pillows for any lumps or stitching that might betray the presence of something hidden. Nothing there. I remade the bed, then looked round for likely hiding places.

There was nothing behind any of the pictures or the mirror, nothing stuck on to the back of the dressing table, or underneath it, nothing but a few bits and pieces I had left behind in the drawers.

In the fitted wardrobe, I looked for a floor safe, but the tiles were all cemented solidly to the floor. Where else could I look? The wardrobe was empty apart from the few things I had brought with me . . . and a pair of jeans I had left behind because Carla had put them in the wash and they weren't dry when I was ready to leave.

'It doesn't matter,' I'd told her when she'd apologized. 'I don't need them. Just leave them in the wardrobe until I come out next time.'

I took the hanger out and felt in the side pocket of my jeans. A tingle went down my spine as my fingers closed over the metal key. Drawing it out, I knew at once that it had to be the key to Athena's floor safe; it was long and heavy, too large to belong to a safety deposit box.

Athena must have slipped it into my jeans as a way of hiding it quickly. She had known that anyone searching the house would go through her things, but would they bother with the guest room?

As it happened, she had chosen the safest place in the house, though whether it would have been discovered if she hadn't come home when she did we should never know.

'Why didn't you stay away just a little longer?' I whispered. 'It would have been better to let them find this, than . . . Oh, Athena . . . Athena.'

Why had she got involved with all this? I had no idea what was going on, but it had to be something nasty, something dangerous. There was so much I didn't know about my sister's life. Carla had spoken of her having 'bad times' – what did that mean? I tried to remember if she had ever spoken of having been in trouble, but her letters to me had always given the impression that she was doing well, making a success of her life and her career.

Yet she had said something about a man . . . a man who had walked all over her. Had he hurt her badly? Is that why she had turned to blackmail – to be revenged on someone who had hurt her?

The questions were going round and round in my head as I walked across the hall to her room. Carla had worked a minor miracle. There was a new fresh cover on the bed, her clothes – those that were not in shreds – were restored to the wardrobe, her shoes neatly stacked in place.

I removed the pile of fashion magazines and slid out the loose tile as Carla had shown me. The key fitted perfectly, just as I had expected. I turned it and opened the heavy door, laying it back so that the contents of the safe were revealed.

There was a large stack of money. I didn't bother to count it, but most of it was in green one-hundred-euro notes and at a rough guess I thought there must be around fourteen-thousand in total – about nine thousand pounds. Beneath the money were two flat jewel cases: one contained a matching diamond pendant and bracelet, the second had a row of valuable rings, diamonds, emeralds and rubies. I thought they were probably worth quite a lot of money, but it was the envelope beneath the boxes that caught my attention, because it had my name on it.

'For Julia,' I read. 'If you're looking at this you'll need to know where things are. Everything is inside, babe. Keep your chin up and do what you think is right. Love always, Athena.'

I rocked back on my heels, shocked and numbed by the message. My sister had known she was about to die! She must have been fairly certain of it if she had written this for me.

My eyes burned with tears, but I blinked them away. Crying would only make me weak, and I was determined to be strong.

I opened the envelope. It contained a key and the name of an exclusive bank in London together with the number of a safety deposit box.

'Oh, Athena,' I choked as the emotion caught at my throat. 'Athena . . . why? Why did you get involved in this?'

I didn't yet know quite what was going on, but it was becoming more and more clear to me that Athena had been mixed up in something unsavoury. I thought she had probably been blackmailing someone and that someone had killed her.

A cold shiver went down my spine and I felt frightened. Just what had my sister been mixed up in? I recalled the hints Nick had made about drugs and related crimes. It seemed he might have been right. Yet I was reluctant to think that Athena had delved into something as rotten as drugs. Despite my denials, I was already beginning to realize it might have been true. Her last phone call had told me that she regretted much of it, that she wished things could have been different. What else had she said? Something had been nagging at me for the last day or so. I remembered her telling me she loved me, that she was afraid for her life . . . but there was something else. Something I ought to remember but couldn't. If only I hadn't wiped that tape!

It would probably come back to me in time. Once things had settled down and I was back to normal, but I wished I knew what the other thing was, because I had a feeling it might be important.

I replaced the jewellery and the money. I didn't feel like doing anything about them for the moment. Until I'd read Athena's will I couldn't legally lay claim to her belongings, nor did I want to just yet. They could stay where they were for the moment – and the key might as well go back where I'd found it.

I slipped the envelope into the pocket of the shorts I was wearing. I wasn't sure where to hide it, but for the moment the safest thing was probably to keep it somewhere on my person, because I had no doubt that whoever killed my sister had been looking for this key. When I opened her safety deposit box I would know who he was – and if he suspected I had it – he might kill me next.

We got through the night without any sudden alarms, and Hans took me into Marbella the following day as promised. The meeting was a revelation, and a lesson in what real power and money can achieve. Where I had come up against a brick wall, everything was suddenly magically possible.

Within half an hour all the necessary papers had been signed, permission given for the removal of my sister's body after the autopsy, which was being undertaken even as he drove me back to the villa, and the case closed. The police would continue to investigate, but they had accepted her death had been caused by person or persons unknown in the course of a burglary.

'I'm so grateful,' I said as Hans drew his car into the drive of the villa. 'I don't know how to thank you enough.'

He got out of the car to open the door for me, his manner

correct, polite and caring. 'It was a small thing,' he said, and reached out to take my hands in his. 'You can go ahead with the funeral now, Julia. I shall of course be there, and you may reach me at any time on this number.' He gave me a pristine white card with elegant black engraving. 'I shall let you know when I am arriving, but if you give me the name of the funeral directors you have chosen, I shall arrange everything.'

'It was fortunate for me that you were here.'

His eyes did not quite meet mine.

'Athena may have business papers: shares, bonds, investments you do not understand. If you wish, I can see to all that for you. I could liaise with her British lawyers if you give me their address.'

'I don't have it,' I said. A warning bell was sounding somewhere in my head. 'I was hoping she might have told you?'

'No, unfortunately she did not,' he said. 'Perhaps you will come across the information amongst her papers. When you do I shall be happy to save you the pain and trouble of dealing with her business affairs.'

'You are very thoughtful,' I replied. 'When I find something I do not understand, I shall telephone and ask for your advice.'

He inclined his head. 'Do not forget that my only wish is to serve you, Julia.'

I'll just bet it is!

What had Athena got that he wanted? I was becoming more and more certain that she'd had something. An icy chill slid down my spine. Was Hans capable of the kind of destruction I'd seen in my sister's room? He seemed too controlled, too reserved – but would he have risked searching the place himself? Unlikely. He would have sent someone to find what he wanted . . . perhaps the man who had killed Athena. Which would make him guilty of murder – at least in my mind.

I wasn't sure how I managed to keep my smile in place as he drove away. The more I thought about it the more certain I became that Hans Werner was the man behind the break-in – and my sister's murder.

94

He must have come to the villa hoping to find just Carla there. Had he intended to search the one room his henchman hadn't – or was there some other reason for his visit? Had Athena let it slip she had a floor safe? I didn't believe he had come just for my benefit. He had been surprised to see me walk in. And why go to so much trouble to arrange for Athena's body to be flown home – unless he wanted the case to be closed for his own sake?

I was almost certain of his guilt – but how could I prove it? The Spanish police weren't going to be much help, they had already accepted the easy option. I'd been relieved at first, because it meant I could take my sister home – but her murderer wasn't going to get away with it if I could stop him. He would be punished, whether by due process of law or some other form of justice.

Hans had refused my offer of a drink, saying he had other business, so I was alone when I walked into the villa. Carla met me in the hall.

'Mr Ryan is here,' she said. 'I told him you were leaving in an hour and he asked to look at your ticket. I think he has booked a seat on the same flight.'

'Nick is here?' I was so surprised I couldn't think straight. 'But he wasn't coming out unless I telephoned. Where is he?'

'He said he would wait for you on the patio. I took him a drink out, but I was on the telephone to the hospital for a while and I'm not sure if he went for a walk.'

'The hospital rang you? Not bad news I hope?'

'Miguel is getting on well,' she said. 'They said his leg isn't as bad as they thought and he may be out by the end of the week.'

'That's good, Carla,' I said. 'I'm so pleased.' I hesitated, then: 'Will you be all right here? If you need money I can let you have some.'

She looked awkward, then sighed. 'I didn't want to ask, Miss Stevens, but if you could let me have some money to keep the bills paid. Just until you decide what to do about this place.'

'I want you to stay here for a while,' I said. 'I'm sure

95

Athena will have made some provision for you, Carla. When I find her will I'll let you know – until then please think of this as your home.'

'Thank you, Miss Stevens.'

'I'll get the money now,' I said, and went into my room. The patio door was slightly open, and so was my wardrobe. Carla often left them that way to let the air through. I took the key from my jeans pocket and went across the hall to Athena's room. As I bent down to move the magazines, I noticed they were not quite as they had been. Had Carla been cleaning?

I unlocked the safe. Everything was as I had left it: money, jewel boxes, contents – and yet I had an odd feeling someone had been here after me. Nonsense! My imagination was beginning to play tricks on me.

I took a large wad of cash from the pile and relocked the safe, slipping the key into the pocket of my cotton skirt, then I went to find Carla in the kitchen.

She looked at the money, then at me. 'This is too much, Miss Stevens.'

'It is Athena's money,' I said. 'Take it. You and Miguel will need money until everything is settled.'

She nodded and I saw understanding in her eyes. She knew that somehow I had gained access to the safe, but accepted that I had not confided in her.

'I shall keep in touch,' I promised. 'And I'll come out again when . . . when things have settled down a little.'

'Will you let me know when the funeral is?' she asked, a hint of tears in her eyes. 'I should like to come.'

'Yes, of course,' I said. 'I'll ring you when I've made the arrangements – and now I'm going to find Mr Ryan. I haven't seen a car so he must have come in a taxi.'

'Yes, he did. Shall I ring for one for you?'

'We need to leave in twenty minutes,' I said, glancing at my watch. 'I'm going out to the pool now. If you would bring me a nice cool drink, when you've made that call?'

'Of course.' She gave me a long, hard look. 'Be careful, Miss Stevens. I know what you're thinking – but be very careful what you do. And don't trust anyone.'

'Thank you, Carla.' I smiled at her. 'I'll remember what you've said and I shall be very careful.'

I left her and went out through the lounge to the garden and round the corner of the house. Nick was sitting in one of the basket chairs, reading an English paper. He got to his feet and came to meet me.

'I know I said I wasn't coming – and it's my own fault if I've had a wasted journey – but I kept thinking you might need me.'

'I'm glad you're here, Nick,' I said, lifting my face for his kiss. 'I did have a problem but Hans sorted it out for me. He managed to cut through all the red tape and will be flying Athena's body home the day after tomorrow. All I have to do is make the arrangements the other end.'

'Hans Werner?' Nick frowned. 'What was he doing here?'

'He flew straight out when he heard the news.' I turned away as Nick released me. 'I know it sounds ridiculous, but I have a feeling he came here hoping to find the villa empty.'

'Why would he do that?'

Did Nick's voice sound odd or was that my imagination?

'I think Athena had something he wanted.'

'What do you mean?'

I looked at him. His eyes were narrowed, searching.

'I think my sister may have been blackmailing him.'

'Good grief!' Nick's voice was thick with disbelief. 'I can't believe that, Julia. Athena was the last person to black-mail anyone.'

'Why? Why do you say that?'

'Because . . .' He shook his head. 'Don't ask, Julia. You won't like the answer.'

'What are you saying? I want to know, Nick.' I glared at him. 'You can't start something and then refuse to answer.'

He hesitated, then: 'Athena told you she was a model, didn't she?'

'Yes. She was, she showed me magazines with her pic-tures in.'

'Actual magazines?'

'No . . .' I wrinkled my forehead. 'She had them made into proper photographs for me – so that I could keep them.'

'Athena wasn't a fashion model, Julia – at least not for the last eight or nine years. She may have done some modelling at first but she wasn't particularly successful, and that wasn't what earned her this villa.'

'What are you talking about?' I was suddenly cold all over. 'Do you mean she has been blackmailing people for years?'

'Not to my knowledge.' He looked grim. 'The last time I met Athena – before you saw me here at the villa – was five years ago. At that time she was running an escort agency.'

'An escort agency?' I stared at him blankly. 'I don't understand . . .'

His brows rose and I gasped as the penny dropped.

'Athena arranged for men to meet women,' Nick said, nodding as he saw the look in my eyes. 'Her girls were very high class, beautiful, sophisticated, intelligent. They only went out with men of a certain status – which means rich and respectable. Politicians, wealthy business men looking for some fun in New York – you know the kind of thing.'

'You're talking about high class call girls, aren't you?' I felt stunned, shocked. 'Girls who go to bed with men for money.'

'Rather a lot of money in this case,' he said. 'Athena took quite a commission for setting up the meetings. And no, she didn't arrange a girl for me. I met her through an American senator who used her service regularly because she was discreet. She was so discreet that she didn't bat an eyelid when we met. She rang me at my hotel later and asked me to have a drink with her, which I did.'

'Did . . . did she . . . ?' I felt the sickness rising in my throat. 'Was Athena available herself?'

'She may have been at one time,' Nick said. 'I didn't ask and she didn't tell me. She certainly didn't need to sell her own services when I met her. She was doing very nicely.'

'That's disgusting!'

I flung away from him and walked across the garden as Carla brought out a tray of drinks. My mind was whirling with shock. My sister was . . . what did they call it? A madam. She ran a high class escort agency, which was another name for a brothel.

'Julia . . .' Nick came after me, catching at my arm. I pulled away from him angrily. 'Julia! Stop this! It makes no difference.'

'Makes no difference!' I swung round in disgust. 'How can you say that? My sister was . . . it's filthy, degrading. I could just about accept that she might have decided to black-mail someone because she had been hurt in the past, but this . . .'

'Because she had been hurt,' Nick said. 'Think about it, Julia. Before you condemn her. You have no idea what hap-pened to her over the years. Besides, she was only providing the girls with a measure of safety. Agencies like hers vet their customers pretty thoroughly. If a girl reports back that the man hurt her, he is blacklisted by all the agencies.'

'And that is supposed to excuse it, is it?'

'No, of course not. I don't like what she did any more than you do, but people do things sometimes. Things they are ashamed of afterwards.'

'She didn't have to do it!'

'You don't know that,' he said. 'You don't know what drove her into it, Julia. She may have started out quite inno-cently . . . she may have been trapped in a life she hated but couldn't break free of.'

His words were beginning to get through to me. I was remembering the message Athena had left on my answer-phone.

'She said something like that . . . how she wished it had all been different . . . that she wished she had been able to have me with her.'

'Exactly,' he said. 'Don't hate her memory, Julia. Try and understand – for your own sake.'

I nodded but made no reply because I had suddenly remem-bered something else Athena had said on that tape.

'She was going to send me something,' I said, more to myself than Nick. 'I had forgotten – but she said it was important, that I was to keep it for her until . . .' I gave a little sob and looked at him, heart breaking, mind reeling under the shock of what he had told me. 'I still love her,' I said. 'No matter what she did. I still care.'

'Of course.' He smiled. 'You wouldn't be you if you didn't.'

'It may have come while I was away . . . the package,' I said, accepting his compliment with a smile but still puzzling over that message. 'I wonder what it was?'

'You didn't get anything before you came away?'

'No. There was some post I didn't bother with, but nothing from Spain.'

'Then it will probably be waiting on the mat when you get back,' he said. 'I shouldn't worry about it. I don't suppose it was that important.'

'No . . .' I was remembering the envelope I'd found in Athena's safe. She must have put it there intending to send it. 'I don't suppose it was.' I reached out to take his hand. 'We'd better have that drink and then get ready. The taxi will be here at any moment – that's if you managed to get a seat on my flight?'

'Yes, I was lucky,' he said. 'As it happens they were able to move us both into business class.'

'That must have cost!'

'It was worth it,' he said. 'Besides, you'll have to get used to travelling in style, Julia. I don't know if you realize it yet – but you're going to be quite a wealthy young woman.'

'Am I?' I hadn't thought about that side of things, but I supposed he was right. If Athena had left everything to me. 'I'm not sure I want money earned that way.'

'That's your decision,' Nick said, 'but don't make it too hastily, Julia. You may not like the way it was earned, but Athena was a good business woman. Why throw it all away?'

I didn't answer as I poured myself a cool drink. I was too confused to think clearly just yet. I hated the idea of money gained from prostitution, but perhaps I should think about it before I made any decisions.

Eight

Nick took me home in a taxi from Heathrow airport. He asked if I wanted him to come in, but I said I would rather see him later.

'I've several phone calls to make, but if you want to come over this evening?'

'I'll take you out for dinner.' He kissed me softly on the lips. 'Don't worry too much,' he said, his fingers just flicking my cheek. 'I've been thinking about spending a few days in the country. We could go down after the funeral. What do you think?'

'Yes, perhaps,' I said. 'We'll talk this evening.'

I let myself into the flat after Nick's taxi had driven away, then stiffened as I noticed a strange smell. What was it? It had a tang – rather like stale cigar smoke. It couldn't be! None of my friends ever smoked in my flat, because they knew I didn't like the smell.

I bent to pick up my letters. A couple of circulars went straight in the bin, apart from that there was my electricity bill and a card from a friend on holiday in France. Nothing from Spain. I wasn't really expecting anything. If Athena had left that message on Sunday she must have intended to send the envelope she'd left in her safe for me. Unless the package hadn't arrived yet? Post from Spain sometimes took a while. No, no, I was sure she'd meant the envelope I had already found.

I dumped my cases on the bed, then, just as I was about to head for the bathroom and a shower, I froze, my spine tingling. Someone had been in this room! One of the dressing table drawers was slightly open where a silk scarf had caught in the top, a tiny fragment peeping out. I hadn't left it like that; I was sure I hadn't.

I began to look round more carefully. The collection of soft toys I kept sitting on top of a pine chest had been moved by the merest fraction. I was quite certain now. I always arranged the bears in a certain way and they were set at the wrong angle.

Someone had searched my bedroom, but very carefully. It had been done in such a way that made it difficult to be sure – but I could see little things out of place.

Why had someone been here? How had they got in – and what were they looking for?

I supposed it must be connected to my sister's murder. Nick hadn't believed in the blackmail theory, because Athena had plenty to hide herself, but I thought her involvement with the escort agency made it even more likely. She would know things about important men – men who might be willing to pay significant amounts of money to keep their secrets.

Perhaps she had saved up her knowledge, waiting until the moment was right, thinking she was in control – but someone had killed her. Why? Had that person got what he wanted? Or had he struck her in a panic? And if he had found what he was after, who had searched my flat and why?

But that still left the question of how the intruder had got into my flat. My security was basic, but as far as I could see the windows hadn't been forced and the door had certainly been locked when I came in.

'The mystery of the locked door,' I murmured to myself as I checked the windows and garden door to be certain. 'Sounds like an Agatha Christie.'

I had a horrible feeling that someone was still in the flat watching me, but it was my imagination, like waking from a nightmare and seeing giant spiders at the foot of the bed. If someone had searched my flat they had been extraordinarily considerate. Nothing had been damaged. Nothing stolen that I could see. In fact I couldn't prove anyone had been in there, though I was quite sure in my own mind.

Could someone have a key? I'd heard tales of people turning up months after a property had been sold with a key the estate agent had given them. It was possible, I supposed, but not probable. Besides, nothing had been taken or damaged. No, this was someone looking for something they thought Athena might have given me to keep for her.

I remembered the threatening phone call a few days before Athena's death and shivered. The sooner I discovered what was in her safety deposit box the better. In the meantime I needed a safe place to hide the key.

'Aren't you going to stay?' I sighed as Nick released me from a close embrace. As usual his kisses left me wanting more. 'I was hoping you would.'

'Sorry.' He gave me a rueful look. 'I have to catch an early morning flight, but I'll be back before the weekend. And we'll have those few days in the country together.'

'All right.' I smiled up at him. I'd always known he wasn't the kind of man you could tie down. If our relationship was to have any chance of working, I had to know when to let go. 'Ring me when you can?'

'Of course.' His fingers traced the line of my throat, making me shiver with pleasure. 'Make sure everything is securely locked, Julia. Just in case.'

I'd told Nick I suspected my flat had been searched. He'd thought it unlikely, but suggested I get the locks changed first thing in the morning.

'It may be just your imagination working overtime,' he said, 'but that's understandable in the circumstances. In your hurry to leave you could have left things differently without realizing it – but to be safe call in a good locksmith. And have a chain put on the door while he's changing the lock.'

After Nick had gone, I checked that the key to Athena's deposit box was still where I'd left it. Finding it untouched, I wondered if perhaps Nick had been right. Perhaps I had let all this play on my mind.

I was certain of one thing. I was going to find out what was in Athena's box as soon as I could the next day.

I had the locksmith in first thing, then rang the bank to make sure I would be able to gain access.

'Yes, Miss Andrews,' the female clerk said. 'You will

need your key and some form of identification – perhaps a driving licence and one other document.'

I had brought Athena's personal papers with me, which included an international driving licence and a medical card as well as her passport. The licence had a photograph of her, but it was quite easy to remove it and replace it with the photo from my own licence. It was illegal, of course, but if I applied for probate before seeking access it was bound to take weeks. I couldn't wait that long.

I felt nervous as I presented my identification, my heart pounding. Supposing someone here knew Athena? Supposing they knew I was impersonating my sister?

'Ah yes, Miss Andrews. You rang earlier.' The smart, efficient-looking woman in a grey business suit smiled at me approvingly. 'You have your key? Good. I'll take you down myself.'

My mouth felt dry with fear as we went down together in the security lift. I kept thinking I would be caught out at any moment. Supposing there was a password or a secret procedure?

'You place your key here, Miss Andrews. Mine is first – then yours. I'll leave you to open your box in private. Please press this button when you have finished.'

'Thank you.'

I drew out the metal box. There was one large brown envelope that felt quite chunky. I stared at it, feeling slightly sick and knowing I needed to be alone to cope with this. I replaced the box and pressed the button. The woman came through from the next room.

'Finished?'

'Yes, thank you.'

We went upstairs again. My knees felt like water and I could hardly breathe.

'Oh, Miss Andrews,' she said just as we left the lift. 'I need you to sign this form please – just to show that you have had access.'

'Of course.'

I signed, hoping it would pass for my sister's hand. Forgery was new to me, but I'd practised Athena's signature several times earlier that morning. I need not have worried. The woman gave it a cursory glance and laid the pad on her desk before turning away to answer the phone.

I had to get out now before I fainted! I wanted to run, but I managed to walk at a normal pace until I was out of the door and in the sunshine of a busy London street. I felt like a criminal. I'd lied, tampered with official documents and forged my sister's signature. I could be in a lot of trouble if anyone ever found out, but why should they?

The envelope felt as if it were burning a hole in my leather shoulder bag, which I'd slung crossways over my body so that it couldn't be snatched. I glanced over my shoulder to see if anyone was watching me, but the people walking by all seemed in a hurry, hardly looking at me as I stood still for a moment to recover my breath. I felt nervous, anxious to be home so that I could see what was inside the envelope – and yet I was also uneasy. What was I going to find?

When I got in, I locked my door and used the new thick steel chain the locksmith had fitted. I was becoming paranoid! No one was going to break in in the middle of the day.

I laid the envelope on the sofa and went to switch on my coffee machine. A part of me wanted to read the contents of that fat envelope, but another side didn't. If it was proof that Athena was a blackmailer . . . There was no point in delaying this any longer! I had to know the truth.

Inside the large envelope were four smaller ones, all sealed. Each had a name printed on them in black ink. I read the names curiously: Lady Catherine Romsey-Black. Senator R. Stiggerson. Ruth Simpson. Hans Werner. There was also an official-looking envelope which I guessed contained my sister's will.

I opened the envelope with Hans' name on it first. It contained a piece of paper with some dates and the name of a hotel, a receipt for a bill at that hotel with what seemed to be his signature on it, and six negatives.

I took them to the window, holding them up to the light to see what was on them. They all seemed to be of the same girl, but rather odd in that they seemed to be close-ups of various parts of her body, but not one of them showed her face. Without the finished pictures I could not be certain, but I thought it looked as if she had been bruised or injured badly. I couldn't be sure, but I had a nasty feeling she was dead.

What was the significance of the negatives? And why had they been put in the envelope with Hans' name on it? Unless? I remembered something Nick had said when I was shocked because Athena had been involved with call girls. If the girl in the photos had been working for Athena when she was injured . . . ?

What had she said about meeting Hans for the first time a year earlier? She must still have been running her agency then. Had she supplied Hans with a girl? Were the girl's injuries a result of some time spent with him at the hotel?

It was horrible! Hans Werner was a respectable businessman. He wouldn't go around beating up women – or would he? Some men got their kicks that way. And yet Athena had been having an affair with him, hadn't she? Surely she wouldn't if . . . ? Yet it might explain that odd excitement I'd sensed in her. Carla had told me she liked to play games. She enjoyed flirting with danger!

What did I know of the real Athena? Perhaps she had thought she knew how to tame him? Besides, I couldn't be sure he was responsible for what had happened to this girl – or even what had actually happened. I was jumping to conclusions.

I looked inside the envelope again, but there was nothing else, nothing that told me any details. Of course Athena hadn't needed them. She'd known what she was selling.

Had she tried to blackmail Hans into divorcing his wife and marrying her? That was a very dangerous game to play with a man who was capable of doing terrible injuries to a woman he had paid for sex. Surely my sister would not have been that foolish? She ought to have known he would never give in to blackmail.

Cold chills were running through me. I felt very frightened, though I wasn't sure why exactly. I'd suspected Hans might have had something to do with my sister's murder, but it was one thing to suspect, quite another to hold the possible proof in my hand.

I made the coffee and drank some of it to steady my nerves. What did the negatives prove? Perhaps that a girl had been hurt. Athena might have been able to connect Hans to her but I couldn't. And I was fairly certain it would be impossible to prove he'd had anything to do with my sister's murder.

He wasn't going to get away with it! I would find a way of making him pay somehow.

I could blackmail him for the negatives, of course. What good would that do? He could afford to pay whatever I asked. Besides, I wasn't interested in his money. If he was responsible for Athena's murder I wanted him to suffer. I wanted him dead.

What was I thinking! I couldn't kill anyone . . . but there were men who killed to order. Men who would take life for money.

'Julia Stevens! Are you mad?' I had to say out loud to myself.

No, no, I couldn't have Hans killed, but I was determined to discover the truth – to make him pay in some way. If he had beaten up that girl perhaps the best way of taking my revenge would be to expose him for the callous brute he must be.

I reached for the other envelopes, opening the one marked Ruth Simpson first. It contained a cancelled cheque for a thousand pounds, made out to someone called M. Ashton and was signed by a Phyllis Barker. I looked again but there was nothing else, nothing to tell me what it meant.

In the envelope marked Senator R. Stiggerson I found more negatives and hotel receipts. One glance at the pictures showed a man in bed with two women. Pretty obvious what that was all about. There was also a business card with a telephone number written on the back.

The fourth envelope contained more negatives and an article cut from a society magazine. It announced the marriage of Catherine Chalmers to Lord Edward Romsey-Black and had a picture of a smiling couple standing outside a fashionable church in London. The negatives were of a woman having sex with three different men – again the reason for blackmail was obvious.

Senator Stiggerson and Lady Romsey-Black had reputations to lose if these pictures fell into the wrong hands. The cheque was more puzzling. Unless . . . ? I remembered forging my sister's signature that morning. Perhaps this cheque was a forgery and perhaps Ruth Simpson had falsified the signature?

But how had Athena come by it and what had she intended to do with it?

More importantly perhaps, what was I going to do with the contents of Athena's envelope? It was a bit like opening Pandora's box and letting the evil out. Perhaps I ought simply to burn everything?

I laid the envelopes aside and opened my sister's will. It was very simple. Apart from a bequest of ten thousand pounds to Carla, everything was left to me. There was the villa in Spain, a cottage in Cambridgeshire, several issues of American bonds that meant nothing to me, some shares, and five hundred thousand pounds in a bank in Jersey. The will had been made by a London solicitor only six months previously.

I sat staring at it in a state of shock for a long time. Athena must have been in London to sign the will. Why hadn't she telephoned me so that we could meet? Why had she never told me about the cottage in Cambridgeshire?

I got up and went into my bedroom, picking up a framed, signed photograph of my sister. She was posed as if for a fashion still, smiling and confident.

'Who are you?' I asked. 'I don't know you anymore. I'm not sure I want to. What kind of a person were you really, Athena?'

I stood at my sister's graveside as her coffin was lowered into the ground. My throat felt tight with emotion but I didn't cry. I felt as if all the tears had been drained out of me. It was almost as if I were watching a stranger being buried. As if the sister I had adored had never been. And it hurt.

It was cooler than it had been. I shivered as the earth trickled through my fingers to rattle on the wooden box that contained the body of a stranger.

'It's nearly over,' Nick said, holding my arm, drawing me

back from that yawning hole. 'Come on, Julia. You've had enough. I'm taking you home.'

As we left the churchyard I saw Hans Werner. He was wearing black as always. I stopped in front of him, gazing up into his eyes. A nerve was flicking in his cheek as if he sensed my hostility. Somewhere behind him I could see Carla, draped in black with a veil over her face to hide her red eyes. There were other people, some I didn't recognize. I was looking for someone . . . a man I had met only once at my sister's villa. He wasn't there. Perhaps it was too far to come from America.

'Perhaps we could talk sometime, Julia?'

'Yes, perhaps. Please call me.'

'I shall . . . very soon.' Hans' smile sent a trickle of fear down my spine. 'You may be certain of that, Julia.'

Nick's hand tightened possessively on my arm and he drew me away to where his car was parked. In town he usually went everywhere in taxis because it was easier, but we were driving down to the country that afternoon.

'Julia – wait a moment!'

I turned as I heard Sandy's voice. She came hurrying up to me, looking puzzled and slightly put out.

'Sandy. Sorry. I meant to say goodbye.'

'Can we talk, Julia? I don't want to be a nuisance, but we do need to sort out a few things.'

'Yes, I know. Can I call you next week? I'm going away for a few days, but I should be back by Tuesday.'

'All right.' She relaxed, giving me an odd look. 'Are you OK? You look dreadful.'

'Yes, I'm fine. I'm feeling much better now,' I lied.

'Good.' She leaned forward and kissed my cheek. 'I thought you might have rung before this?'

'I've been busy. Don't worry about the business, Sandy. I'll be in touch next week.'

Nick had the car door open. I got in, turning to wave at Sandy as he drew away from the kerb.

'Are you all right?' he asked. 'Your friend was right, you do look pale. I thought you were going to faint earlier.'

'No. I'm better now.'

109

He shot a puzzled look at me. 'Something on your mind?'

No, not really. Just feeling a bit tired, I suppose. I haven't been sleeping that well.'

'That's natural. You're sure you're not worried about anything in particular?'

'It has been a strain, that's all. I shall be better now this is over.'

I hadn't told Nick about the contents of Athena's box – or even that I'd found the key. I had taken her will to the solicitor and the envelopes were in a new safety deposit box in my own name. For the moment I was still trying to decide what I ought to do about them.

I had written the senator's telephone number in my address book, and I'd looked up Lady Romsey-Black in the phone book. I had also traced three women living in London with the name R. Simpson. I hadn't tried to contact any of them yet, because I was certain in my own mind that Hans was responsible for my sister's death.

'I hope it turns warmer again tomorrow,' Nick was saying. 'It's much nicer in the country if the sun shines.'

'Yes. Yes, it is.' I turned to smile at him. For the next few days I was going to try and forget Athena. I wanted this chance to be alone with Nick. 'Exactly where are you taking me?'

He smiled and shook his head. 'You'll just have to wait and see. It's a surprise, Julia.'

Nick's house was a converted barn on a beautiful private estate near Holt in Norfolk, which was situated just a few miles from various seaside resorts and surrounded by beautiful countryside.

The main living room was at the top of the house and reached by an open wooden staircase. It had a high, vaulted ceiling with lots of old beams and was furnished with expensive antiques.

'What a lovely place,' I said, going to look out of the window at a tiny stream and some pretty woods. 'If I owned this I think I would want to live here all the time.'

'You would probably find it a bit isolated in the winter,'

Nick said. 'Everything looks better when the sun shines. Besides, London is more convenient for my present lifestyle.'

'Yes, I expect so. You don't stay put much, do you?'

'Not a lot.' He smiled ruefully, then reached out to draw me close, his arms going around me in the possessive way I had come to expect. 'That's why the time I spend here is so precious – especially when I can spend it with you.'

'Oh, Nick.' I sighed as I relaxed into his embrace. 'It's so good to be here with you.'

'You've had a rough time,' he said and kissed me lingeringly, tenderly. 'I'm going to look after you for the next few days. I want you to forget all the nasty things, Julia. Think of your sister as you knew her and forget the rest.'

Just for that moment I did truly long to forget. Athena was dead, nothing would bring her back. Why should I cause myself so much heartache? Yes, perhaps Nick was right, perhaps I should let it all go.

For three days I almost succeeded. We went for long walks in the countryside and on the beach at Cley, throwing rounded pebbles into a grey sea and watching them skip the waves. At night we found tiny restaurants tucked away in secret places where we ate wonderful fresh sea food and drank delicious wine. Then, back at Nick's home, we lay together in the warmth of his bed and made love.

Our loving was sometimes warm and comforting, sometimes as wild and stormy as the sea as it rushed against the Norfolk coastline, but always satisfying and complete.

I knew I had never felt like this about a man before. When we were together I was so happy I was almost afraid – because nothing perfect ever lasts.

After our love-making I lay in his arms, my face pressed against the damp saltiness of his sweat-drenched skin, and talked in low voices. I told him about my childhood, about the accident that had killed Athena's and my parents, forcing us to live with Aunt Margaret.

'She might never have gone to America if our parents had lived,' I said on our last night together in Norfolk. 'Aunt Margaret was such a prude. She was always getting at Athena, complaining about her clothes, her manners – everything she did. I'm sure that's what drove her into running away.'

'I think you're probably right,' he agreed. 'I know she was unhappy when we first met. She had been living in London for six months then. She'd had a few modelling jobs but wasn't getting anywhere. Then she had this promise of a glamorous job in the States.'

He was frowning. I sensed something . . . anger, frustration, guilt?

'Was that why you parted, because she wanted to go to America?'

'In a way – but there was more.'

'Won't you tell me? Please, Nick?'

He hesitated, then reached for his dressing gown, getting out of bed to go and stand by the window. 'She had a friend, a girl called Ruth Simpson. She was what your aunt would have called a bad woman and she led Athena into things she would have been better to leave alone.'

'What sort of things?'

'They went to parties where they could meet rich men. I wasn't rich then, Julia – just starting out in a small way in computer software. So I didn't qualify for a serious date . . . just a coffee when Athena was feeling lonely, which she often did in those early days.'

Nick turned to look at me and I was caught by the expression in his eyes.

'She got into trouble, didn't she?'

He nodded, seeming to consider for a moment. 'She rang me one night, late. She was in the country, at a phone box, alone. She begged me to go and pick her up. She was in tears . . . almost hysterical.'

'What did you do?'

'I drove out there – it was about thirty miles outside London, a small village. I can't recall the name . . .' He paused, then looked at me. 'She was in a terrible state, Julia. Her clothes were torn and she had cuts on her face. I asked her what had happened. She said she'd been staying with someone and that he had raped her. She said she thought he would kill her so she ran away and phoned me for help.'

112

'Athena was raped?' I felt sick and shaken. 'Oh, Nick . . . I had no idea. She never told me.'

'She didn't tell anyone else,' he said. 'Even when she discovered she was pregnant. She was frightened of the man and she hated him. She said she would get even with him one day.'

'She was pregnant with his child?'

'Yes, that's what she told me. She asked me to lend her the money for an abortion. I offered to marry her instead, but she wanted the chance of fame in America, so I gave her the money.'

'She was a fool. She should have married you when she had the chance.'

Nick smiled wryly. 'I was just starting out then, Julia. I didn't have enough money to satisfy your sister's ambitions.'

'You sound bitter?'

'No, not really. It was a long time ago, Julia.' He came back to the bed and sat on the edge, looking down at me with a question in his eyes. 'Besides, I have you now, don't I?'

'Nick . . .' My heart raced wildly. 'Of course you do – if you want me?'

'Surely you know the answer to that?'

For answer I reached up to kiss him on the mouth. I was far from certain of him, but now wasn't the time to talk about the future or the doubts that plagued me from time to time.

It was a long, long time later that I said, 'Do you know the name of the man who raped her, Nick?'

'No, she never would tell me that,' he said. 'Why? It doesn't matter, does it?'

'No. Of course not,' I lied.

It mattered quite a bit, because if the man happened to be connected to someone in one of those envelopes it would explain an awful lot about what I had found in Athena's box.

Nine

I rang Sandy on Monday evening after Nick had dropped me off at the flat, and arranged to go down to Cambridge with her the next morning.

'I want to have a look at those samples,' I said, 'and it's time we sorted out a few other things. Have you done anything about the shopfitters yet?'

'I've had three estimates as we agreed,' she said. 'One of them is almost twice as much as we'd budgeted but their design is the best – at least I think so.'

'We'll probably use them, but we could try getting the price down a bit at first. And I want to talk to Bernard about that pattern cutter. We can afford the best now, Sandy, and I don't see why we should settle for anything less.'

'What do you mean? Has . . . I mean . . . ?' She stumbled to a halt, obviously embarrassed.

'Money isn't a problem, if that's what you mean,' I said. 'I don't want to talk about it just yet, Sandy, but you don't have to worry.'

'OK. If you say so.'

She didn't sound certain, but I wasn't ready to tell her all of it yet. I hadn't made up my mind what to do about the money or the envelopes – though I was sure I wanted Athena's murderer punished. That thought was growing steadily in my mind day by day.

Now that I knew at least a part of my sister's story I was inclined to feel slightly better about the things she'd done. A man had brutally raped her and she'd had an abortion to get rid of an unwanted child; that was quite enough to make any woman bitter. And yet somehow it didn't fit with the call girl agency. Having suffered humiliation and brutality

114

herself at the hands of a man, wouldn't my sister be against other women selling their bodies for money?

How could I know what had gone on in her mind? Maybe the girls would have sold themselves anyway and Athena had simply taken care of them? Such an explanation made the idea a little more acceptable to me. After all, if I'd been through her experiences, maybe I wouldn't feel quite so high-minded. I didn't think I was a prude, but perhaps some of Aunt Margaret's teachings had rubbed off on me.

I tried to put it all to the back of my mind and get on with some work, trying out various ideas I'd been thinking about for the autumn range. I rather liked the idea of interchangeable silk shirts, a basic cut we could use over and over again with slim and easy fits, changing it slightly to match the current range.

Decisions had to be made soon. If we wanted to get started on time, both Sandy and I were going to have to work flat out – and that might be a good thing as far as I was concerned, because I wouldn't have time to think.

It was about eleven o'clock that evening before I was ready to pack up for the night. I put down my shears as the telephone shrilled. Was that Nick? He'd said he wouldn't stay the night but might phone last thing. I picked up the receiver, a smile on my lips.

'Hi . . .'

There was silence, then heavy breathing. A prickle of fear started at the nape of my neck.

'Who is this?' I asked. 'Nick, is it you?'

The phone went down at the other end. I stared at my receiver before replacing it and dialling the call back service. I was half expecting it when the operator told me the number had not been registered.

Had someone rung just to find out if I was home? The last time this had happened the caller had threatened me with what would happen to my sister if she didn't back off – and now she was dead. Was someone about to break into my home and attack me?

My mouth was dry and I was trembling as I went to check the safety lock on my door and the new window locks I'd had installed as a further precaution.

Everything was secure. I was as certain as anyone could be that no one could get in, but that didn't make me feel much better. If someone wanted to hurt me they would find a way.

Whoever it was must suspect that I had Athena's safety deposit key. They must fear that I was going to continue blackmailing them. The idea came to me like a blinding force, sending an electric shock running up and down my body. Of course! Why hadn't I seen it before?

This problem wasn't going to just go away, no matter how much I tried to ignore it. Something had to be done and I thought I knew how to get things moving. I would make each of the people named an offer they couldn't refuse: the return of those envelopes for information. Every one of them must have known Athena; they must each have a story to tell – and from their stories I should be able to piece together my sister's life, or as much of it as I needed to know.

I wanted nothing from these people except information. The only person I wanted to punish was the man who had killed my sister. If I was satisfied of their innocence I would return the envelopes to them. But when I found Athena's murderer, what then? I would think about that when I got there, when I had proof of the person who wanted to kill my sister.

'So you're satisfied with the samples then?' Bernard asked, after I had examined the two jackets and matching skirt thoroughly. 'You want to go ahead with the range?'

'Yes, but can you increase the size range to sixteens?' I asked, glancing at Sandy, who nodded agreement. 'And I've brought you a pattern for some jeans, which we'll want making up in colours to tone with the jackets. I think we need slightly better finishing on the pockets, but you've promised to sort that out – and you're interviewing a new pattern cutter tomorrow?'

'Yes. I can promise you he's good. The best available.'

'OK. We'll have the contract drawn up then and you can start producing as soon as we've got the colour range fixed with the cloth manufacturers. I'm pleased with the browns and oranges – but I think the blue needs to be a little deeper. Don't you think so, Sandy?'

'I've been trying some new shades,' she said, 'and I think I've found the perfect contrast. I'll show you and if you agree we can get it off to the textile firm this afternoon.'

'I'm glad it's all settled,' Bernard said. 'I'll start on the autumn range tomorrow.'

'Good. The blues and blacks are for winter so we can wait a bit longer for those.'

We shook hands and I wandered outside to where we'd parked our car, leaving Sandy to have a few words with Bernard in private. She was looking thoughtful as she came out to join me.

'Would you mind dealing with the shopfitters yourself?' I asked. 'There's somewhere I want to go this afternoon. If I could drop you off and meet you at the shop later?'

'I was hoping you would be there,' she said. 'I'm sure you would handle it better than me.'

'Just say you're prepared to accept their offer if they give us ten per cent off the asking price,' I said. 'If they won't, leave it and I'll have another go at them tomorrow.'

'What is so important that you can't be there?'

'I have something to do, that's all. If it wasn't important I wouldn't ask, Sandy.'

'Oh, all right,' she said, looking a bit sulky. 'I'll do it, but I don't think you're being very fair, Julia.'

'No, perhaps I'm not,' I said. 'If you really want me to come with you I can do this later.'

She looked awkward, as if she had suddenly remembered the reason I hadn't been pulling my fair weight for the last few days. 'No, I can manage. I suppose this has something to do with Athena?'

'Yes, it does,' I said, knowing she resented not being taken into my confidence. 'But I can go this evening if you need me?'

'Take no notice of my moaning.' She grinned at me, suddenly coming out of the sulks. 'Go off and do whatever it is you have to do and we'll meet later.'

117

'Thanks.' I started the car. 'I'll make it up to you somehow.
I promise'

Athena's cottage was at a place called Wicken Fen. I had
traced it on the map the previous evening, but finding the
actual cottage took longer than I had expected. It was quite
isolated, at the end of a country lane and completely on its
own.

I checked the address with the one her lawyers had given
me when I'd inquired about the property earlier that morning.
As far as they knew the house was unoccupied, but they
didn't have a key and they had no idea where it might have
been kept.

I was at the right place. The name was on the gate: Windrush
Cottage. The garden looked as if it hadn't been touched in
months, the grass was long with thin stalks that had seeded
and would need a scythe to cut them down, and the flower
beds were choked with weeds. It didn't look as if anyone
had been near for a while, but to make certain I wasn't
intruding, I rang the bell a couple of times and waited.

No one came. So the problem was how to get in? I looked
round for any possible hiding places for a key. I noticed a
flowerpot near the front door, but there was nothing under
it. I felt along the ledge at the top of the front door, still
nothing. There was a path leading round to the back door,
which had a porch over it. In the porch there were several
pots and a mat. I looked under them all but found nothing.

The back door had a glass panel; I picked up a metal
doorstop and smashed the glass, then put my hand through
to release the Yale lock. The door swung open and I walked
into the kitchen. It was quite pretty and modern, which
came as a surprise after the neglected garden. I tried the
electricity and discovered it was actually working. The
fridge door was open, the inside clean and empty. So no
one was living here.

I went through to the hall, which smelt faintly of something flowery, and then into the front sitting room.
Immediately I was caught by its prettiness and its sense of
peace. The colours were pale pastel shades of yellows, greens

and a deep bronze, rather like those huge chrysanthemums that cost the earth at Christmas.

The large, comfortable sofa had piles of silk cushions in toning shades and the chairs were like Victorian button-backs, but probably reproductions. A lot of the furniture was also possibly reproduction, but pretty and made out of unusual woods with some marquetry around the edges of tables and the top of the chiffonier.

It wasn't just the prettiness of the room that appealed, though. It had a warmth and charm about it that made me feel instantly at home. I didn't know if my sister had spent much time here, but I felt that she had been happy in this place.

I went upstairs to the bedrooms, of which there were two, plus a tiny boxroom, which was filled with boxes and crates, some of which seemed to have things stored in them. One of them was open and I saw a collection of old records and books. Lying on top was a faded photograph album. I opened it and my heart stood still with shock.

The first pictures were of Athena, our parents and me at the seaside when I was no more than two or three years old. I hadn't seen them for years, and now realized she must have taken them with her when she left that night. I closed the book but didn't return it to the tea chest, taking it with me as I explored a little further.

It was easy to see which was Athena's own room. Her clothes were hanging in the wardrobe, still smelling faintly of a perfume I recognized as one she often wore.

'Oh, Athena,' I whispered, my throat closing with emotion. I felt somehow closer here to the sister I had known in what must surely have been her secret hideaway. 'Where are you? I'm trying so hard to find you.'

I checked to see if there was a floor safe in the wardrobe, but I couldn't find anything. Would Athena have left anything important here? How often had she been here? Why had she wanted a cottage in a little country village like this when she could have lived anywhere in the world?

It was yet another unsolved mystery. I was in two minds whether to stop and search the cottage for clues. The electricity was still connected, but I hadn't come prepared to stay – and Sandy was expecting me back at the shop.

I might come down one weekend, I decided. Meanwhile, I would have the locks changed, and get the electricity account sent to my own bank. I didn't want to come down and find it had been cut off all of a sudden. And I'd better have the back door fixed, too – perhaps a new one that wouldn't be quite so easy to break open.

I took the photograph album with me, laying it on the back seat of the car. Looking at the pictures might be painful, but perhaps I would learn something from them.

It was late when I returned to my flat that evening. The green light on my answerphone was flashing madly, so I pressed the play button and waited.

'I have to fly to the States tonight.' Nick's voice sent the customary tingle down my spine. 'Sorry to have missed you, Julia. I'll ring when I get back at the weekend.'

The next two messages were from textile wholesalers answering my inquiry about certain shades I wanted for special cloth I had ordered.

The fourth was a call I had been instinctively waiting for.

'Is that Julia Stevens?' the man's voice asked. 'Look, I'm not sure if you will remember me. We met briefly a few weeks ago at Athena's villa. Robert Lee – her business adviser. I've just heard . . . God! I hate these damned machines. How can I tell you how I feel? If I had known sooner I would have been at the funeral. You're probably wishing me to hell by now and you may not want my trampling all over your life, but I really would like to see you. I can't get away for a couple of weeks, but I'd like to talk then. I'll give you a ring when I'm sure about times . . . Oh, you might like my number in case . . .'

I picked up a pen and wrote the number down.

Robert Lee. He had finally got in touch. I'd been waiting for some sign that he knew about Athena's murder. When he hadn't come to the funeral I'd wondered if I would have to find a way of contacting him, but he'd found me.

Although Hans was still my number one suspect, Robert

Lee came a close second. He had been very angry when Athena turned him down that day. She'd told me their argument was over a modelling contract, but that seemed unlikely after Nick's revelations.

Mr Lee was obviously involved in Athena's business, which meant they had both been lying when they talked about a modelling contract. That gave me a nasty taste in my mouth.

I had instinctively disliked the man, but now I felt closer to despising him. It might be possible to find excuses for my sister, but I wasn't inclined to look for any for Robert Lee.

Could he be responsible for my sister's murder? I now had five suspects and I thought it was time to start a little investigating of my own.

It seemed safer to start with a woman. I tried ringing Lady Romsey-Black but her secretary told me she was busy and asked if I would like to make an appointment.

'Thank you,' I replied, giving her my name and telephone number. 'I really wanted to speak to her personally. I'll try again later.'

I looked at the list of R. Simpsons I'd taken from the phonebook, and began to dial the first number.

'May I speak to Ruth Simpson please?'

'Sorry, you must have the wrong number. My wife's name is Rosalind.'

'I'm sorry to have troubled you.'

I dialled the next one on the list.

'May I speak to Ruth Simpson please?' I asked as a woman answered. The phone was slammed down so loudly it made me jump.

I dialled the third number.

'May I speak to Ruth Simpson please?'

'Speaking. Who is it?'

'You won't know me – at least I don't think so. Unless Athena mentioned me. Athena Andrews . . . ?'

I heard her quick indrawn breath. 'I was at the funeral. You looked right at me but you didn't see me.'

'I'm sorry. I wasn't seeing anything very clearly.'

'No, I don't suppose you were. What do you want?'

'Can I come and see you?'

'When?'

'Today, if possible?'

'You can't come here. I'll meet you somewhere.'

'St James's Park – on the bridge?'

She hesitated, then, 'Yes, all right. Half past twelve. Don't be late, I've got things to do.'

'No, I shan't be late. Thank you for seeing me.'

She put the phone down without answering. I glanced at myself in the hall mirror and smiled. It was easier than I'd thought.

I was on the bridge by a quarter past twelve. At a quarter to one I was almost ready to give up and go home, then I saw her. She had long bleached hair, a tight black dress and high strappy sandals. If I had seen her loitering outside Kings Cross station, I would have thought she was a prostitute. She approached me reluctantly, a half-smoked cigarette dangling between nicotine-stained fingers.

'You're Athena's sister,' she said. 'I saw you the other day.'

I'm sorry I didn't notice you.'

'Why should you?' Her eyes narrowed. 'Did she tell you about me?'

'No, not exactly.' I hesitated, finding it suddenly difficult to put my idea into practice. 'Shall we go and have a drink somewhere?'

'Say what you've got to say here.' She took a drag on her cigarette. 'You've found it, haven't you? The cheque. I knew Athena must have taken it, but I never thought she would use it. It's no use asking me for money. I'm broke.'

'I don't want money. I don't even want to know about the cheque or what you did, Ruth. I just want you to tell me about my sister.'

'What kind of things?' She looked at me suspiciously. 'I'm not the sort to split on a friend.'

I wondered about Ruth. What was her background? At times her speech seemed to border on being common, at others there was an almost cultured ring to her voice. I had the feeling that her behaviour was a deception. Perhaps she was acting out the part of a common tart? Athena and Ruth had first met working together in a dress shop, so she must have been acceptable to an employer who was obviously particular about the staff she employed. And she had been my sister's friend.

'You knew Athena before she went to America, didn't you?' Ruth nodded, drawing on the cigarette again. 'You knew the men she was seeing.'

'Might have done. There were quite a few of them. Athena liked a good time in them days. We were always out at some party. She liked the rich ones and they liked her.'

Ruth was clearly protecting her identity. She didn't want me to pry too deeply into the past.

'Was there one in particular? Please, Ruth, think about this. Was there a man she used to talk about – and then suddenly didn't see anymore?'

'Might have been.' She wrinkled her brow. 'A lot of them were just one night stands. I told you, there were a lot of them . . .' She broke off and frowned. 'There was one she was keen on – a toff, I think. He was a bit older and rolling in money. He bought her a diamond ring and she talked about marrying him, then . . .' Ruth nodded. 'It was just before she went to America. I asked her why she wasn't seeing him and she snapped at me, bit my head off. It wasn't like her . . . at least she changed a bit just before she went off to that modelling job, wasn't as much fun as she had been.'

'Can you remember his name, Ruth?' I asked, feeling frustrated at being so near yet still so far. 'It is important.'

'No . . .' She wrinkled her brow. 'Sorry. We didn't bother about names much, he was just her bloke.'

'Is there anything else you can tell me, Ruth? Anything that has puzzled you?'

'No, except that she started drinking more. She used to tell me off for getting drunk, but all of a sudden she started knocking it back. I wondered why but I didn't ask; she would have told me if she'd wanted me to know.'

I believed her. There didn't seem to be much point in her lying, even though I didn't quite believe in the image she clearly wanted to portray. But no doubt she had her own

123

reasons for that . . . reasons that were private and nothing to do with me or Athena.

'Thank you,' I said, and took the envelope from my jeans pocket. 'I think this belongs to you.'

She looked inside, then smiled wryly. 'I worried about that for a long time,' she said, 'but then I worked out that Athena must have taken it. Phyllis Barker was our boss, you see. She owned a little dress shop in Kensington, had plenty of money. So much of it that one little cheque shouldn't have made a difference, but she noticed it, when they sent it back from the bank. They used to send all the cancelled cheques back then, you see. She knew it wasn't her signature and she blew her top, said she was going to the police . . . but then it disappeared. She couldn't do anything, not without evidence. I hadn't taken it so I knew Athena must have done. Phyllis sacked us both, but she couldn't prove anything – not without the cheque. She was always paying large bills. She wouldn't even have noticed if she hadn't seen that signature. It was just bad luck that she noticed.'

'Athena never threatened to blackmail you with it?'

'Blackmail me?' Ruth looked indignant. 'We were friends. Some kind of a sister you are! Athena wouldn't do a dirty trick like that.'

'But you thought I might? You told me you hadn't any money.'

'Well, I didn't know you, did I?'

'No, you didn't,' I said. 'Thank you for telling me all this, Ruth. You didn't have to.'

'It doesn't matter much now anyway. Phyllis Barker died last year and there's no one left to care what happened to one cheque nearly eleven years ago. It all went to a charity anyway. Bloody cats' home! They are not going to bother, are they?'

'No, I suppose not.' I hesitated, then, 'Tell me, why did you want the money?'

'A friend of mine was in trouble,' she said. 'I did it for him. And then the bastard left me for someone else.' She grinned wryly. 'Men! They're all the same, love. Never trust

124

them, that's my advice to you. There isn't one of them worth spitting.'

'I'll remember what you said.' I smiled at her, liking her because of the way she had stood up for Athena. 'Maybe we could meet again sometime?'

'I doubt it, love,' she said. 'I'm on the game and you're not. I saw that right away. You wouldn't want to be seen with the likes of me often. No, best forget you ever met me.'

'I shan't do that,' I said. 'Thank you for telling me everything, Ruth. You don't know how grateful I am.'

'If I think of a name I'll ring you,' she said. 'I've got your number. Checked it on the call back after you rang. You can't be too careful in my business you know. You could have been the vice squad.'

'No,' I said. 'I don't suppose you can.'

I watched her walk away, hips swaying provocatively. So that was Ruth Simpson and one I could cross off the list.

When I got back to my flat I saw a man standing outside, his manner that of someone who was clearly prepared to wait for as long as it took. My heart sank as I realized it was Ben. Not relishing a confrontation, I almost walked away, but then he turned and saw me.

'Julia,' he said, coming to meet me. 'Your neighbour told me you would probably be back soon. I had to come. I wanted to see you, to explain . . .'

'There's nothing to explain, nothing we haven't said.' I sighed as I saw his expression. 'It's over, Ben. You lied to me, cheated both me and your wife. I'm not prepared to put up with that . . .'

His eyes narrowed angrily. 'I suppose there's someone else? That's why you're not prepared to give me a chance to make it up to you.'

'If there is someone new – and you're right, there is – that's my business. I've tried saying it every way I know how. I'm sorry, but I don't want to see you again, Ben.'

He made a move towards me, as if he wanted to grab hold of my arm. I stepped back and almost collided with Philip and Terry, who had come from the corner delicatessen, their arms full of bags spilling over with fruit, exotic vegetables and spicy foods.

Philip took my arm to steady me. He noticed my flushed expression, his eyes narrowing as he saw Ben and summed up the situation.

'Need any help, Julia?'

'I think Ben was just going . . .' I met his furious stare defiantly. 'Would you and Terry like to come in for coffee? I'm going to make some.'

'Why not come and try some of this delicious cheese flan I've just bought.' Philip looked at Ben. 'You'll have to excuse us, we must get this food in the fridge. Come along, Julia, love. I've got something special to show you . . .'

'Please don't ring me anymore,' I said to Ben. 'And don't bother coming round. I have no wish to see you ever again.'

'Bitch . . .' He glared at me, then backed off as Terry took a menacing step towards him, his mouth curling in a spiteful sneer. 'Enjoy yourself with these two, do you?'

'They are friends, good friends,' I said. 'Bye, Ben.'

He turned and walked off, clearly in a temper.

'Not quite your style,' Philip said. 'I like your new man better, darling. Saw him leaving one morning . . . much nicer. Much more your sort.'

'Yes, he is,' I said and gave a shaky laugh. 'I'm glad you two came back when you did. Thank you for scaring Ben off; he has been making a few threats recently, and I was feeling nervous.'

'We're always here,' Philip said. 'Any time you need us, just call . . .'

The incident with Ben had been unpleasant, but I had far more troubling things on my mind, things I found almost too painful to face.

That evening, I forced myself to look through the photograph album I had brought from the cottage. Most of the pictures were of our family before our parents were killed, but there were some of Athena in London, posing with friends. I saw one of Ruth when she was younger and had mousy brown hair; she looked pretty.

On the very last page of all there was a picture of a man. He was good looking, dark-haired, lean-faced and had a rather aristocratic manner. One corner of the photo had lifted from the page so I took it out and turned it over. My sister had written something on the back.

'I'll get even, Teddy – if it takes forever!'

'Teddy . . .' I spoke the name aloud. Why did that seem to ring a bell? 'Teddy . . . Edward.' The penny dropped. 'Sir Edward Romsey-Black!'

Ruth had said the man Athena was seeing regularly was a toff. It all fitted together nicely – but why keep pictures of his wife and not of him? Surely it was Teddy she wanted to hurt, not his wife. Granted it might hurt him to know that his wife had slept around a bit, but it would hurt Lady Catherine even more. Athena wouldn't do that, would she?

I got up and started to walk around the flat. A picture of my sister was beginning to emerge, but the trouble was she seemed to be two people. There was the cold, callous woman who got rich off the immoral earnings of other women – and there was the good friend Ruth had spoken of who had swiped a forged cheque to stop her going to prison, thereby making herself an accessory to the crime.

Athena had taken the cheque and kept it. But Ruth had seemed certain she would never have used it against her. Why keep it in her safety deposit box if she wasn't going to use it?

Maybe it was just insurance? Because she thought Ruth might know something . . . something she didn't want to come out. It would have been simple to do a straight swop.

So what had Athena needed to hide when she was still living in London?

Was it the fact that she'd had an abortion? Somehow that did not seem enough. Many women had abortions these days, and the fact that she had been raped would secure most people's sympathy.

From what Nick had told me, the escort agency had been something which came later, something Ruth Simpson might not have known about.

I sensed a deeper mystery. Athena's decision to go to

America had been made in haste. That was understandable if she had been offered a modelling contract, but what if that was just another lie?

What if she had left England for quite another reason?

Ten

That thought kept me restless for most of the night, but I was no nearer to solving the mystery when morning came. Feeling heavy-eyed and on edge, I decided to try and concentrate on my work that morning.

Besides the basic ranges of skirts, jackets and tailored shirts, I had drawn a few sketches of special tops, which would interchange with the tailored shirts, for evening wear. And I had purchased several lengths of plain white and cream silks, which I intended to hand print and make up myself. These tops would be my signature pieces, and available only through the boutique itself.

I had just spread out a roll of cheap white fabric to practise on before using the silk, when my intercom buzzed. I picked up the receiver.

'Yes? Julia Stevens. Who is it please?'

'You won't know me' – the woman's voice was soft and husky – 'but I think Athena must have told you about me. You rang my home some days ago. I was away at the time . . .'

'Are you Lady Romsey-Black?'

'Yes. Yes, I am.' She sounded awkward, unsure of her welcome. 'May I come in? It is important that I speak to you personally, Miss Stevens.'

'Yes, of course.'

My heart was beating faster than usual as I glanced at myself in the mirror. Obviously Lady Romsey-Black knew that Athena had those revealing photographs of her, and I suspected she was about to ask for their return. Until this moment, I had been certain in my own mind who had murdered my sister, but now I wondered.

I supposed it was possible that Athena could have been

killed by a woman. She had supposedly been struck from behind with a blunt instrument. A woman was capable of such a blow.

Catching sight of my cutting shears lying amongst some patterns on the sideboard, I concealed them beneath the material I was going to print. They might come in useful, should I be attacked, I thought as the paranoia set in.

My nerves were jangling as I went into the hall and opened my front door. I was a little surprised by the appearance of the woman who stood there. In her pictures she looked striking, her hair an enhanced blonde that was very attractive. Now her hair had been allowed to revert back to a much darker shade, which made her look ordinary. She was dressed in conventional, classic clothes in dull browns and camel; she didn't look particularly smart or beautiful.

For a few seconds I wondered if it was the same woman. Yet as I looked closer, I saw her bone structure was good, and she might still have looked more attractive if she had tried. It was almost as if she had deliberately played down her looks, as if she was trying to be someone else.

'You're Julia,' she said as I stood back to let her enter. 'I'm Catherine. Athena showed me photographs of you when you were still at school, and she talked about you a lot.'

'Did she? Were you a close friend of hers?'

'Yes, we were good friends.' She seemed to seize on my words eagerly. 'Particularly before she went to America, but we kept in touch for a long time after that. I was shocked when I read the report of her funeral. And then I received your message . . .'

I could see the hesitancy in her eyes. She was itching to know if I had found the photographs, but didn't want to ask straight out. Was she embarrassed, or was there another reason altogether?

'Your name and number was in Athena's address book,' I lied, not wanting to tell her everything at once. 'I rang you on impulse. I'm trying to trace people my sister knew – people who might have some idea why she was murdered.'

'Why . . . ?' she said in an odd, strangled voice. 'I thought

'. . . the papers said she was killed by an intruder who ransacked her villa.'

'Yes, that's what the Spanish police think happened.'

She looked really disturbed now. I wasn't sure if it was guilt or fear reflected in her eyes.

'But you don't think that's what happened, do you?'

'She was killed by an intruder, but I'm not sure why he was there or what he was looking for,' I said slowly. 'I think Athena might have known whoever killed her. I think that person might have believed she had something he or she wanted.'

Her face had gone very pale, and her hands trembled. She shoved them into the pockets of her camel coat. For a moment I thought she might faint.

'You . . . you're talking about blackmail.' She seemed half angry, half fearful now. 'You think someone killed Athena to stop her blackmailing them . . . ?'

'What do you know about this?'

She had sunk down on to a corner of my sofa, which was littered with patterns and bits of material. Now she looked up at me, her eyes wary. She was anxious, perhaps a little frightened.

'You've found the photographs of me, I suppose?'

There was no point in lying now.

'They were in an envelope with your name on them.'

'My name?' Once again, she seemed defensive, unsure. 'You're certain it was my name and not my husband's?'

'Yes. Why? It amounts to the same thing, doesn't it?'

'No . . .' She flicked her straight, shoulder-length hair back behind her ear. 'The idea was to blackmail Edward. Athena wanted revenge on him for what he did to her. He was a bastard to her, Julia. He led her on, got her half drunk, then raped her. I married him for his money. I gave Athena the pictures, because I knew he would pay anything to stop them getting into the wrong hands once we were married. He would do anything to prevent a scandal, he's that kind of a man. The rape was out of character. He . . . he lost his head that night . . .'

'You're telling me you were helping Athena to get her

revenge on your own husband?' I stared at her in disbelief. 'But why? I don't understand.'

'It's very simple. Edward had no idea I'd been a call girl. We met by accident, and he fell in love with me. He was quite literally besotted. I . . . I come from a decent family, who also had no idea what I'd been doing for the previous couple of years. Edward wanted to go to bed with me, but I said it was marriage or nothing. I wanted the money, to get away from all that. It was my chance to make a new life – and I knew what he'd done to Athena. I thought he deserved to be punished. We decided I would marry him and she would blackmail him. Afterwards, when he asked for a divorce, I would make him pay through the nose for it. That way she would get her revenge and I would have a large slice of his money. It seemed a perfect set-up.'

'How long ago was this?'

'Eleven years. I was married the day before she went to America.'

I was surprised that she could even think of sleeping with the man who raped her best friend, and I wondered how they had arrived at such an idea. Maybe they were both drunk . . . or was there more to it?

'So what changed your minds? Why didn't you go ahead with your plans?'

'I'm not sure. At first I meant to sleep with him a few times, just so that the marriage couldn't be annulled . . . really take him to the cleaners. It wasn't so very different from sleeping with the punters, if you see what I mean. Some of them are beasts. They think they can treat women like dirt if they're paying. I was just going to lie back and think of England, it wouldn't have been the first time. But Edward was so sweet to me, so generous and considerate.

'I didn't expect that. He wasn't a bit rough when we made love, in fact it was surprisingly good between us. I think he just lost his head with Athena that night. He isn't really like that . . . at least, not with me.' A flush came on to her cheeks. 'I discovered I was pregnant soon after we got back from our honeymoon. Edward was overjoyed and I discovered I cared for him in my own way. He sounds a right bastard, but he isn't . . . not really. Besides, he's given me security. I know what he did to Athena was despicable, but he'd had too much to drink . . .'

I frowned. 'Does that make it all right?'

'No, of course not. I'm not condoning what he did. He told me about it, told me he had regretted what happened. He said he'd tried to put things right . . . that he had done something to help Athena, something which more than made up for his behaviour. I asked him what he meant, but he wouldn't tell me what it was. He never has . . .'

'Did Athena know you'd changed your mind?'

'Yes. We met in London a few years ago. She said it was all water under the bridge, that she was over it, that she would return the photographs.'

'But she never did?'

Why hadn't the photographs been returned? Something didn't sound right to me.

'No. I expect she was too busy. Or she just couldn't be bothered. Athena was like that sometimes.'

'Did that worry you? Weren't you afraid she might go ahead on her own? After all, Athena had something to gain, didn't she? You said your husband would do anything to avoid a scandal. Particularly if he loves you. I should imagine he would have been willing to pay quite a lot.'

'I didn't kill Athena,' Catherine Romsey-Black said defensively. 'I've told you the truth, Julia. Your sister was a friend. I trusted her. Yes, I did worry that the photographs might fall into someone else's hands, but not that she would use them against me. The whole thing was my idea, because I wasn't a very nice person in those days. I would never have given her those pictures if I hadn't trusted her. Athena would never have hurt me.'

'You are sure? She might have changed recently.'

'You obviously didn't know her very well, Julia.'

'I hardly knew her at all, that's why I'm trying so hard to find out what made her keep these things . . . I need to know what she was going to do and why.'

Catherine's brows rose. 'You mean she had more envelopes?'

'Yes.' I hesitated, then, 'Have you heard her mention a Senator Stiggerson?'

'Stiggerson? No. No, I've never heard the name before.' She frowned. 'I can't believe Athena would blackmail someone just for money. It doesn't sound like her, Julia. She wanted to get even with Edward, but the blackmail was my idea. Besides, she had money . . .'

'Do you know how she earned it?'

'Modelling and an agency, I believe?'

'I've been told it was an escort agency – she supplied girls for men. High-class call girls . . .'

'That's ridiculous! Athena wouldn't . . . she *wouldn't*, Julia. She worked for a legitimate agency here in London. So did I, for a while. We were warned against having sex with clients, but some of us did – because the money was good. But that was up to us. We did it at our own risk, and if the agency found out they let us go. I moved on before Athena went to America – some months earlier in fact. I had been left a small legacy by my grandmother, and of course I was marrying Edward.'

'I've been told Athena's agency in New York arranged for girls to have sex with men in a safe environment . . . at least, I thought that's what he meant. Yes, I know he did.'

Nick had been very clear about what he was saying.

Her gaze narrowed. 'Who told you that?'

'Someone who knew her well . . . Nick Ryan.'

'Nick!' Catherine frowned. 'He might say anything. You shouldn't believe him, Julia. There was something between them in the old days. I don't know what Athena did to him, but I think he ended up hating her. We met once, after she went to America. He hadn't a good word to say for her. Of course, he was mad about her for ages, and she hurt him.'

I stared at her, feeling slightly sick. 'You're saying Nick hated her enough to lie about her to me?'

If he hated her that much . . .

'Let's just say she wasn't his favourite person. I think she did something . . . asked for one favour too many.'

'What do you mean? I know he helped her over the abortion.'

134

'No, this was something else. Something he was angry about, but I don't know any more. I remember him saying she was a selfish bitch who cared about no one but herself . . .' Catherine shrugged. 'What can I say? He wasn't talking about the Athena I knew.'

I turned away from her. An icy coldness was spreading down my spine. Nick *had* mentioned Athena's selfish behaviour a few times, but he hadn't seemed to hate her, only to tolerate her for what she was – likeable but self-centred. Unless he was hiding his true feelings?

I remembered thinking that if I could solve the mystery of Athena, I would also discover the real Nick. Now, I felt certain that something in the past linked them in a way that neither had been able to forget. They shared a secret, a secret that might have damaged one or the other – or perhaps both.

Had Athena known something about Nick that could cause him harm? Had she kept something he wanted back – something so important that he would . . . ?

I stopped short of the final conclusion. Nick had not hated Athena enough to kill her. I could not, would not believe that! I was in love with him. He could not be a murderer. The very idea made me want to curl up and die. Besides, I only had Catherine Romsey-Black's word for any of this; she could be lying for reasons of her own.

'What about your pictures?' I asked. 'Do you want me to destroy them, or send them to you?'

'Couldn't you give them to me now?'

'I am sorry, I don't have them here. I thought it best to put them in a safe place. After what happened to Athena . . .'

She looked horrified. 'Surely you don't think . . . ?'

'Someone has already searched my flat.' I shrugged. 'Who knows what they will do next?'

'Have you been to the police?' I shook my head. 'Surely you should, Julia?'

'What could they do? They can't put a twenty-four-hour watch on me, can they? Besides, I've no proof of anything – and I don't particularly want to be under surveillance.'

'Then what will you do?' She seemed genuinely anxious on my behalf, but I wasn't sure I believed her concern.

'Contact the people Athena may have been blackmailing and offer to return their property in return for information. The innocent ones will give it freely the way you have, and the murderer . . . may betray himself.'

She looked at me oddly. 'Is that why you telephoned my home?'

'Yes. You don't imagine I wanted to blackmail you?' My gaze intensified as I saw her flushed face. 'You did wonder, didn't you? You thought I might capitalize on what Athena had left me.'

'I wasn't sure,' she replied awkwardly. 'Now I've met you, of course, I realize you wouldn't do anything of the sort – but you could have got the wrong idea. You might have thought Athena had a score to settle and . . .'

I lifted my head proudly, giving her a cold stare that made her drop her own gaze.

'Even if she had, I should not have asked you for money. All I want to know is who killed my sister and why. You say you can't help me with that, and I have to believe that. So, what do I do with your property?'

'Don't send them,' she said, opening her shoulder bag and taking out a card. 'Post can so easily go astray or be opened by the wrong person. This is my mobile number. Ring me when you have the photographs and we'll meet somewhere.'

'It might not be for a while. I'm going to be busy this week, and I'm going somewhere this weekend. Perhaps I can manage it when I get back next week?'

'It isn't a matter of life and death,' she said, smiling as she stood up. 'I am sure I can trust you, Julia.'

'Yes, you can. I'm sorry. I might have offered you coffee or tea?'

'Thank you, no,' she replied. 'I must go. I have a lunch appointment. I wanted to see you first, just to set my mind at rest. I'm glad we've had this little talk, Julia, and I should think about going to the police if I were you.'

'I've had all my locks changed,' I said. 'Besides, whoever it was who searched my flat knows I've nothing here they want, so they're hardly likely to come again.'

She nodded, smiled again and left, the strong aura of her expensive perfume lingering after her.

Another name to cross off my list? If I believed everything she said, I had no need to consider her as a suspect, but I wasn't completely convinced. The whole thing could have been a pack of lies. If only I knew what Athena had been up to, I might have had a clearer picture. Had I been home when she telephoned that last time . . . but everything could have been different if she hadn't been so reckless.

Why had my sister been killed? The question kept going round and round in my head. Was it because she had been trying to blackmail someone – or had the contents of her safety deposit box misled me?

The rest of the week passed without incident. I worked on my hand-printed silk vests and tops, producing six individual designs that I was really pleased with when they were pressed and finished.

Sandy went mad over them when she brought over some mock-ups of the leaflets we were thinking of having printed, prior to opening at the boutique.

'You were always much better at actually producing this sort of thing than me,' she exclaimed. 'I love them all, Julia. If you can come up with a few more exclusives, we shall really have something to shout about when we open.'

I showed her a couple of preliminary sketches of long, floaty skirts I had been working on that morning, and a very special dress I wanted to make a feature of in our first window display.

'We both have our own talents,' I said. 'I like the suede pants and waistcoats you've come up with this week. Do you think Bernard can cope with suedes and leathers?'

'He is just about to install a special machine for fancy stitching on leathers, that's what made me rough out these sketches for the winter range. I thought we could reserve them for the boutique this time, then include them in the mail order brochure next year if things go well.'

It was all looking good so far. Sandy's experience with a chain store had given her a practical grounding in costing the lines and how to size the basic range. Some of her ideas could be adapted over and over again; they were modern classics, the kind of garment that could sell in large numbers if we managed to get the mail order side of the business up and running. Yet they were still different, not the kind of clothes you could buy at any of the main stores. My own designs were more individual, and some of my silk prints would never be repeated, which meant they would sell at quite a high price.

'We're a good team,' I told Sandy. 'If we're lucky, we may be able to open other boutiques much sooner than we thought. I want to come to London as soon as possible. I still think it's the place to be.'

'Using Athena's money?' Sandy frowned. 'I can't put in equal capital, Julia. You know that. I would prefer to go slowly at first – if it's all right with you?'

'It just means we don't have to worry as much as we might otherwise have done,' I said. 'I don't want to rush anything. We'll work it out together.'

'You could have gone out all on your own now, couldn't you? Started up your own fashion business in your own name.'

We had decided on 'Alexandria Stevens', combining our names as a brand. I thought it sounded good and now that Sandy and I had started out together, I didn't want to change.

'I would rather it was this way,' I assured her. 'It's more fun having someone to share it all with – and you've had more experience of actually working in the trade than me. Besides, it would be too much hassle for one person. I should have to get a team together, and why change when we get on so well?'

'We do seem to complement each other, don't we?' She looked pleased. 'If you're sure you don't want to go it alone?'

I laughed. 'I couldn't at the moment. I don't have the time. You do most of the running around, Sandy. How is the shop-fitting going?'

She launched into a description of builders and electricians, but before she had got very far my telephone rang.

'Hi,' I said. 'Julia speaking . . .'

138

'Your bitch of a sister got what was coming to her. You've
got something that belongs to me. I want it. Don't even think
about blackmail, or you will be sorry – that's just before you
die.'

It was a harsh voice, perhaps vaguely American? But almost
certainly disguised so that it was impossible to be sure.

'Who the hell are you? What do you want?' I cried, almost
dropping the receiver.

My whole body was shaking and I must have gone white
because Sandy was staring at me. She jumped up from the
sofa and came towards me, obviously concerned.

'What's wrong, Julia? Who the hell is it?'

'You've got someone there,' the harsh voice said in my
ear. 'I'll be in touch again. And remember what I said . . .'

Sandy snatched the phone from my hand. 'Who the hell are
you? We're going to the police, sucker, so don't try this again!'

She replaced the receiver, then dialled the recall number,
pulling a wry face as she heard the operator saying the number
had not been recorded.

'This isn't the first time this has happened, is it?' she
asked, looking at me as I sat down.

'No . . . but it's the first time he has made threats against
me. The first time it was Athena . . .' I pressed my fingers
to my mouth. 'It has to be him, Sandy. The man who ransacked Athena's villa . . . he says I've got something he
wants.'

'Have you?'

'I don't know . . . I don't know who he is. Or what he
wants . . .'

'But you do have something that belongs to someone
else?'

'Yes . . . I have a couple of things . . .'

'Something Athena left for you?'

'Yes. They were in her safety deposit box . . .'

Sandy stared at me, her face white with shock. 'What's
going on, Julia? Are you being blackmailed?'

'In a way, I suppose. I think Athena knew some rather
unpleasant people, Sandy. And one of them killed her for
something she had that he wanted.'

'You've got to do something – go to the police.'

'No, I can't do that . . .'

'You can at least get your phone number changed, go ex-directory.'

'That's such a nuisance. Besides, he would get to me somehow. He knows where I live . . . he knows *me*, Sandy. If he is determined to get to me, he will.'

'I think this all sounds a bit dangerous. Can't you move in with someone for a while? You could come to my place, although I'm moving next week.'

'No, I don't want to involve you in this, whatever it is.' I stared at her thoughtfully. 'There is somewhere I can go, though. It's away from London, and quiet. It would be a good place to work and think things through. I've decided to buy myself a mobile phone. I'll ring you, give you the number, but keep it to yourself, Sandy. And if anyone asks you where I am, just say you don't know. OK?'

'Yes, all right.' She looked at me anxiously. 'I still think you ought to move in with a friend. What about Nick?'

'He's away a lot of the time,' I said and frowned. He hadn't phoned for several days and I was wondering why. 'It isn't that kind of a relationship, Sandy. Not yet anyway.'

In my heart, I was beginning to think it might never be anything more than just a casual affair. If Nick really cared, he would surely have been in touch before this?

Nick still hadn't phoned by the time I was ready to leave my flat. I rang him and put a message on his answering machine.

'I'm going away for a few days,' I said. 'Leave a message for me if you want to meet next week. Hope you had a good trip. Bye.'

It wasn't a very satisfactory way to leave things, but I had always known an affair with Nick wouldn't be easy. He might turn up at my door over the weekend, but I wasn't prepared to hang around on the off chance. I needed to get right away for a couple of days. And I had been wanting to visit Athena's cottage again.

I had arranged for the electricity to be put into my name,

and I was taking enough food for the weekend with me. It was a convenient place to hide and work; besides, I wanted to have a good look through my sister's things. I was fairly sure that no one knew she owned the cottage – at least, no one who might be searching for something she had been using as blackmail. I should be safe from abusive phone calls, or unwelcome visitors.

I'd found those envelopes in her safety deposit box, but what I was looking for was a clue to whatever lay behind them – and I was sure there had to be something else. Athena had meant me to know what was going on, she wouldn't have intentionally left me hanging in the dark this way. She must have known there was a possibility that I might be in danger because of her secrets.

Ruth Simpson had been sure Athena would never have used that cheque to blackmail her, and Catherine Romsey-Black had said more or less the same about her photographs. In my heart, I felt the Athena I had known would never have done anything so horrible – and yet she had kept those incriminating pictures for some reason.

What was the meaning behind those four envelopes?

As I caught the train to Cambridge, I was trying to remember what we had talked about in Spain. She had spoken of people owing her something . . . she had told me that her one bad experience had made her decide love wasn't for her . . . and I knew she had enjoyed living on the edge. Carla had told me she was reckless, and I'd seen the excitement in her eyes when she was beginning her affair with Hans Werner.

If I was right, the photographs in his envelope showed a naked woman who had been beaten and might possibly be dead. Had Hans been the man who did that to this woman, whoever she was?

Surely Athena could not have wanted to have an affair with a man who did things like that? I could understand that she might try to blackmail him if he had harmed or killed one of her girls . . . but not that she would want to make love to him. Indeed, despite Hans' denials to me, she had been hoping for marriage. Had she imagined he might be willing to divorce his wife as the price for those pictures?

If so, I thought she was fooling herself. He did not seem to me to be the type of man who would give in to blackmail. Thinking about it, I could not see him paying for sex or beating up a woman for kicks either; he was dangerous, but I wasn't sure he was a deviant. Somehow I thought Hans Werner would find plenty of women willing to go to bed with him, and I thought him too proud to pay for the privilege.

So perhaps he was not responsible himself – but in some way connected to the man who had beaten the girl? I felt a tingle at the base of my spine, and I believed I was beginning to get somewhere. This new theory made sense.

Hans Werner was a businessman, a very wealthy, respected man who was financially involved in a wide span of international companies. He must have a lot of men on his payroll, official and otherwise. Men who were able to do him some kind of a favour. And favours had to be returned, didn't they? Wasn't that the way it worked in the world of high finance? Supposing . . . just supposing he had arranged the girl for someone else? Someone he needed in some way . . . someone he was willing to protect, because they were important to a business deal of some kind.

I wasn't sure the girl in the photograph was dead. Supposing the man who had beaten her up had been frightened by what he'd done and asked Hans Werner for help? Hans might have covered up for him. Maybe he had paid the girl off, persuaded her not to go to the police, got the man he was protecting away from the hotel – that might explain the hotel bills, which bore his signature.

I warmed to my theme. If the girl wasn't dead, only badly hurt, she might have gone to Athena afterwards. Perhaps she was frightened that the man who had hurt her would do it again . . . perhaps he had threatened her about what would happen if she didn't keep her mouth shut?

The pictures would then be easy to arrange, but how did Athena get hold of the hotel bills? They must have been stolen from Hans . . . by whom? My sister or someone else?

It was all so ugly, so sordid. And it still added up to blackmail, which must surely have been planned in cold blood.

142

I did my best to shut it all out of my mind as I went through the motions of hiring a car and driving to the cottage in Wicken. At least here, I could be alone for a few days.

I arrived at about two in the afternoon, letting myself in with the key to the new lock I'd had fitted to the front door. The glass I'd smashed to get in last time had been repaired, and the electricity was working.

I made myself a pot of coffee, then rang Sandy.

'I'm at the cottage,' I said and gave her my mobile phone number. 'I'll ring you when I get back to London, but if you need me I'll be here. I'm going to work on some sketches and patterns.'

'Are you sure you're all right, honey?'

'Very sure. Don't worry. I'm quite safe. No one knows I'm here.'

'And you don't want me to give this number to anyone?'

'No, not yet. Not until this bother is cleared up.'

'And when will that be?'

'Soon,' I promised. 'It's all right, Sandy. I think I'm beginning to get somewhere. I'm not certain yet, but I believe I know what this is all about.'

'So what are you going to do about it?'

'Nothing for the moment. But next week I'm going to speak to someone about this – and if I'm right, he may be able to help me sort things out.'

'Are you talking about Nick?'

'No, someone else.'

'I'm still worried, Julia. Are you sure you don't want me to come down and stay with you?'

'No. I'm safe here. No one knows about this place. I'll ring you next week. OK?'

'OK, if you're sure.' Sandy sounded reluctant as she rang off.

I drank my coffee, unpacked my bags, and went upstairs to examine the contents of Athena's boxes.

It took me an hour to go through everything, and when I got to the bottom of the last box, I found what I realized I had been looking for all the time. It was a diary and, as I opened it, I saw that part of it covered the period of my sister's life from the time she slammed out of Aunt Margaret's house until she left for America. She had written on most pages, and the tingling sensation at the nape of my neck told me I was about to discover at least a part of my sister's past.

Eleven

I sat curled up in an armchair, a bag of grapes, some chocolate biscuits and a glass of orange juice on the table beside me. I had a feeling this was going to be a long session, and I wanted to read the whole diary in one go.

The first few pages described my sister's feelings at being free of Aunt Margaret's grumbling at long last:

> I should have left long ago. I would have – except that it means Julia has to bear the brunt of it now. I must do something for her. If there weren't so many years between us, I could have taken her with me, but it's no use worrying. She will have to stay where she is until I can have her with me.

So Athena had planned to have me live with her at the start – what had changed her mind? I frowned as I read on, especially when it got to the part about her losing her job at the dress shop, as Ruth Simpson had said, after the cheque had been stolen. They had certainly been friends at the time. It was true that Athena had taken quite a risk for Ruth's sake:

> I don't think the old bitch thinks I took it. She really had it in for Ruth. Of course she shouldn't have done it, but I couldn't let her go to prison for something like that, but it means I'm out of a job. I think I might try the escort agency – the one Catherine told me about last week. She thinks she could get me on the books – and it sounds a lot more exciting than working in another shop. Besides, I need a reference and the old bitch certainly won't give me one. Catherine says she'll forge some for me, but maybe I shan't need them . . .

By the next entry it was obvious Athena had been taken on at the agency. She was full of it; how exciting it was being escorted to various nightclubs and parties by rich and often lonely men:

I feel sorry for some of the men. Despite what people think, there's nothing strange or unpleasant about most of them. They are lonely and some of them are trapped in unhappy marriages they haven't a hope of getting free of, poor devils. Some of them are desperate for sex. We're not supposed to go back with them to their hotels, of course. The agency would kick us out if they knew, but Catherine does it all the time. She says they give her wonderful presents. She won't take money, she wants jewellery and clothes. One of them gave her a sports car, would you believe it? I'm tempted to do it, not with all of them, but there are one or two I like, and I know they would be generous. I'm fed up with having no money. I want to be rich. Of course, Nick would kill me if he knew I was even thinking about it. He wants to marry me . . . but I can't stand the thought of being tied to a kitchen sink like any downtrodden housewife. I don't want to be like Aunt Margaret. I want excitement. I want to live dangerously . . .

I stopped reading at that point. My heart was hammering against my ribs and I felt sick. This was the confirmation if I had needed it, that there was a close relationship between them.

I began reading again. It was mostly details of Athena's life, where she had been and with whom. She had been to bed with some of her clients, and they had given her presents. Expensive jewellery and designer clothes. The first time she had confessed to a feeling of shame, but she seemed to shrug that off after a few more men. It seemed she felt she was doing them a favour, and the presents were just proof of their gratitude. She wrote that she didn't feel as if she had been paid, that the men were her friends.

'Oh, Athena . . .' My throat felt tight as I read between the lines. She was lonely – desperately lonely and looking for love. She mentioned me quite often, and spoke of wishing that I was older so that I could have lived with her.

'Athena . . .'

I could feel the tears trickling down my cheeks and taste the salt on my lips. It hurt to know Athena had fallen into that particular trap. I didn't condemn her, I just felt pain for her sake, because I knew she was beginning to dislike herself and what she was doing.

Suddenly, the tone of her writing changed. She had met someone through the agency. Someone she liked very much. He was an important man, a businessman and he had ambitions to become a politician. He had hinted that he would like to go to bed with her, but Athena had told him she wasn't allowed to, that she wasn't that sort of a girl.

> I know I'm a fool, but I can't help it. I've fallen in love with Teddy. I should leave the agency now. I should go home and make it up with Aunt Margaret – or take up the offer John Stiggerson made me.

I stiffened as I read the name. This was her first mention of Stiggerson. Had he been an American senator then? She certainly hadn't recorded it here. But he had made her some kind of an offer:

> I know Teddy would never marry me if he found out that I'd been with other men who paid to go out with me. He would think I was a prostitute – but it wasn't like that. Oh hell! Of course it was. I wish I'd never done it, but it's too late now. I'll just have to risk it, because I love him so much . . .

The next two weeks had no entries, then I came to some very smudged, close writing. I was sure this was the entry that would tell me about the rape.

I read Athena's scrawled writing with a lump in my throat. She had gone with Sir Edward Romsey-Black to his country home, there she had drunk rather too much wine and . . . she had told him the truth about herself, begging him to forgive her.

147

He was so angry. It was all my fault. I knew he had been
drinking. I should never have told him. As soon as he knew
what I'd done . . . what I am . . . he changed. I could see
what he was going to do and I tried to run . . . but he caught
me. He hurt me so much. Afterwards, I ran out and I took
his car . . .

Took his car? Nick had told me about the rape, but hadn't
said anything about Athena taking Sir Edward's car. She had
been drinking . . . she hadn't even passed her driving test as
far as I knew. Why hadn't Nick told me the rest of the story?
What was he hiding from me?

I read the next few lines, hoping to discover many things
which had puzzled me.

I shouldn't have done that, I wasn't fit to drive. Nick was
furious when he came and got me . . .

So Nick *had* known about the car. I turned the page, but
the entry stopped abruptly. Oh, come on, Athena! I thought
as I flicked impatiently through the next pages, but there was
nothing . . . until much later. This time her words made me
catch my breath. I sensed I was close to discovering the
reason for her sudden departure to America.

I've been so frightened since I read about it in the papers. I
had to tell someone. I didn't know what to do. Nick says it's
all right. He says he has squared it with Teddy. They've fixed
it between them. It's best that I go to America and forget it
ever happened. After all, there's nothing I can do – and it
was Teddy's fault. If he hadn't raped me . . .

Again the entry ended abruptly. It was as if Athena had
not been able to bring herself to write about whatever it was
that had happened the night she was raped. What could be
so bad that it was worse than rape?

I flicked through the rest of the pages, but there was nothing
more. Athena had obviously left the diary here with her
things. But she hadn't had the cottage then, so she must have

stored them somewhere. She had bought the cottage only a couple of years or so ago. I wished she had left some more diaries for me to read, more recent ones that might give me an insight into her life in America. Perhaps she hadn't kept a diary after this one. I wished she had and that I had it here with me now.

Yet what was there to learn that I wasn't already halfway to discovering? From Athena's confessions, I knew that it was likely her agency in America had been exactly what Nick said it was . . . or at least, she hadn't actively discouraged her girls from going to bed with the customers. After what she had written about the men being her friends and feeling sorry for them, I felt there might have been more than a desire to make money behind her actions. It was immoral, of course, but in some cases Athena could have believed she was providing a worthwhile service – even protecting the girls from the wrong kind of men: the kind who might beat them up perhaps? Or was I just desperate to find excuses for her?

No, no, I didn't think my sister was evil. I couldn't approve of what she had done, but I could begin to understand.

Yet she would surely have needed money to set up such a business? She had mentioned a John Stiggerson, but now I remembered that the man named on the envelope in my possession was Senator R. Stiggerson. Was he perhaps John's brother?

I was beginning to fathom the way Athena's mind worked now, and I believed the envelopes were some kind of an insurance.

Perhaps she was a little afraid of the senator? She had obviously liked John, but his brother might be a different man. Had one of them set her up in business? I imagined things were done that way. They might not have wanted to be involved in a business of that kind, not directly. She might have fronted it for someone else – and she would have needed someone with influence to help her get established in America. She must have been granted regular work permits to stay there for as long as she did, because she had not taken American citizenship. Was that the reason she had kept the

149

photographs of the senator, just in case one day he decided he didn't want to help her any more?

Athena might have been reckless at times, but she had learned to protect her back. So why had someone killed her? Had she decided to use the contents of one of her envelopes to blackmail the wrong person? There were some people who would kill rather than submit to blackmail.

All these thoughts were going round and round in my mind, forming patterns then breaking apart to make new ones. I couldn't be sure of anything. I only had tiny pieces of all the puzzles.

Even before I had come down to the cottage and found my sister's diary, I had suspected that there was some mystery behind her decision to go to America – something that Nick knew and would not tell me. Why? What had he fixed for Athena?

Something had happened the night Nick rescued her – after she had been raped. The night she had stolen Sir Edward's car . . . a car she was not fit to drive.

Had there been an accident?

Some thought was triggered at the back of my mind. There was a scrapbook in Athena's boxes. I laid the diary down on the floor beside my chair and went upstairs to look for it. If I could find that book I might find the key to the mystery – or at least a part of it.

I began to search through the boxes. I had just found what I was looking for when I heard the noise downstairs . . . like breaking glass. My first thought was milk bottles, then I remembered that there were no houses close enough to the cottage for it to be anywhere but here. And there were no milk bottles outside my door. Someone was breaking into the cottage . . .

Who knew I was here? No one . . . except Sandy, and she wouldn't break in. Had someone followed me down here? Who? It had to be the man who had killed my sister. No one else would go to such lengths to find me. I had thought it would be safe, coming down on the train and hiring a car. But someone must have followed.

I could hear the person downstairs moving around. My

spine tingled with fear. I believed it was the man who had killed my sister and he was here to kill me. Surely it had to be. Why would anyone break in unless it was for some sinister purpose?

I remembered Athena's gun. I'd seen it in the chest beside her bed the first time I came down. It had sent cold shivers down my spine then, but now I was glad it was there.

Slipping off my shoes, I walked barefoot across the floor, taking care to make as little noise as possible. I pulled open the drawer and picked up the gun. The metal felt cold and the gun itself was heavy and awkward. I had no idea whether or not it was loaded, but as I had no real intention of using it, I hoped that the mere sight of it would frighten off any intruder.

What I was going to do if it didn't was a bridge too far for me at that moment. I was too scared to think properly. All I knew was that I had to go down and confront whoever it was or he would kill me.

As I crept down the stairs, I heard a door open and a spasm of fear went through me. The intruder had come into the hall, and as he stopped and looked up at me standing halfway down the stairs, my heart stopped for one terrible moment. This was my worst nightmare come true.

'No!' My hands were shaking as I levelled the gun at him, and I could hardly hold it still. 'Why did it have to be you, Nick? I was praying it would be anyone but you.'

'Julia!' Nick stared at me, guilt and shock written all over his face. 'So it was *your* car parked outside in the lane. I thought it must belong to one of the other houses. I was sure this place was empty'

I was hardly listening, my thoughts whirling in confusion. 'Why did you do it? Why did you kill her?'

'What the hell are you talking about?' Nick's eyes narrowed as he suddenly seemed to realize I was pointing a gun at him. 'And what are you doing with that thing? Put it down, Julia. Guns have a nasty habit of going off whether you mean them to or not.'

'Why have you come here? Did you follow me from London?'

'Aren't you listening to me? Calm down, Julia. I'm not

151

here to harm you, whatever you might think. I told you, I thought the cottage was empty. I tried to use the key Athena sent me; it didn't work so I broke the glass. You ought to have a different door fitted if you're going to come down here alone. It isn't safe. Anyone could get in.'

I lowered my arm, suddenly feeling empty, drained of emotion. What did anything matter? If Nick *was* the murderer, he might as well kill me and get it over, because I wouldn't have much to live for anyway.

'You scared me,' I said, a little sob escaping me. 'A few days ago someone made a threat to kill me . . . I thought he had followed me here. When you broke in, I thought it must be you . . .'

'Why did you think I would hurt you?' His gaze narrowed and I could see he was angry. 'You thought I might have killed Athena, didn't you? Even now you're still wondering. I can see it in your eyes, Julia. I thought we meant something to each other . . . that you trusted me?'

I laid the gun down on the hall table and walked past him into the sitting room without speaking. He followed, catching my arm and swinging me round to face him. His expression was controlled, but I could sense the anger simmering inside him.

'You asked me why I killed her. Obviously you meant Athena. Why, Julia? What have I done to deserve that?' He seemed defensive. 'Just tell me.'

'You lied to me, Nick,' I said. 'You know a lot more about what's been going on than you've told me. And yes, I have wondered if it might have been you. Catherine Romsey-Black said you hated her. She thinks Athena asked you for one favour too many . . .'

'Catherine was always a bitch,' Nick said, running his fingers through his thick hair. 'I blame her for getting Athena into all this in the beginning. If she hadn't turned Athena's head with her talk of expensive jewellery and sports cars . . . but that was a long time ago.' He sighed heavily. 'I suppose I ought to have told you all I know from the beginning, but I didn't think it mattered anymore. I can't believe it has anything to do with Athena's death.'

'I found an old diary amongst her boxes upstairs,' I said. 'When you got here I was upstairs looking for a scrapbook . . . Athena mentioned reading something in the papers that frightened her. I wondered if she had kept the cutting. She said you and Teddy had fixed it. I think she meant Sir Edward Romsey-Black . . . the man who raped her: the man whose car she stole that night.'

'You *have* come a long way.' Nick looked at me with a wry admiration in his eyes. 'I seriously underestimated your powers of detection, Julia. How much of this was in the diary?'

'Athena's diary confirmed some of what I'd already worked out,' I said, sitting down and gesturing for him to do the same. 'Relax, Nick. You're obviously not going to murder me. I am sorry I reacted like that, but I've been in turmoil since my sister was killed.'

'It's natural enough in the circumstances, but I thought you knew how I feel about you?'

'I'm all mixed up,' I said, pushing my hair back as it fell across my face. 'Athena was beginning to be close to me again and then . . . well, her death threw me off balance. I know we have a strong physical thing going, but . . .'

'I thought it was more.' He still looked angry. 'Maybe I was wrong.'

'Please, Nick. Don't let's argue about us. I was startled earlier and I couldn't think properly. I do care about you, but I have to get this business of Athena sorted in my head.'

He nodded, his eyes a kind of wet, slaty grey. 'You said someone threatened to kill you – how?'

I took a deep breath. 'Over the phone. His voice was disguised, odd. He said I had something that belonged to him, that my bitch of a sister had got what was coming to her – and that if I attempted to blackmail him, I would be sorry before I was dead. It scared me, Nick.'

He swore, his expression changing, becoming grim. 'No wonder you were in such a state when I broke in. I'm sorry, Julia. I didn't think you even knew about this place. I came down to get something Athena apparently hid here. A package was waiting for me when I got back from the States yesterday evening. Athena had sent me a key to her cottage. She told me I would find the tape here.'

'She sent you a key?'

'Yes. It arrived while I was away and a secretary at my office signed for it. Athena must have sent it a day or so before she died. It took ages to get here.'

'What is on the tape, Nick?'

'A conversation we had just before she left London for New York.' He wrinkled his brow. 'She taped it without my knowledge – for insurance, or that's what she told me later. In case either Romsey-Black or I tried to blackmail her. The tape made us accessories.'

I felt a tingle at the nape of my neck. 'What do you mean? What had Athena done that you and Sir Edward covered up for her, Nick? Was it an accident? Did she hit someone the night she stole that car?'

'Who told you that?' He looked at me hard. 'Or is this more guesswork?'

'It stands to reason, doesn't it? She was drunk. I'm not even sure she knew how to drive.'

'Athena did have a licence. She'd passed her test just a month earlier.'

'But she had been drinking – and she had just been raped by a man she thought she loved.'

He nodded, looking serious. 'She was crying as she drove, out of her head with grief and shame. Afterwards, when she saw the report in the paper, she told me she had been driving with just the side lights on. It was misty and she was in no fit state to be at the wheel. She did feel a slight bump but she swore she didn't see anything . . . she wasn't sure she had hit anything . . .'

'Did she knock someone down?'

'We think so. Athena drove on after that, so we couldn't know for certain, but someone witnessed an accident that night at about the right time, although they didn't see who was driving. The witness just saw a large, expensive black car go rushing past her gate, and she found the girl lying in the road.'

'A girl lying in the road . . . Was she dead?' I felt sick

154

and shaken as I looked at him. 'Go on, Nick. I have to know it all.'

'No, not dead, but badly injured. She was seventeen, a foreign student over here to study at college. It was a long time before she was identified. That's why the story made the national newspapers. She had no papers with her, nothing to tell anyone who she was. In the end, they discovered she was Spanish and living part-time with an English family. They had all gone abroad for two weeks, believing she was at college. She – her name was Maria Rodriguez – had had a row with her boyfriend that weekend. She hitch-hiked back to the family's house but must have found it empty. They think she was trying to get back to college that night and . . .'

'They think?' I stared at him, trying to control my horror. 'Did she die, Nick?'

'Not for some months. She had head injuries . . . she never came out of the coma.'

'Oh, my God!' I felt the colour leave my face. I was sickened by what I was hearing. 'Athena knocked that poor girl down and didn't even stop?' I stared at Nick in bewilderment. 'And afterwards, when she knew what she had done . . . No wonder you said she was selfish!'

'She was frightened,' he said. 'Don't be too quick to condemn her, Julia. It wasn't as cold-blooded as it sounds, believe me.'

'But surely . . . if she had stopped . . .'

'It probably wouldn't have made much difference. From what the witness said, Maria rushed at the car. I suppose she was trying to stop it – to get a lift. It was a lonely road, late at night, and the mist was coming down. Athena didn't see her. Yes, she should have stopped when she felt something, but she was in too much of a state to realize what it might be. Even afterwards, she didn't know for sure that she had hit Maria – it just seemed to fit what had happened in the report.'

'But what about the car – surely there was a dent of some kind?'

'Athena crashed it about twenty minutes later. She went

off the road into a tree, which wrecked the whole front of the car. That's why she telephoned me to come and get her. She was shaken and dazed, but managed to walk up the road and find a phone box.'

'If she crashed the car . . .' I frowned at Nick. 'Didn't the police connect the two incidents?'

'Not immediately. She had been driving for twenty minutes, remember. In any case, there was nothing to indicate that Athena was driving. Romsey-Black reported the car as stolen by an unknown person, and I wiped her prints from the steering wheel that night.'

'You did what?' I was stunned, disbelieving. 'Nick! Why? What made you do such a thing?'

He shrugged. 'She was in enough trouble, Julia. I didn't know then that she'd knocked someone down, but she had stolen and wrecked an expensive car. I thought Romsey-Black might prosecute, but when I went to see him about it he was too frightened of being accused of rape. I made a deal with him. If he stuck to his story about the car, Athena would keep quiet about what he'd done to her. Otherwise, the whole thing would come out. He was running for election as an MP that year and couldn't afford a scandal.'

'That's horrible. So sordid.' I shuddered. 'Didn't any of you think about that girl . . . Maria Rodriguez?'

Nick glared at me. 'Of course we did. Athena cried herself sick over it, but what good would it have done if she'd gone to the police? They would never have believed she didn't know she'd hit Maria – and she still wasn't sure. None of us ever knew for certain. There was no real evidence. It would not have stood up in court, unless she confessed. It would just have caused a scandal – and ruined her chances of making a new life for herself in America.'

'So she just went off and left Maria to die in a hospital bed?'

'She had been offered a modelling contract. She wanted to go. I told her I would help Maria if she ever came out of the coma – but she never did. Don't look at me like that, Julia! There was nothing I could do. Nothing Athena could have done if she had stayed here. I did visit Maria twice in hospital . . . but it didn't help.'

'But you blamed Athena, didn't you? You were angry with her for involving you?'

'Yes. After Maria died. I felt guilty, even bitter. I did speak harshly of Athena to Catherine.' He frowned. 'It took me a long time to get over it. Something like that haunts you, leaves a nasty taste in the mouth. And when I met Athena in New York, when I realized what she was doing, then I was very angry. I covered up for her, Julia. I did something I shall always feel ashamed of, and for what? She was back doing the very thing I'd tried to get her away from – prostitution!'

His tone carried the sting of a whiplash, making me wince.

'Catherine said the agency was legitimate, Nick? Are you sure Athena knew what was going on? Even if she did, might it not be that she was trying to protect the girls, because of what had happened to her?'

'Not with Stiggerson behind it,' Nick said, looking grim. 'He is a very unpleasant person, Julia. Believe me. If he was backing the agency, he knew what was going on. I should imagine there was a lot more besides the call girl side of it: drugs, blackmail, the works. I think that's why Athena wanted out.'

'Yes, I expect you are right. Carla told me they had a break-in at the New York apartment. A janitor was killed. It frightened Carla. Athena was frightened, too. I think that must be why she kept the photographs . . . for insurance.'

'What photographs?'

'In her safety deposit box.' I explained what I had found and Nick's look darkened. 'Catherine said she gave her photographs to Athena, but I think now she was lying. After what you've just told me, I don't think Athena would have dared to blackmail Sir Edward. I think she must have got hold of them somehow and kept them as insurance – in case someone tried to blackmail her.'

'Yes . . . I see your point.' Nick nodded. 'But that still leaves Hans Werner and Senator Stiggerson. I've met Stiggerson several times, Julia. As I said before, I consider him dangerous. I believe he put up the money for Athena's agency. She was certainly afraid of him. I saw that when we met in New York.'

'Do you think he could be the one who threatened me?' I wrinkled my brow. 'I had thought it might be Robert Lee, because the voice sounded vaguely American, but now . . .'

'Robert Lee was Athena's agent,' Nick said. 'He had been in love with her for years. He did sometimes find her modelling contracts, nothing wonderful but enough for her to pretend that was how she earned her living. In the last few years she had become too involved with the other business to risk becoming well known. She knew too much about too many people, Julia. That's why she sold her share of the agency and went to live in Spain.'

'But she put her insurance in a safe place – and I think she must have tried to cash in on some of it.'

'That was very foolish of her. Are you sure she was really trying to blackmail someone?'

'I think she may already have done so. She had a large amount of cash in her safe at the villa, and she told me a lot of people owed her. Whoever killed her that night was looking for something, Nick. Carla thought she must have been sleeping when the murderer broke in, but my sister was nervous. I think she would probably have set the alarms before she went to bed. Somehow it seems more likely that Athena returned unexpectedly and found whoever it was . . .'

'I promise you it wasn't me, Julia. I asked her for the tape several times. It was the reason for the quarrel you witnessed. She always said she would return it when she got around to it – and in the letter she sent me just before she died, she said it was here. Upstairs in a jewellery casket of some kind. I came here to get it today, because I knew you would find out about this place soon, and I wanted to keep the worst of it from you, if I could.' He looked me in the eyes. 'I didn't tell you all this, because I thought it would hurt you. I would rather you hadn't had to face this. You do believe me, don't you?'

'Yes, I do,' I said. 'I'm sorry for doubting you, Nick. I understand why you didn't want to tell me, and why you were angry with Athena. There's a jewellery box on the dressing table, a sort of Chinese cabinet. I've looked inside, but I didn't see a tape.'

'She hid it inside the lining. We'll look in a few minutes.' He reached out for me as we both stood up, putting his hands about my waist, gazing into my eyes. 'You should have come to me when you found the envelopes, Julia.'

'You weren't around that often,' I said huskily. 'Besides, I wasn't sure how far this thing was going to go between us, Nick.'

'As far as you want, I think.' He smiled as he bent his head to kiss me lightly on the mouth. 'I might as well stay over now I'm here,' he said. 'I have a week or so free before I need to dash off. Perhaps this is as good a time as any to explore just what we do feel about each other . . .'

Twelve

I don't ever remember talking to a man the way I did to Nick that night. His revelations about Athena had broken down the barriers between us. For the first time in my life I told someone what it had been like after my parents died – the years with Aunt Margaret, before Athena left and afterwards.

'It was so awful the way they argued,' I said as we lay curled up in each other's arms after making love. 'My aunt sometimes seemed almost to hate Athena. When she was ill, she told me it was because Athena was so like our mother. It seems that she took our father away from Margaret. Bill was Margaret's boyfriend until he saw Mum. Her name was Helen. She was beautiful, clever and funny. Poor Margaret was always the plain one, the one who somehow always got left out. She never married. I think she always loved my father. She never found anyone else. She just got plainer and older – and bitter.'

'Yet she took you both in when your parents died.' Nick touched my face with gentle fingers. 'She cared sufficiently for that, didn't she?'

'I think she did care for us, and her sister,' I said, 'deep down. But she couldn't show it. She tried to restrict Athena's freedom too much. She was nearly eighteen, remember. I was just ten when Mum and Dad were killed in that air crash in America. Athena stuck it out for just over two years. I believe that was for my sake. She didn't want to leave me alone with my aunt, but in the end she couldn't take it any more.'

He looked at me sympathetically. 'Was it very bad after she went?'

I moved my head negatively. 'No, not all the time. Aunt Margaret was strict, and she was always grumbling, but she gave me all she could. It was a lot better than being in an orphanage. And that last couple of years she seemed to change, to soften somehow. I suppose she knew she was ill, though she didn't tell me. She let me go to art school without a word.'

'That was brave of her,' Nick said. 'And generous. Some people would have expected to be repaid for what they had done for you.'

'Yes, I know. She was generous in the end. She left what she had to me. I didn't even know she was so ill until the last few months, and even then she wouldn't let me do much for her. She was very strong-minded. She fought the cancer until the last.'

'You sound as though you were fond of her?'

'I suppose I was. She was always nicer to me than she was to Athena. Yes, I did care for her in a way. I missed her after she died. At least while she was alive, there was someone there waiting – a home.'

Nick's arms tightened around me. For a while we lay close together without speaking. The warmth of his body was comforting, and I became sleepy, drifting away gradually so that I hardly knew I slept. When I awoke it was to the aroma of freshly brewed coffee. Nick had brought a tray up to the bedroom and was standing smiling at me from the foot of the bed.

'What shall we do today?' he asked as I yawned and sat up, stretching my body lazily like a contented cat. I felt so good! 'Do you want to go out somewhere – or shall we just stay here? I've been looking at the garden. It could do with some tidying. If you've got work you want to get on with, I'll have an hour or so out there.'

'Do you really want to do that?' I raised my brows at him teasingly. 'I don't see you as a gardener somehow. I've always thought of you as a definite townie.'

'Living in town suits my present lifestyle,' Nick said, 'but you know I like to get away when I can – and I don't mind the occasional spot of gardening.'

'I do have some work I ought to finish,' I said. 'It's going to be an awful rush to open the boutique on time as it is.'

He nodded, his eyes thoughtful. 'Carry on as you intended to if I hadn't surprised you by barging in. I'll work for a couple of hours, then cook us some brunch.'

'We'll do that together. I'm not going to work all the time.'

We drank our coffee, then Nick left me to get dressed. When I went down, he was in the garden at the rear of the cottage. I could see him attacking some overgrown bushes with the shears as I started work on a set of patterns. I wanted Bernard to make samples of a dress and coat I had designed for our winter range. It was an expensive set, but I thought it might sell to women who needed something really smart, which was also serviceable but different to the clothes they could buy in any large chain store.

I had finished most of what I needed to do by the time Nick came in to wash his hands at the sink. His skin was glowing from the fresh air, and he looked as if he had found his self-appointed work invigorating. Together, we made a salad and grilled steaks, sharing our task with a pleasing companionship that was very comfortable.

We sat for a long time over that meal, talking, drinking wine, getting to know one another even better.

'My father would have liked you,' Nick said as we did the dishes a little later. 'You've got what he called gumption. He was always telling me I should find a woman with a bit of go about her. Mary needed someone around to hold her hand – and I wasn't here often enough.'

'Mary was your wife?'

Nick had never mentioned his wife before, but I had sensed instinctively that there had been someone in his past. I hadn't asked, because it hadn't seemed to matter, but now I was interested, perhaps because he had never opened up like this before.

'Yes, for two years – though it was never right from the beginning. I think we both realized that soon after the wedding. She wanted a man who came home at five every night, and I wasn't that man. After a while she got tired of waiting for me to come back from a trip and found someone else. I came home one day and discovered she'd left, taking most

162

of the furniture and all the money in our joint account.'

'Ouch!' I said, looking at him with sympathy. 'That was a bit rough. What did you do?'

'I gave her the divorce she wanted.' Nick smiled wryly. 'It was never a huge romance. We drifted into marriage, perhaps because our families knew each other – and we drifted out again. After that, I realized there wasn't much point in looking for a steady relationship. I've been too busy flying here and there. What woman is prepared to settle for that?'

'Maybe a woman who knows she's going to be pretty busy herself for the next few years.'

'You?' He leaned towards me, the scent of his body enticingly familiar. We kissed, tasting the wine on each other's lips. 'Do you think we can make it work, Julia?'

'No one ever knows that for sure,' I replied, meeting his eyes. 'I do know I feel more for you than I've ever felt for a man before. I miss you when we're not together, and I love being with you – but I want to make the boutique work, Nick. I need to see if I can be successful as a designer. One day I'll probably long for a house in the country and a couple of kids, but I'm not ready for that yet.'

'I don't think I am either,' he said. 'Besides, I'd have to be sure we were going to stay together before I changed our lives around to that extent.' His gaze was serious, very intent now. 'But I think we might make some changes, don't you?'

'What kind of changes?' My pulses were racing wildly as I waited for his answer.

'We might consider living together for a start. We could look for somewhere different. A larger flat – with an office for me and a studio for you.'

This was important! I felt a tingling sensation at the nape of my neck. Nick's suggestion both excited and frightened me. He was talking about making a real commitment now.

'We could start looking,' I agreed, a little breathless. 'My flat isn't big enough for both of us on a regular basis. It's hardly big enough for me when I'm working.'

'That's what I'd thought,' he said, an amused gleam in his eyes as he glanced round the little sitting room.

'I have spread out a bit,' I agreed and laughed. 'One day I suppose I'll need special workrooms – if I ever get to the stage when I want to put on a show of my own.'

'Is that what you intend eventually?'

'Yes, I suppose so, in time, though at the moment I'm more interested in ready-to-wear than haute couture. I want to design and sell the kind of clothes women like me wear, or would if they could buy them. Good quality basics with a difference – and a few crazy things for when we feel like having fun.'

'You're really into all this, aren't you?'

I blushed as Nick's brows went up. 'You've got me on my pet subject now. I'm talking far too much.'

'No, you're not,' he said. 'I enjoy listening to you. Business of any kind fascinates me. What you're doing is exciting – risky but with potential. If you need help with the financial side of things, I'm here: advice or money.'

'We could do with some advice,' I said. 'Neither Sandy or I have any experience in running a business. So we shall need help setting up the accounts, and regulating our budget. But Athena's money is more than sufficient to get us started . . .'

He nodded, then frowned. 'You shouldn't feel guilty about using it, Julia. Most of what she left you was probably earned honestly. I'm still not convinced about this blackmail thing – unless Athena was trying to get even with someone.'

'I've wondered about that, but someone is definitely worried about something I'm supposed to have. Worried enough to threaten me.'

'Yes, I hadn't forgotten,' Nick said, still thoughtful. 'But I can't see her getting involved in anything like that, unless she had good reason. She was always careful. She taped that conversation with me for insurance, nothing more. I found it where she said in her letter, in the lining of that box you mentioned. Athena was straight with me. If she *was* blackmailing someone he – or she – must have done something to make her angry.'

'Yes, I think you're right.' I smiled at Nick. 'I feel much better about all this now. It upset me to discover that she might have been blackmailing people – and that she was involved in a sordid business. I still feel uneasy about what happened the night she drove that car . . .'

'It was an unfortunate accident,' Nick said. 'Athena didn't mean to hurt that girl. I don't think she ever stopped feeling guilty over it, though.' He frowned, hesitating. 'She said something odd the last time I spoke to her . . . the day you heard us quarrelling . . .'

'What do you mean, odd?'

'I'm not sure. We were interrupted and I never did get round to asking her for details. It was something about having made reparation for what she'd done.'

'How? Maria died in hospital,' I said. 'There was nothing anyone could do – no way of putting things right.'

'Not for Maria . . .' Nick hesitated. 'But she had relatives. I know they came over for the funeral. I saw them, but I did not speak to them. Athena wasn't here then, of course, but I suppose she could have traced them if she had wanted . . .'

'You think she might have done that? Given them money or something?'

'I am just suggesting that she might have done, if the accident was playing on her conscience.'

'Yes, I suppose that's possible. Yet she made no mention of anyone in her papers. Perhaps she never dared to try and contact them, because she was afraid of what might happen if they guessed she was responsible for Maria's death. Somehow I don't think she meant it that way, Nick. No, I think she probably meant she had paid her dues to society.' I looked at him thoughtfully. 'If I knew who Maria's family were, I might be able to do something.'

'Don't get involved,' he warned. 'The accident wasn't your fault, Julia. If you feel you owe somebody something, make a donation to a charity that supports the families of accident victims. I can give you a few addresses of people you might like to contact.'

There was something in his voice then, and as I gazed up into his face, I knew it was what he had done himself. A way of easing his own guilt, though he surely had nothing to blame himself for anyway.

'Thank you,' I said and reached for his hand, feeling a little guilty myself, because for a while I had wondered if he might have killed my sister. I had seen his detachment, his reserve, as somehow threatening, but now I understood what made him keep a protective barrier in place. He had been hurt more than once and he would rather not get involved in an unsuitable relationship again. 'Yes, I would like to do that, Nick.'

'Good.' His fingers closed over mine. He looked at me with concern and something more. 'Are you going to be all right living by yourself for a few weeks? We could manage at my place for a while – if you felt it might be safer? I can always stay with you at your flat when I'm here, but I'll be off again first thing Monday morning. And this time it will be for the best part of two weeks.'

'Two weeks? I shall miss you.'

'Think you can stand it?'

'Yes.' I met his slightly anxious gaze steadily. 'But if you're going to be away for that length of time, I think we should make the most of this weekend.' I stood up and held out my hand to him. 'Let's go to bed.'

Nick smiled his slow, lazy smile. 'I thought you'd never ask . . .'

We returned my hire car and Nick drove me back to London on Sunday evening. He insisted on staying the night and on having my telephone number changed to one that would remain ex-directory.

'It's a nuisance,' he said when I protested, 'but you can give your new one to friends, and this will save you being terrorized by whoever has been trying to upset you. If you have any reason to think you're being followed, ring this number. Terry owes me a favour or two. He will arrange protection if you need him.'

I glanced at the card Nick had given me, feeling a chill down my spine as I saw it was from a special security agency. 'I'm sure I shan't need this. Anyway, who is he?'

'Ex army,' Nick said. 'He's into private security now. I helped him set up for himself. I've already talked to him

166

about what's going on, Julia. If you're worried, just ring him. Promise – for me?'

'All right, thank you.' I kissed him, feeling a pang of regret as we parted. 'Take care of yourself, Nick. I love you.'

'I love you, Julia,' he said, and touched my cheek. 'This *is* going to work, Julia. I have a good feeling about us.'

'Me too. Ring when you can, but don't worry if I'm not here. I shall probably go down to Cambridge for a couple of days. It's going to get hectic from now on. I'll try ringing your number every so often.'

Nick nodded, his expression thoughtful as he took me in his arms to kiss me again. 'We'll have some time together soon,' he promised.

I let him go, trying not to let my reluctance show. This was the way it had to be for the time being. We were both busy people. We needed our own space. A relationship like ours was never going to be easy, but we were prepared for that – and we loved each other.

I had never been as close to anyone as I had to Nick these past couple of days. Sometimes in life you have to take a risk, and I believed that this time it might just be worthwhile.

Sandy rang the doorbell as I was about to have lunch the following day. She had come up with a batch of new designs for jeans, skirts and tops for summer. The skirts had slits both sides almost to the waist and were worn over matching shorts; the tops were soft knitted cotton and ranged from a wrapover style to a very sexy number that cut over one shoulder, leaving the other bare.

'These are wonderful,' I said. 'You didn't mention you were working on them last week.'

'Bernard showed me some fabulous samples of a new stretch denim,' she replied. 'It started me thinking – and this is what happened.'

'I feel very lazy,' I said. 'I managed a few patterns – but Nick showed up and somehow I didn't get as much done as I thought I would.'

'So, tell me about it.' Her brows went up. 'I thought your being down there was supposed to be all hush, hush?'

There was an odd note in her voice, as if she was put out over the fact that I'd been with Nick after telling her not to give my whereabouts out to anyone.

'Apparently Athena had told Nick about the cottage. He came down and . . . there I was.' I held back from telling Sandy the whole story. 'Anyway, he came and we talked . . .'

'Is that all?' Her brows went up in disbelief.

'No, but it was important. We needed to get to know one another better. We've sorted a few things out – and we may try living together. When Nick can find a flat big enough for the two of us, that is. He has to have an office, of course, and I could do with a proper studio.'

'That sounds serious?'

'I hope so. It's too soon to be sure – but I love him and he loves me.'

Sandy looked doubtful. 'Didn't you say he was away a lot?'

'Yes. But I'm busy too, Sandy. It might be best for us both this way. We both need space at the moment. One day – when the business is more developed – it might be different.'

'At least he doesn't want you to give up work and have a family.'

'I couldn't, not yet. This is too important to me – and you. This is our chance, Sandy.'

Sandy's attention seemed to have wandered. She was looking at a sketch I had been working on that morning. It was a slinky evening gown, made of raw silk, heavily beaded on the bodice and meant to be expensive.

'This is fabulous,' she said, frowning slightly as her gaze transferred to me. 'It's too good for the boutique, of course. Something like this deserves to be in a show for London fashion week.'

'I was toying with the idea of making it up as an eye-catcher for the window,' I said. 'I could make it up in my own size. If it doesn't sell I could keep it for myself.'

'But it will take a lot of time . . .' Sandy's expression showed she thought I ought to be working on something more practical. 'I could never come up with anything like that . . .'

'But your stuff is going to sell in large numbers.' Sandy

168

nodded, but I could see she was doubtful about something. 'Honestly, I think the combination of our two styles is going to be a terrific success.'

'Maybe, but you could put on your own show. Get out there with Zandra Rhodes and Vivienne Westwood. You have the flair to knock them dead, Julia.'

'I'm not ready yet, Sandy. When I am, I'll tell you. Anyway, I would still want to be part of our business.'

She shrugged, avoiding my eyes. 'OK. If you say so.'

After lunch Sandy left, intending to go down to Cambridge. She would be moving into her new flat soon, and she wanted to supervise some changes there. I should miss her popping in when she felt like it, but Cambridge wasn't that far and we would be meeting often because of the business. Yet I felt something had changed between us recently, though I wasn't sure just what was different.

I tried to settle down to my work again, but somehow my heart wasn't in it. I was thinking too much about Athena, and what Nick had told me that weekend.

My sister had caused a girl's death by recklessly driving a car she had taken without permission. It had been an accident, of course, but she would never have been able to forget, never quite managed to put the consequences out of her mind. Perhaps I hadn't known her well, but I was sure it must have haunted her.

I tried to put myself in her shoes. What would I have done? She must have tried to forget, to get on with her own life, but if she couldn't, she would have needed to atone in some way. Perhaps by doing something for Maria's relatives. Or for other girls. I wondered if that was why she had become involved in the escort agency, if she had believed that she was helping girls who might otherwise have found themselves in dangerous situations. Or was I just trying to make excuses for her again, because I couldn't face the truth? Was I merely trying to absolve my own conscience?

I thought about the pictures of Senator Stiggerson, and the contents of the envelope with Hans Werner's name on it. I had no way of contacting the senator, but Hans had given me his card.

169

It was still in the bag I had taken to Athena's funeral. There were two numbers, one in Germany and obviously an office, the other a mobile. I could ring him, tell him my own number had been changed, and ask for a meeting to discuss some business.

Athena had owned various shares, some of them in American companies of which I knew nothing. I could ask Hans for his advice, then turn the conversation to the agency; I could give him the envelope with his name on it and ask if he knew how I could return the pictures to Senator Stiggerson.

It would probably mean I should never know for certain who had killed Athena, but at least it might stop the threats from whoever had been making them.

I reached for the phone, dialling the mobile number first. It was answered almost immediately.

'Hans,' I said, a little breathlessly. 'It's Julia Stevens here. You said to ring you . . .'

'Julia,' he said, sounding surprised but interested. 'How are you? I tried to ring you a couple of days ago but there was a fault on your line, the number was unobtainable.'

'I've changed it, gone ex-directory. Some idiot has been making odd calls, so I thought it best.'

'That's such a nuisance, especially for young women who live alone.' He paused, then: 'Would you like to meet this evening? I'm actually in London for a few hours. I leave again in the morning.'

'Could we? I should be so grateful, Hans. I do want to talk to you.'

'We'll have dinner,' he said, a catlike purr in his voice. 'Then we can talk privately in my suite – if that suits you?'

'Yes, please.' Suddenly, I decided to come right out with it. 'I'm worried, Hans. I think Athena may have been in some trouble. I have some things – some envelopes I want to get rid of, to give back to their rightful owners.'

There was silence for several seconds, then, 'I'm not sure I perfectly understand you, Julia.'

'I'm not asking for anything, Hans. I don't want money – or revenge – though I would like to know just what happened to my sister. Most of all, I want all this bother to be over, to get on with my own life.'

'I'm sorry, the line seems to be fading,' he said. 'I must go. I'll pick you up this evening at seven thirty. We'll talk then.'

I felt a little shaken as I replaced the receiver. Hans had to know what I was talking about. Why had he pretended otherwise?

Oh hell! My thoughts were going round and round in confusion. I almost wished I hadn't rung Hans, and yet I knew that this had to be faced. A new life was opening out for me. I did not want it to be overshadowed by mysteries from Athena's past.

Thirteen

I worked throughout the afternoon, though when I glanced at my sketches later there was nothing worth keeping. Giving up in a fit of despair, I rang the number Nick had given me. There was no answer. Of course there probably wouldn't be at this time of the day, he would be in a meeting somewhere, his mobile switched off.

I was thoughtful as I went to take a bath and change for the evening. Nick would probably be furious if he knew what I was doing, but I wanted this thing settled. And Hans was still my number one suspect. Especially if Athena had been foolish enough to try and blackmail him.

My doorbell rang at precisely seven thirty. I opened it expecting to see Hans, but found instead my neighbour, Philip, who was holding a small package in his hands, looking at me, obviously expecting to come in.

'This arrived for you on Saturday,' he said. 'It was insured post so I signed for it. I would have brought it round before, but I've been busy these past few days and it slipped my mind.'

'Oh, Philip, thank you,' I said, glancing at the Spanish postmark. I felt a tingle down my spine. *This must be the package Athena had rung me about! I couldn't take it now, not when Hans was due at any moment.* 'I'm going out now. I would rather not leave it here, because it might be important. Would you do me a favour? Would you hang on to it until tomorrow, please?'

'Hang on to it . . . ?' He looked puzzled, then, as we both heard footsteps outside my door, he slipped it into his inside jacket pocket. 'Yes, of course. I'll be seeing you then.'

My doorbell rang twice, imperiously. The door wasn't shut, but I opened it wider. The man standing there was wearing the dark uniform of a chauffeur. He touched his peaked cap in a salute but did not smile.

'Miss Stevens?' I nodded. 'Herr Werner sent me to fetch you, miss.'

'Oh . . . I thought he was coming himself?'

'Unfortunately, he was delayed at a meeting. Rather than keep you waiting, he asked me to—'

Whatever he was about to say was lost as we all heard a series of short, sharp bangs that made us all jump.

'What the hell was that?' Philip glanced round as the chauffeur swore and ran back up the steps to the pavement where his car was parked. 'It sounded like automatic gunfire!'

We both started towards the steps, but before we had got very far the chauffeur was back, looking down at us. He held up his hands to warn us not to come up. As we hesitated, he came down, pushing both me and Philip into my hallway.

'What's wrong?' I asked. 'What happened?'

'Go in please, both of you,' he said, looking shaken. 'Miss Stevens, if I might use your phone please. Those shots were meant for us. Someone thought we were in that car . . .'

I felt the sick tremors run through me as I saw the expression on the chauffeur's face. He wasn't joking. Someone had fired at the car in an attempt to kill whoever was inside it – and that could have been me.

I went inside, followed by Philip, who was looking pale and shocked.

'I don't understand,' I said, my throat tight. 'Why should anyone shoot at the car? Why should they think we were inside?'

'The Mercedes has tinted windows. I was a few minutes late. Had I been on time, we should have been about to leave.' The chauffeur glanced towards the telephone. 'I must ring Herr Werner – with your permission?'

I nodded, feeling too shaken to answer. This was frightening, much more so than the threatening phone calls, which could have been just a crank. Someone had actually fired at the car I was due to get in at any moment!

'Shouldn't you ring the police?' Philip asked, looking at him suspiciously.

'Herr Werner will advise the right people. He will not want this to become generally known; it would be harmful if it were to get into the papers.' He gave us both a very meaningful stare.

'It's all right,' I said, sinking on to the sofa with a bump. 'Let him do what he wants, Philip. That was too close for my liking, I'm out of my depth.'

'Poor Julia,' Philip said, sitting beside me to hold my hand. 'This isn't nice for you, love. In fact it's bloody terrifying. It has made me feel quite odd, I can tell you.'

I nodded. Behind us, the chauffeur was speaking in German. I had no idea what he was saying, but after a few minutes of rather urgent conversation he turned and held the receiver out to me.

'Herr Werner would like to speak to you, miss.'

I took the receiver from him.

'Hans, what is going on?'

'Are you all right, Julia? You were not hurt?'

'No, just shocked. What happened? Who tried to shoot us?'

'It was a warning for me, Julia. Don't be frightened. My man will stay there with the car. A taxi will come for you in a few minutes and the police will be there soon. Leave all that to Klaus. There is no need for you to be involved in this unpleasantness. This was meant for me, not you. I shall explain when you arrive at my hotel.'

'You have quite a lot of explaining to do, Hans.'

'Forgive me. I would not have endangered your life for the world. Please believe me, Julia. Had I known this would happen, I would not have sent Klaus for you.'

'I'll try to believe you, but this was too close, Hans. Unless you can explain properly, I shall have to tell the police.'

'You would be foolish to do that, Julia. They will be told all they need to know. Silence is golden. Your taxi will be there shortly.'

I glanced at the receiver as the line went dead. Was that a threat? My spine was tingling and I must have looked pale as I turned to Philip, because I could see the concern in his eyes.

174

'Do you want me to come with you, Julia?'

I forced a smile as I picked up my jacket. 'It's all right. I'll see you tomorrow, Philip. I have an appointment I have to keep at the Savoy Hotel – and that sounds like my taxi arriving now.'

'What about this place?'

'Will you lock up for me?' I asked, giving him a pleading look. 'Just pull the door to after you – and Klaus.'

Philip looked puzzled, uncertain, then nodded as the front door bell rang. 'I'll answer it – just in case.'

It was the taxi Hans had promised, arriving promptly. So promptly that I wondered how he had managed to arrange it in such a short time.

Something didn't seem right to me. Had those gunshots been no more than a charade for my benefit? If so, what did he hope to gain by frightening me?

I kept my spare key in the drawer of my telephone table. Had Klaus been part of an elaborate plan to get hold of that key? Would I return home at the end of an evening spent in Hans Werner's company to find my flat had once again been carefully searched?

These thoughts and many others of a similar vein went through my mind as I was driven to the prestigious hotel. Hans was waiting for me in the lavish reception area. He greeted me with a look of concern, kissing my cheek on either side.

'You are pale,' he said. 'As lovely as always, but upset. This is my fault. Forgive me. Please, come to my suite. I have arranged for dinner to be sent up. After what happened earlier, I must take more care of you.'

'Yes, you should do that.'

Did I sound as if I was threatening him? I was too angry to care. He heard the sharp note in my voice, but other than a faint lift of his brows gave no sign until we were alone in his suite.

'You are very angry,' he said as I threw my jacket on to a sumptuous silk brocade sofa. 'I think you blame me for many things, not just what happened this evening. You suspect me of having a hand in Athena's death, do you not?'

'Were you responsible? I met his narrowed gaze, reckless and beyond caution. 'And what was all that about tonight? If you wanted access to my flat so that Klaus could search it, you're wasting your time; the envelopes aren't there.'

'Of course not.' Hans laughed, disarming me. He was a very attractive, and charming man after all. His brows went up. 'Do not underestimate me, Julia. I respect your intelligence. I know you would not be so careless as to leave something like that lying around. I expect the envelopes are quite safe – indeed, I trust so, for all our sakes. In answer to your question, no, I was not responsible in any way for your sister's death. I was not in love with Athena, but I was fond of her. I found her attractive. She was an exciting lover – a little dangerous to know but quite fascinating as a woman.'

His bluntness took my breath away. I studied his face in silence for a moment, then I said, 'You never had any intention of marrying her, did you?'

'None at all.' He looked surprised. 'Did she hope for that – surely not? She must have known it was out of the question.'

'Why was she killed? Was she blackmailing you – or Senator Stiggerson?'

'You have seen the photographs, of course?' I nodded and his eyes narrowed, his expression intensified, his pupils almost silver, seeming to penetrate my mind. 'Yes, I imagined you must have done. I wonder what you made of them?' He smiled oddly. 'The mind is so fascinating, don't you think? Everyone has their own fears, their own phobias. Please sit down, Julia. Will you have some champagne?'

'I would prefer an explanation, before the champagne.'

His brows arched. 'You have never quite trusted me, have you? A pity. Believe me, I mean you no harm. Nor did I arrange to have Athena murdered. Someone did murder her. You are quite right to suspect it was not just a casual break-in. She told me she thought she was in danger . . .'

'She told you? When?'

'A few days before her death. She telephoned to assure me the envelopes would be perfectly safe with you if anything happened to her. She said I was to leave you to sort

176

things out and not interfere – that you would come to me in time. I advised her to employ another bodyguard if she felt nervous, but she said Miguel would look after her.'

'Unfortunately, she was wrong. Someone made sure he wasn't around when she needed him.' I was still angry, but the prickling sensation was easing from the nape of my neck. 'Do you know who might have killed her?'

'It wasn't Stiggerson,' he said. 'I know she had those pictures, but that business was finished a long time ago.'

'Are you certain? Athena was expecting money. You don't think she might have tried to blackmail him?'

'He was made to pay for what he did at the time.' Hans frowned, but looked thoughtful. I sensed something beneath the surface, something he wasn't prepared to tell me. 'You saw the girl who was beaten?' I nodded and his mouth thinned in distaste. 'It was very unfortunate. In business it is sometimes necessary to help people you would rather not know. Do you understand me, Julia?'

'He was useful. You repaid a favour with a favour.'

'How sensible you are. Athena was not so accommodating. She made a big fuss, threatened to ruin the senator if I did not see her point of view, and that would have rebounded on me. Stiggerson was drunk that night, of course. What he did was regrettable, but these things happen. He phoned me from the hotel in a panic. I did what was necessary, but Athena insisted the girl must be compensated, and she was, putting an end to the affair as far as I was concerned.'

'She wasn't dead then? I couldn't be sure from the pictures.'

'Had she been, I would not have helped Stiggerson,' Hans said. 'He is useful to me, but not important enough for me to become an accessory to murder.'

'So, he paid the girl off. Or did you do that?'

Hans inclined his head. 'It was me, of course. Again, you surprise me by your grasp of the situation. But perhaps I should not be surprised by anything you say, Julia. You are a remarkable young woman.'

'Supposing Athena wasn't satisfied, supposing she decided she wanted Stiggerson to pay himself? I'm almost sure she was blackmailing someone. She told me some people owed her, and I'm sure she meant money. I think she might have wanted to punish Stiggerson.'

'That would have been unwise. Once crossed, he is a most unpleasant man.'

'Someone has been threatening me,' I said. 'Unpleasant telephone calls, telling me what will happen if I try to take over from Athena. I want to finish this, Hans. If I give you the envelopes, would you square it with him? I'm not interested in blackmail – or revenge. At first I wanted to punish whoever killed her. Had I known who it was, then . . .' I shrugged. 'Things are different now. I just want to forget all this.'

'Good. This is what I wanted to hear.' He looked at me with approval. 'Give them to me. I promise you will hear nothing more from the senator – if it was he who threatened you. Believe me, Julia, he will not harm you. You have my word on that.'

'Thank you,' I said. 'I don't have the envelopes with me. I can get them first thing in the morning and bring them here.'

'It is a pity you do not have them now. I leave for the States very early tomorrow.'

'Then I'll keep them until you return, shall I? Believe me, I'm not going to suddenly demand money from you – or anyone else.'

'Yes, I do believe you,' he said and smiled. 'Could we not be friends, Julia? Surely you trust me now?'

He was not the kind of man I would ever really trust; there were too many layers, too many shady deals and secrets in his past, but I half believed him. He had no real reason to want Athena dead, at least none that I knew of.

'Yes, I trust you,' I said and accepted the glass of champagne he was offering me. 'I am relying on you to sort this mess out for me, Hans.'

'As I shall,' he assured me. Then, as I sat down on one of the huge sofas, he added, 'You wanted some advice on Athena's investments? Or perhaps that was merely an excuse?'

'I am thinking I might sell Athena's shares. I don't understand them. Is it a good time to sell now?'

'If I were you, I would hold on to them for a while. Things are unstable in the financial market just now. If you are in need of money, I could help. A loan for your new business venture perhaps?'

'Do you know everything about me?'

A flicker of amusement showed in those unusual blue eyes.

'I make it my business to know anything that may be useful to me in the future, Julia. Besides, you interest me. You are very different to Athena – but perhaps even more charming.'

A tingle of unease went through me. 'Thank you – for the compliment and the offer – but I have no need of a loan. Nor do I want you to give me anything. If Athena owes you money, or if there was a gift I should return, please tell me.'

'How independent you are.' He laughed softly. 'You owe me nothing, Julia. I should thank you for coming here this evening – especially after that unfortunate incident earlier.'

'Was it really meant to be an attempt on your life?'

'It was not the first, I dare say it will not be the last,' he replied coolly, seeming unperturbed. 'It is a hazard of my business. Believe me, had I wished to frighten you, Julia, I should have been more subtle.'

'Then I am sorry. It must be unpleasant to have such a threat hanging over you – frightening.'

He shrugged. 'A man in my position makes enemies. I have learned to accept that. I am only angry that it should have touched your life, threatened your safety. Please forgive me for putting you in some danger. Had you been hurt I should never have forgiven myself.'

'You couldn't have known it would happen. It was just as well you did not come yourself. You might have been killed.' I shuddered at the idea.

'Your concern is gratifying. If I did not know your affections were otherwise engaged . . .' He arched his brows as I stiffened. 'Do not worry, Julia. I never push my attentions on a woman. I am not like Stiggerson and his kind.'

'I don't imagine you need to ask very often,' I replied, the tension easing all at once. 'I expect most women fall over themselves to catch your attention.'

'It is a pity we did not meet at another time in another place,' he murmured, a gleam in his eyes. 'I should have liked to have known you better, Julia. Yes, I should have liked that very much . . .'

Hans Werner could be an extremely pleasant companion when he wished. We dined together on all manner of expensive and delicious trifles he had ordered to please me, then he sent me home in an executive taxi, promising to contact Senator Stiggerson as soon as possible.

'I shall tell him I have the envelopes in my possession,' he said before I left. 'Trust me, Julia, he will not bother you again. I give you my word.'

I thanked him and said I hoped to return his property very soon. He told me he would be returning to London the following week and would contact me.

Riding home in the taxi, I wondered if my flat had been searched. However, nothing was out of place, my spare key still in its box, my possessions undisturbed. So perhaps Hans hadn't been responsible for the first very careful attempt to find Athena's papers. Who then? Not Stiggerson, he would have torn the place apart. Could it have been Catherine Romsey-Black – or her husband?

She might have lied about her own photos. If Athena hadn't been blackmailing the senator, could it have been Catherine? Despite her denials, I still felt something didn't quite fit there.

'Oh, Athena,' I sighed. 'Why didn't you talk to me while there was time? Why didn't you tell me what was going on?'

I remembered the package Philip had signed for on my behalf. It must surely be from Athena. Was it too late to claim it this evening?

Glancing at the clock, I saw it was nearly eleven. I couldn't go round now. I would just have to wait for the morning.

As I went in to the sitting room, I noticed the light flashing on my answerphone and pressed the play button, smiling with pleasure as I heard Nick's voice.

'Where are you, Julia? I'm missing you. I want you, love you, need you. Talk to you soon, my love.'

I played it through again, noticing the hint of impatience in his voice. He had phoned at ten thirty, obviously expecting me to be in. He wouldn't be pleased if he knew I'd been alone with Hans at his hotel suite. Until this weekend, I wouldn't have thought twice about seeing anyone as a casual friend, but things were different now.

I was about to go to bed when the phone shrilled again. I snatched it up to hear Nick's voice at the other end.

'You're back then?'

'Yes. I just got your message. I miss you too.'

'Where were you? I was worried.'

'I had dinner with Hans Werner. I talked to him about giving those envelopes back, because this business has to be finished. I want us to be happy, Nick. I don't fancy the idea of looking over my shoulder all the time, waiting for something to happen.'

Nick was silent, obviously digesting this, then he spoke. 'What did Werner have to say?'

'Much what we expected. He swears he wasn't personally involved in any of it – and that he will sort it out for me. He says I'm not to worry, that I won't get any more trouble from the senator.'

'Good. I might speak to Stiggerson myself while I'm out here. I know a few people myself, and I can probably pull a few strings – make him back off.'

'If you think you should. Be careful, Nick.'

'I can handle him. As long as you're all right? No more upsetting phone calls?'

'I'm fine, honestly. Hans was very straight with me this evening. I don't like him much, Nick, but I think I believe him when he says he had nothing to do with Athena's murder.'

I said nothing about the shooting incident outside my flat. Nick would only worry, and there was nothing he could do. It was Hans Werner's problem, not ours.

'I wish the Spanish police would come up with something. Maybe it *was* just a burglary, Julia. I've never believed Athena was a blackmailer, she had too much to lose herself. She might have been talking about something entirely different when she said she was owed – maybe she loaned money to a friend?'

'Perhaps. I'll keep looking through her things. I might find the answers somewhere.'

'Just take care of yourself – and keep away from Werner. He may be charming, but I wouldn't trust him. I love you, Julia.'

'I love you too.'

'I'll ring soon.'

'Love you . . .'

I smiled as I replaced the receiver. Perhaps Nick was right. Perhaps the answer was in Spain after all.

The next morning I collected the package Athena had sent me only a few hours prior to her death. Philip was clearly concerned for me as he handed it over, and I realized the incident of the shooting was still very much on his mind.

'What's going on, Julia? Something I should know about? Are you in some kind of trouble?'

'No. At least, I don't think so. Athena might have been murdered for reasons other than those suspected at the time, but I think it is all sorted now.'

'You ought to tell the police,' Philip said, looking worried. He knew there were things I wasn't telling him. 'Or someone who works for an investigation agency. You could have been hurt last night, even killed. I didn't much like that chauffeur chappie – or the way he hushed things up. The police who came after you left weren't like any police I've ever met, they took it all too calmly. The car was badly damaged down one side, but the whole thing smells odd to me.'

'It was just a warning apparently,' I said. 'Herr Werner says he has enemies. It isn't the first time an attempt has been made on his life – and they were probably special police, Philip. The kind who deal with international incidents like this. Sometimes they have to keep things quiet for political reasons. Hans is an important man in the world of high finance. When he snaps his fingers, others do as he says.'

Philip wasn't convinced, but he was in a hurry to leave for work. I thought about what he'd said as I opened the insured packet. What could be so important that Athena had decided it was safer not to leave it at the villa?

182

I wasn't sure what I would find. I hoped it wouldn't be more compromising photographs, and I was relieved when I discovered the package held a letter and some papers but no pictures. The letter looked quite substantial, so I decided to make a pot of coffee before I settled down to read it.

I'm sorry to land you with all this. I never expected things to get out of hand this way. These papers might be significant, but only if something happens to me. Sorry to be so cloak and dagger, Julia. You must be wishing me to blazes by now. I just hope you aren't in trouble because of me. I do care what happens to you. I know I've been a bit of a selfish bitch at times, but I always loved you. Do you remember the day I took you to Yarmouth? Just after Mum and Dad were killed . . .

Tears stung my eyes as I recalled that summer day, when I was ten and she had taken me on a day trip to the seaside. Memories of lying in the sand dunes, eating candyfloss as we walked along the promenade and a rather scary ride on a huge roller coaster made me smile despite the lump in my throat.

'Oh, Athena,' I whispered. 'What happened? What made you do all these things?'

I concentrated on her letter once more.

I've done some things I'm not proud of. The worst was causing the death of a young student. It was an accident, Julia. Believe me, I didn't see her. I wasn't sure I had hit anything, but I must have done. I was driving too fast and crying. I'm not making excuses, but there were reasons for the state I was in that night. One day you may hear all about that from Nick. What he doesn't know is that I managed to trace the girl's family. I've done what I can to make up for what happened, though I know that isn't really possible. But I have tried . . . honestly, I have tried.

Athena's writing was becoming more and more difficult to read. It looked as if she were in a hurry or perhaps a panic.

These papers won't mean anything to you, Julia. They are just my insurance, in case I ever need them. A back-up to some envelopes in my safety deposit box. You won't need to bother with any of this – unless I'm dead by now.

I've been foolish. I thought I could get away with something I ought never to have started. It wasn't as though I needed the money. I wanted to punish someone, but it's more dangerous than I imagined. Christina was my friend. What I've done was for her sake – what she would have wanted. If it all goes wrong, take the papers and photos to Hans and let him deal with the situation. He will know what to do. He isn't whiter than white, Julia, but I trust him.

Forgive me for involving you in this mess. I shouldn't have done it, but I didn't know what else to do. I love you, Julia. Try not to think too badly of me when it all comes out.

Athena. x

I blinked as the tears stung my eyes once more, then laid her letter to one side. There was a lot of personal stuff I had skipped over but would read again when I felt up to it.

Looking at the papers, I saw there was a death certificate for a young woman of twenty-three, a doctor's report – and also some bills for what I took to be a private school.

I began to read the report, which outlined the reasons for the death of Miss Christina Hale. As I came to the end, I was aware of a bitter taste in my throat and a feeling of sickness in my stomach. Miss Hale had suffered a brain haemorrhage, caused in the doctor's opinion by a vicious blow to the head some weeks earlier. He had examined her after her beating, and believed the damage must have been caused then, although it had not shown up at the time.

Hans had lied to me. I knew instinctively that Christina Hale was the woman who had been beaten by Stiggerson. She had not died that night, but the injuries she had sustained at the time had led to a sudden deterioration of her condition some weeks later – and this report was in effect evidence of murder. Delayed, difficult to prove in a court of law perhaps, but still murder.

Now I understood why the senator had been so desperate to discover this dangerous report. This was why, if he suspected Athena might have sent these papers to me, he had made those threatening phone calls. The photographs might have damaged him politically, but this was far more serious. If Athena had given this to the police he might have been facing a charge of manslaughter, at least . . . Why hadn't she?

Surely it would have been the best way of punishing Christina's murderer? Athena had chosen to extort money instead – why? It hardly made sense. Unless . . . I looked at the other papers and saw that they were receipts for school fees for a Miss Jane Hale.

Christina had had a daughter! I read the details. Jane was eight years old and being cared for at a very expensive boarding school. Suddenly everything slid into place and I began to understand why Athena had decided to try blackmail.

She had sold her interest in the escort agency and moved to Spain. And her career as a model was over, she had been definite about that despite the promise of a new contract. She hadn't been short of money, but Christina's daughter was going to need support for several years. I realized Athena must have been paying for the child's keep since her mother's death. For some reason, she had decided that Stiggerson should contribute to Jane's future education.

'Oh, Athena . . .'

My throat caught with emotion. Blackmail was such a horrible thing, but now I could understand. I could empathize with what my sister had done. It still wasn't right, of course, but I saw the temptation. I saw the reasoning behind it.

Athena had money but she was no longer working. She wanted to make sure Jane was secure without committing her own resources – perhaps because she wanted to spend some of her own money on me.

For several minutes I sat staring at the papers my sister had entrusted to me. What was I going to do with them?

Athena had said I should give them to Hans, and I had already agreed to pass the envelopes on to him – but this had changed things. Christina had died because of the beating Stiggerson had inflicted. The doctor's report seemed to confirm that, yet it would be difficult to prove.

It wasn't right that the senator should get away with murder. I had been willing to let it go, because the whole idea of blackmail had shocked and sickened me. Now I was thinking of an eight-year-old child who had lost both her mother and her only friend. Surely she deserved something?

Hans was an accessory to murder. He was also a very rich man. He could quite easily set up a trust fund for Jane Hale.

Julia be careful!

I seemed to hear my sister's voice. For a moment I almost felt her presence in the room beside me.

'There's no need to worry, Athena,' I said aloud as I folded the papers and stood up to put them away. 'I know what I'm doing.'

I wasn't going to blackmail Stiggerson or Hans, but if I spoke to Hans, asked him for help, he might respond to a suggestion that Christina's daughter was owed something.

Surely there could be no harm in trying?

Fourteen

After I had put the papers away, I finished my coffee and tried to settle down to some work. Sandy was already producing far more ideas than I'd managed, and she had every right to feel aggrieved over my preoccupation with my sister's affairs. It was time I pulled myself together and came up with a winning idea for next summer's range.

I spread out a pattern I had drawn the previous day and began to trace round it. Bernard would make his own copies, but I wanted to keep my master pattern as a reference. Trying very hard to block out everything else, I began to cut the outline. I had almost finished when the telephone rang.

'Hi,' I said, feeling oddly apprehensive though I wasn't sure why. 'Julia Stevens speaking.'

'Julia . . .' Carla sounded hesitant. 'You left your new number on the answerphone . . .'

'Yes,' I said, relief flooding through me at the sound of her voice. 'It was necessary to change the number, but I wanted you to have it in case you needed to contact me.'

'I was wondering . . .' She faltered, sounding muffled.

'Yes? Is something wrong, Carla?'

'My brother . . . we wondered what you had decided about the villa. He thinks he should look for work elsewhere. Had you thought about coming out soon?'

I'd been too busy, too wrapped up in all I was discovering about Athena's life to think about Carla.

'I'm sorry. I should have told you before. Perhaps the solicitors have written, I don't know. Athena left you some money in her English will, Carla. As soon as we get probate you will receive a cheque for ten thousand pounds.'

187

She made a sound halfway between a sob and a protest. 'No, no, it is too much. Always she was so generous.'

'Look, I'll try and get a flight this weekend,' I said. 'Just for a couple of days. I can come out on Friday by Iberia and fly back on Sunday. It's time we talked, Carla. I'm not sure about the villa, but I may sell it.'

'You must do as you wish.'

'I was thinking you and Miguel might stay on until it is sold? Then we can work something out. But we'll talk this weekend, all right?'

'Just as you wish, Miss Stevens.'

Carla replaced the receiver abruptly. She sounded so strange. I thought she must be crying again, still blaming herself because she'd been at the hospital with her brother the night Athena was attacked.

I knew in my heart I didn't want to keep the villa, because it would always make me think of Athena being murdered, but I wanted to make sure Carla was secure. She had been a good friend to my sister, and ten thousand pounds wasn't so very much these days. Especially as she would be losing both her home and her job. Perhaps I could buy her a small apartment or something once the villa was sold, something of her own.

Replacing the receiver, I went back to my work. If I was flying out to Spain that weekend, I would need to get these patterns finished and delivered to Bernard before I left. And then perhaps I could relax in the sunshine for a couple of days.

It was a hectic week as far as work went, but apart from that nothing much happened. Going ex-directory seemed to have halted the threatening calls, and I had stopped jumping out of my skin every time the phone rang.

Nick called me twice from New York. I told him about my trip to Marbella.

'I suppose it's best to get things sorted,' he said. 'Just make sure all the alarms are set every night.'

'Yes, of course I will. I don't want anything unpleasant to happen. I've got so much to look forward to, Nick. Life is so much brighter now that we're together.'

188

'Bless you for that,' he said. 'Take care, my darling.'

There was a thoughtful note to his voice as he replaced the receiver, and I knew he still believed Athena's murder had more to do with her being in the wrong place at the wrong time than blackmail – and perhaps after all he was right.

Sandy pulled a face when I told her I was flying out to Spain that weekend. I asked her if she would like to come with me, take a break and enjoy some swimming and lying around in the sun.

'My treat, all expenses paid,' I offered. 'It would be good to have some company, Sandy.'

'I'd like to, Julia, but I'm seeing Bernard this weekend.'

'Then I'll see you when I get back,' I promised.

She smiled, nodded, and looked at some sketches I'd been working on that morning. I sensed a withdrawal in her, a kind of holding back, and I knew there was something she wasn't telling me. I almost asked, then changed my mind.

After this weekend, I ought to be able to put the past behind me. I would ask Sandy what was on her mind when I went down to Cambridge the next week.

I took my sketch pad on to the plane, roughing out a few ideas I'd had when I was in the bath that morning. Our summer range would have to go into production almost as soon as we opened the boutique. We were very late with our autumn and winter stock; the only reason we were even able to consider a production run so late in the season was because Bernard was also just starting out in business. No one else would have been able or willing to drop everything else just for us. We had been lucky to find him.

Sandy was becoming more and more involved with Bernard. I wondered if that might be a part of the reason for her withdrawal from me.

My thoughts were drifting. I discovered I was sketching far too many impractical designs and closed my pad with a sigh. Sandy was right, a lot of my stuff was too exclusive for ready-to-wear and would be too expensive to sell from the mail order line. Perhaps I might have to consider doing

189

a show of my own one day soon when all this worry over Athena was finished.

I supposed that was what was really getting to me. I had so much on my mind. I couldn't forget Christina or the child in that boarding school. Her fees had been paid for some months ahead, but sooner or later I was going to have to sort it out. So far I hadn't told Nick what I'd discovered. I wanted to wait until he was home and we could talk properly.

First of all, I had to talk to Carla. At least I could do something practical for her. She had been devoted to my sister and I didn't need or want the villa. I would put it up for sale and ask the estate agents to find me a suitable apartment for Carla.

Carla was waiting for me when the taxi drew up outside the villa. She took my cases and I followed her inside, sensing there was something trembling on the tip of her tongue.

'It was good of you to come out, Miss Stevens. I did not like to trouble you, but Miguel said it must be done.'

She looked nervous, uneasy. I thought she had lost weight and I was concerned for her. There were dark shadows beneath her eyes, as though she hadn't been sleeping. Perhaps she was nervous living here at the villa? It made me feel guilty. I had been so wrapped up in my own life that I'd forgotten Carla, forgotten how upset she had been over Athena's murder.

'I should have done something before. Forgive me, Carla.' I moved towards her, impulsively kissing her cheek. 'Look, I might as well tell you at once, I'm going to sell the villa and buy you a small apartment of your own. It's only fair after all you did for my sister. And I don't need this huge place.'

'No!' Carla's face was white and she looked as if she were about to burst into tears. 'You are too generous. Just like her! You must not. I do not deserve it.'

'Don't be silly, Carla. You can't keep on blaming yourself for what happened. It wasn't your fault.'

'Excuse me. I make you some tea.'

She almost ran from the room. Obviously, she was in a nervous state, brought on by her remorse over not being there when Athena needed her – and possibly fear of another break-in. It was just as well I had come out, the sooner the villa was sold the better for all concerned.

I went into my bedroom, then opened the sliding patio door and stepped out on to the terrace. We were at the end of August now, just over two months since I had first visited the villa. So much had happened, it felt like a lifetime away.

It was very hot despite the late hour, and I decided I would have a swim before unpacking. There was no one to see me so I stripped off my clothes, grabbed a towel from the bathroom and ran to the edge of the pool, diving naked into the silky coolness of the water.

I swam two lengths of the pool and then climbed out. Reaching for my towel, I dried myself and wrapped it around me sarong style. I was about to go in and dress when I heard a sound behind me. Whirling round in alarm, I saw the man watching me and was reminded of my first visit to the villa. How long had he been standing there?

'What are you doing here?' I demanded, angry at being caught at what was meant to be a private moment.

'I flew out a couple of days ago to see Carla. She told me you were arriving this evening, so I came over.'

'Without phoning first, to ask if I was prepared to see you? That was rather presumptuous of you, wasn't it, Mr Lee?'

'I did telephone you in London, asking if we could meet – didn't you get my message?'

His eyes had an odd glitter in the light of the pool, and I shivered feeling suddenly cold.

'Excuse me, I have to dress.'

He moved towards me. 'Did Athena tell you much about me?'

'No, not much. You were her agent once, weren't you?' I held my towel tightly around me, feeling nervous. 'Please don't come any closer. If you do, I shall scream for Miguel. He is armed and he will use the gun if he thinks I'm in danger.'

'Good grief!' He looked at me incredulously. 'You don't imagine I had anything to do with Athena's death?'

'Someone killed her. You were angry when she sent you away. It could have been you.'

'I was in New York by then. I can prove it. I *was* angry, because I didn't want her to throw her life away out here. She was still beautiful, there were plenty of things she could have done.' His mouth thinned with anger. 'She was having an affair with Werner. He was using her. I loved Athena. I would have married her if she . . .' He shrugged, but his face was torn with grief. 'Oh, to hell with it! Think what you like.'

'Don't go,' I said as he turned to leave. 'At least, would you come back tomorrow? Please? I'm rather tired this evening, and perhaps I was rude just now – but I would like to talk. You must have known my sister very well. I should like to talk about her, if we could?'

He hesitated, then gave me a rueful look. 'All right. I'll take you to lunch tomorrow. It will have to be early, because I'm flying to London in the afternoon. That's why I came over this evening. I'll pick you up at twelve thirty.'

'Carla will prepare lunch here,' I said. 'It will give us more time to talk. Come at twelve – or earlier if you wish.'

'OK. If that's what you want.' He hesitated, then: 'Sorry if I was staring earlier. You are a very attractive woman. I couldn't help noticing. I didn't mean to upset you.'

'My partner thinks I'm attractive, too,' I said, warning him, still wary. 'I shouldn't have jumped at you the way I did. I was startled. Since Athena was killed . . . well, things have been happening, frightening things. But come tomorrow and we'll talk.'

He nodded, his expression grim. 'Perhaps there are a few things you *should* hear,' he said, eyes cold, hard. 'I think Werner knows more about Athena's murder than he is prepared to admit.'

'He says not.' I looked at Robert Lee thoughtfully. 'Have you seen him recently? I thought he was in America?'

'He's here, at his villa. I spoke to him earlier this evening. In fact I asked to meet him but he made excuses. He has been avoiding me for weeks. If I'm honest, that's why I came over. I missed him in New York and I was determined to

192

get to him. He refused point blank to talk to me, put the phone down on me three times. If you ask me, he's afraid I know too much about him and some of his friends.'

'What do you mean?'

'Athena told me most things. She trusted me, even though she refused to marry me.' He smiled wryly. 'Sleep well, Julia. I'll make sure the gate is closed as I leave – and remind Carla to set those alarms.'

'I doubt if she needs reminding.'

'She is on edge, isn't she? I noticed it myself – looks drained.'

'She is grieving for Athena.'

'She isn't the only one.'

I went into the villa as he walked away. A part of me wanted to call him back, to hear everything I was sure he could tell me about Athena and her life, but I was beginning to turn cold despite the warm evening and I let him go.

Carla knocked at my door as I was dressing.

'Supper is ready, Miss Stevens.'

'I'll be there in a moment.'

When I reached the dining area, I found a tray with various cold dishes and a pot of tea. I poured myself a cup and bit into a sandwich. It was delicious, really tasty, as was the salad. Carla had spoiled me once again.

After I'd finished eating, I took the tray back to the kitchen. Carla and Miguel were sitting there together, drinking beer. Miguel stood up as I entered.

'No, don't go,' I said. 'I've told Carla about my plans to buy her an apartment. I want to give you something, Miguel. Athena left some money in her safe. Before I go home, I shall give what's left to you. It isn't very much, but I'm not sure what else I can do – her other property is tied up in shares. You might like to have her cars perhaps?'

'You owe me nothing,' he said, his dark eyes sombre. 'I worked for the señora. She was a generous employer. I regret that I was not here the night she was killed. I would have given my life for her.'

'Thank you.' His simple words spoken with such sincerity made my eyes sting. 'Neither you nor Carla were to blame.'

'I was careless. I should have checked the brakes myself.'

I met his brooding gaze, and realized that he too had been a little in love with my sister.

'Do you think they had been tampered with – that you were meant to have an accident?'

'No, señorita.' He frowned, looking angry. 'I tell the police this. They blame me for neglect, they say the pads were worn, but I take the car to the garage the week before the accident. They say the brakes were checked as always, but I do not believe.'

'So it was just a careless mechanic?'

'If I know for sure I make him sorry. The senora was good to me – and to Carla. She not deserve to die like this.'

Carla made an odd, choking noise. The air was charged with emotion. I sensed she was close to tears.

'Mr Lee is coming to lunch tomorrow,' I said, changing the subject for Carla's sake. 'He will be here at twelve. I hope that is all right?'

'Yes, of course. As you wish, Miss Stevens.'

'I shall go into Marbella after breakfast to see an estate agent. I want to sell the villa, as you know, but you will stay on until it is sold, both of you? Please?'

Carla nodded, her face averted.

'I start new job next week,' Miguel said. 'For Herr Werner, but I work here in my own time. I keep everything as always. Until you sell. No problem.'

'Thank you,' I said. 'I'm glad you've found another job, Miguel. It was good of Herr Werner to take you on.' I smothered a yawn. 'Flying always makes me tired, I'm afraid. If you will excuse me, I shall go to bed now.'

I was thoughtful as I returned to my room. It *was* good of Hans to take Miguel on – and I was being very silly to even imagine it might be some kind of a bribe.

I drove into Marbella the next morning. The sun was very bright, the sea an unbelievable blue as it lapped lazily against the curving shoreline, palm trees waving their fronds in a gentle breeze.

I had been recommended to an estate agent in the main street. As I glanced in their windows I saw they dealt in

194

properties very like Athena's villa, most of which seemed to be reaching a high price.

Going inside, I stated my business to the receptionist. She asked me to sit down at an impressive desk, which I did, giving the details of the villa to the man who came to sit opposite. He was dressed in a cream linen suit and a yellow shirt, very cosmopolitan, very tanned, and fluent in English.

'Ah yes,' he said as I told him what I wanted. 'I do know those particular villas well. They are very sought after, Miss Stevens. I am sure I can get you a good price, especially as things are moving well at the moment.'

'I also want you to look for a small apartment, somewhere nice and safe, easy to look after, but not too expensive to keep up,' I said. 'It is for my late sister's housekeeper.'

'Ah yes, I read about the unfortunate incident. It was a terrible thing, Miss Stevens. Terrible . . .' He shook his head over it. 'Your housekeeper can take her choice of properties. I shall prepare some leaflets for her and go out to take photographs of the villa myself. If your solicitor has power of attorney you will not need to come out again yourself.'

I thanked him, we shook hands and then I emerged into the sunshine once more. I considered wandering down to the front for a stroll along the pleasant promenade, which was very smart and had in the past couple of years been laid out with a pinkish marble that was kept scrupulously clean. There were many small cafes where one could sit in the sun and sip wine or coffee, and on the beach little boats filled with sand had wood fires over which sardines were being smoked.

It was tempting, but if I went straight back to the villa I would have time for a swim before Robert Lee arrived.

I had swum the length of the pool several times when I heard the sound of a male voice. Hauling myself out at the shallow end, I towelled vigorously and slipped on a robe. I was about to go in and change when Hans Werner came out on to the patio.

'Hello,' I said. Somehow I wasn't surprised. I had sort of been expecting him. 'I heard you were here. I thought you had urgent business in America?'

'It was over sooner than I expected.' He frowned as I tied

the belt of my robe tighter around my waist. 'Would you like to change before we talk? I have something important to tell you, Julia.'

'All right. I shan't keep you waiting long.'

I closed my curtains while I changed into a cool white linen dress, slipping on flat-soled sandals, but didn't bother to do more than run a comb through my hair before going back outside.

Hans gave a nod of approval as he saw me.

'That was quick, Julia.'

'You said it was important?'

'It is. Stiggerson is dead. He shot himself.'

I gasped and swayed, feeling sick.

'Why? Was it because . . . he was afraid of what I might do with those photos?'

'No. He was involved in another scandal, a girl died after he beat her. This time there was no covering things up. So he took his own life rather than face what he'd done. My office in New York sent me a fax. I heard about it just this morning. I wanted you to know – in case the police should start asking questions.'

'What kind of questions?' I looked at him hard. 'Why should they come to me?'

'Because Stiggerson was Athena's partner in the agency, of course. He used her to cover his involvement, but it was always there, right from the beginning.'

It was a shock and yet I had suspected it.

'No wonder he was afraid of what I knew – what I might do.'

'It will all come out now, of course. Athena sold out to someone else, but the police may want to dig into the past . . . and that means they may come to you.'

I was silent for a moment, staring at him, noticing the faint signs of agitation in his manner.

'You knew Christina Hale died of her injuries, didn't you, Hans? Not that night, of course – but later. You helped Stiggerson, and that makes you an accessory. That's why Athena kept those pictures and bills, isn't it? She didn't want to use them against you, because she enjoyed your company.

She even hoped to marry you, but she knew you were dangerous – so she kept her insurance just in case.'

'What are you implying, Julia?' His eyes glinted with anger suddenly. 'I thought we had settled this the other evening? You were going to give me the envelopes . . .'

'That was before I read the doctor's report on Christina – and before I knew she had a child. Jane is eight now. She is going to need support for a lot of years, Hans.'

I raised my head, giving him a challenging stare.

'What are you saying? I paid Christina off. She was satisfied. If this is blackmail . . . ?'

'It would be awkward for you if everything came out, wouldn't it? If I were to give the American police all the information I have. Especially now that the senator is dead.' I looked him in the eyes. 'Are you certain it was suicide, or did you decide he was a liability? Did you have him killed? The way Athena was killed . . .'

'You bitch! You're worse than Athena!'

He lunged at me, going for my throat, a look of menace in his face. I gave a squeak of fright, backing away from him as I realized I had gone too far. At the very least, he was going to hurt me, and judging by his expression, murder was in his mind.

'Miguel!' I screamed. 'Help me!'

I backed steadily away from Hans, my eyes never leaving his face. I knew I had to keep him at bay until Miguel arrived. He lunged at me again, but, before he could grab me, there was movement behind him and a shout of fury. Suddenly Robert Lee was there. He had obviously arrived early for our appointment, and had immediately taken in the situation.

'You murdering bastard!' he yelled. 'Touch her and I'll kill you!'

In another moment he had reached us. Hans turned towards him, startled by his timely arrival. Robert went for him without hesitation, his fist connecting with his chin and knocking him backwards. He rocked on his feet, so stunned for a moment that he didn't react. Another hefty punch followed the first, and this time Hans staggered back towards the edge of the pool. He was tottering on his feet, losing his balance finally as he fell into the shallow end.

The noise had brought both Carla and Miguel out to see what was going on. For a few minutes we all watched in a kind of awed silence as Hans spluttered and cursed, floundering about in the water. He climbed out at last, his expensive clothes clinging to him like rags, dripping with water. He looked so furious that I drew a sharp breath.

'You will hear from my lawyer, Lee,' he muttered. 'As for you, Miss Stevens, you will find yourself being charged with blackmail if you try to suggest that I had anything to do with either Stiggerson's or your sister's murder. It wasn't Stiggerson who killed her, and I certainly had nothing to do with it.'

'You were trying to kill Julia when I arrived,' Robert put in. 'We have only your word for it that you didn't have a hand in Athena's murder.'

'I was trying to knock some sense into this foolish woman's head,' Hans snapped. 'I am not prepared to be blackmailed by her for something I had nothing to do with?'

'You lying bastard!' cried Robert, looking as if he would like to finish what he'd started. 'I'd bet my last dollar you were behind the break-in the night Athena was killed . . .' He took a step towards him, preparing to hit him again.

'No!' The anguished cry came from behind Robert, stopping him in his tracks and making us turn. 'It was not Herr Werner. It was me . . . I killed her. I killed Athena.'

I stared at Carla's face, the dread trickling down my spine as I saw the guilt written there, the awful anguish of living with what she had done.

'You . . . ?' Still I was disbelieving, unable to take in what she was saying. 'You couldn't have . . . you cared about her . . .'

'You don't know what you say.' Miguel glared at his sister. 'Be quiet, you foolish woman.'

'No!' Carla came towards me, her eyes pleading with me to listen, to understand. 'Please, you must believe me, Miss Stevens. I did not mean to kill her. She came back when I was searching for something. She challenged me and we argued . . .'

198

'Carla, what are you saying?' Miguel was looking at her, his expression one of horror mixed with disbelief. 'You . . . hurt her? It was you all the time?'

'It was an accident. Nothing was planned, please believe me,' Carla said, smothering a sob. 'She tried to tell me but I wouldn't listen. I flew at her in a rage and we struggled. She fell and hit her head on a stone figure . . . the one that used to stand by the fireplace. I hid it until after the police had finished, and then I washed it clean of her blood.'

'You hid it? Where?' This from Robert. 'Why didn't the police find it?'

'I put it in the garden and smeared dirt all over it. The police did not look at it, they look only for footprints and they find them. I make them with old boots from the gardener who worked here before we came. They believe me when I tell them I came back in the morning, but I left the hospital that night, and went back after I had made it look as if there had been a break-in at the villa. The next morning I came back and started screaming . . . then I telephoned the police . . .'

'But why?' I asked, confused and unwilling to accept what she was telling me. 'Why, Carla? Why did you quarrel with her?'

'It is a long story. Miss Andrews helped me when I was down . . . I had been in trouble with the police. She gave me a job, and stood by me until I had conquered my problems . . .'

'What kind of problems?'

'She drank,' Robert said, his brow furrowed. 'I warned Athena against trusting her too much, but she wouldn't listen. She said she wanted to help her.'

'Why were you quarrelling?' I asked, my eyes intent on Carla. 'What had changed suddenly? You were devoted to her and she had helped you. What made you turn against her?'

Carla's mouth trembled. She looked at me, her face pale and strained. I sensed she was near breaking point.

'I never knew why she helped me,' she said, and now there was a glint of anger in her eyes, 'until the day Mr Ryan came here – and then I heard them talking . . .'

'It was something you heard Nick say?' A tingling had begun at the nape of my neck, and all at once I began to suspect what she was going to say. 'You quarrelled with Athena over something you heard them discussing . . . something that happened a long time ago, that's it, isn't it, Carla?'

'Yes. So you know. Did she tell you about Maria?'

'No. I discovered it after her death. She didn't mean to hurt Maria,' I said. 'It was an accident. She was driving a car she had never driven before that night. She was crying – and she had been raped. It doesn't excuse what she did, but she didn't realize, Carla. She didn't know she had knocked a girl down until she read about it in the paper sometime later.'

'I know. She tried to tell me that night, but I would not listen.' Tears were streaming down Carla's face. 'Maria was my youngest sister. I loved her. It was my fault that she was in England. I told her she should study and make something of her life. When I heard she had been knocked down by a driver who didn't even stop . . .' A sob escaped her. 'I was so bitter towards that person. I hated him, hated him so much that it was like a stone in my heart.'

'Yes, I understand. I can see how you must have felt, Carla.'

'I was living in America,' Carla went on, her eyes staring through me as she looked back into her past. 'I was living with a man, but he left me because I could not stop crying. I started to drink, and then to steal. I took things from shops and one day I was caught. I went to prison for six months, and when I came out I couldn't find work. I drank too much and for a while I went with men for money. Then one day a woman approached me to say that she wanted to help me lead a normal life. I thought she was from some charity. That woman was Miss Andrews. She took me in . . . and she forced me to stop drinking. She taught me to live again.' Carla was suddenly focusing on me once more. 'I loved her . . . You must believe me. I loved her so much, but when I discovered the truth I went crazy. I had to find proof. I knew she kept everything. I thought I would find something . . .'

'But she came home and found you looking; she asked

200

you what you were searching for and you accused her of killing your sister. You quarrelled and then you hit her.'

Carla shook her head. 'I only pushed her off when she grabbed my arm. I was going to leave but she wanted me to stay. I pushed her and she fell and struck her head . . .'

'That was an accident,' I said, a shudder going through me. 'It wasn't murder, Carla. Why did you cover it up, make it look like a break-in? Why did you destroy all her things? You made me think Miguel's accident was deliberate. You convinced me it was all part of a plot to kill her. Why?'

And yet, was that quite true? Athena's desperate phone message had put the idea into my mind. I had been chasing the wrong trail all the time. Yes, my sister had begun to blackmail Stiggerson, and she was frightened he might try to kill her – no doubt he had threatened her even before he made that warning call to me – but her death had been an accident.

Perhaps my flat had never been searched. In my rush to leave for the airport, I might have left that piece of scarf hanging out of my drawer – or perhaps Hans had been behind that very careful search of my home. I would never be quite certain.

'Why, Carla?' I saw the grief and despair in her eyes. 'Why didn't you just tell me the truth?'

'I was frightened,' she said. 'I thought she was dead. I ran out of the house, took the car and went back to the hospital.' Her eyes were stricken as she raised them to meet mine. 'But she wasn't dead then. If I had called an ambulance, she might have lived. I left her there to die . . . and I can never forgive myself. I might as well be dead myself.'

'No, Carla . . .' I took a step towards her, but she backed away, then turned and ran into the villa. I was about to go after her, but Robert caught my arm.

'Let her go,' he said, eyes hard, unforgiving. 'She murdered Athena. She has to come to terms with it herself. You shouldn't believe all that nonsense about it being an accident. She murdered Athena and then covered it up to save herself.'

'It was an accident,' I said, shaking off his hand. 'Just as it was the night Athena knocked that student down; Maria died of her injuries, because Athena was too upset or too frightened to stop . . . and what Carla did was the same. She did not mean to . . .' I stopped abruptly as I heard the shot. 'Oh, my God! No! Oh, Carla . . .'

Miguel was already running into the house. Robert tried to stop me following, but I was determined and he could not hold me. My heart was racing with fear as I approached the kitchen.

'Please don't let Carla be dead . . .'

I stopped on the threshold as I saw Miguel kneeling beside his sister. He looked up at me, his face grey with grief.

'She is dead,' he said in a muffled voice. 'She put the gun in her mouth and . . .' His voice and face reflected the horror he could not put into words. 'I beg you, please. Do not come any closer, Señorita Stevens. It is bad. You should not see this. Go back and ask Herr Werner to telephone for the police.'

'All right . . .' I could feel the vomit rising in my throat as I saw the blood spreading over the tiled floor – the floor that Carla had taken such pride in keeping spotless. 'I'm sorry, Miguel. So very sorry.'

'It is not your fault,' he replied. 'Carla should have told me. I did not know she had done this thing. You must believe me.'

'Yes, I do,' I said, and then I turned away.

Fifteen

Throughout the remainder of that day I seemed almost in a trance. Surely this was a bad dream, from which I would eventually wake?

Robert Lee was forced to abandon his plans to fly to London that afternoon. He was annoyed and spent almost half an hour on the telephone cancelling meetings, but it couldn't be helped; it was necessary for all of us to remain at the villa until the police had completed their inquiries into Carla's suicide.

By the time they arrived at the villa, one of Hans Werner's staff had brought him a change of clothing, and it was he, looking immaculate as ever and speaking fluent Spanish, who dealt with the situation. As I had noticed before with Athena's Spanish lawyer, he had an air of authority that worked wonders with the official red tape out here. Had it not been for him I imagine it would have taken far longer to sort out, as it was, the police were at the villa for five hours.

The stone ornament which had been the cause of Athena's accidental death was taken away for further investigation. And Carla's body was removed in a plain wood coffin; there would no doubt be an autopsy to confirm the cause of death before her funeral could take place. Eventually, after all our statements had been carefully taken down, translated into Spanish, read out to Robert and me in English, then signed and witnessed, the police cars departed one by one and we were told we were free to leave. We would hear from them at our various addresses if required to attend the inquest.

'So . . .' Hans said, looking at me rather uncertainly after they had finally gone. 'Your flight does not leave until midday tomorrow, Julia. You cannot remain here, it would not be comfortable for you. Perhaps I could offer you the hospitality of my villa for the night?'

'No, I don't think so, thank you.'

He frowned, annoyance flickering in his eyes but he did not allow it to show in his voice. 'You cannot still imagine I would harm you? My lapse of manners earlier was regrettable. I hope you will forgive me, and believe me when I say it will not happen again.'

'She's not fool enough to trust you, Werner,' grunted Robert and glared at him. The hostility he felt for Hans had not lessened because of Carla's confession. He could not forgive Hans for having been Athena's lover.

'Please don't argue over me, there's been enough violence today.' I sighed wearily. I was feeling drained and wanted only to be alone. 'I shall call a taxi and ask the driver to take me to a hotel. It's not that I don't trust you, Hans. What happened earlier was probably my fault. I was on edge and spoke hastily. I meant to ask for your help for Christina's daughter, not to threaten you. I'm sorry for that. Somehow things got out of hand. We were all on edge. It is understandable given the circumstances.'

'Exactly.' Hans inclined his head. 'If you contact my solicitor at this number –' he wrote something on the back of his business card – 'he will help you set up a trust fund for the child with a contribution from one of my charitable funds. I have several, and I am sure one of them will suit your purposes.'

'No. No, thank you.' I raised my head, looking him in the eyes. 'I've decided to take care of Jane myself. I was wrong to ask you for anything. As far as I'm concerned this is all over. Senator Stiggerson is dead. You helped him escape punishment the night he hurt Jane's mother, but you couldn't have known that night that Christina would die. It wasn't your fault.' I pressed a hand to my forehead as the throbbing started again. 'All this . . . Athena's death . . . all of it was caused by a series of accidents that were compounded by lies and deceit. Athena made a terrible mistake one night, and because of that she went to America, becoming involved with people she would have done better not to know. If she had faced up to what she'd done, then she might never have been caught up in all these horrible things . . . She might still be alive.'

A sob rose in my throat. I fought it, pressing shaking fingers to my lips. The past few weeks had been a strain and Carla's violent death had taken the last of my mental strength. The scream was building inside my head. I was only hanging on by the merest of threads.

Robert Lee made an awkward movement towards me, as if he would comfort me, but I held out my hand to ward him off. He had cared for Athena and one day we would meet to talk about her but not now. I couldn't take any more for the moment.

'No! Leave me alone. I can manage. Please . . . both of you. Just leave. I'm going into the villa to pick up my bag and order a taxi.'

I walked away from them. I was close to breaking down. I didn't want their help or their sympathy at this moment, I needed to be alone.

I needed Nick.

I telephoned Nick from the hotel I checked myself into. The sound of his voice was so close that I could feel him near me. I smothered a sob, wanting so badly to have his arms about me, to cling to the strong, warm, powerful body of the man I loved.

'What's wrong, Julia? What has happened?'

He listened in silence as I recounted the day's events, but my explanation ended in the tears I could not control.

'Don't cry, my love,' he said. 'It's over now. It's all over. You know the whole truth. You know why Athena decided to try a little blackmail. It wasn't because she was a greedy bitch out to grab something for herself – she was just trying to help Christina's daughter. Perhaps what she did was reckless and wrong, at least in the eyes of the law, but she must have cared an awful lot to have taken such a risk.'

'Yes, I know.' My voice was husky with emotion. 'I've been thinking. I should get at least £450,000 from the sale of the villa, Nick. It may take a while to sell because of what's happened there, but once it is sold I shall use the money to set up a trust fund for Jane.'

'Is that what you want? What about your business? You could have used the money to set yourself up as an independent design house.'

'I can still do that in a smaller way. I can sell my things through specialist boutiques for a start, take them round to the fashion magazines – oh anything, just to get a start. If I'm any good I'll get there, Nick. Making sure Jane is safe is more important. It's what Athena would have wanted. And I need to do it; I need something good and wholesome to come out of all this ugliness. You don't mind, do you?'

'It makes no difference to me either way. I just want you to be happy, my darling. Whatever you decide is fine with me.'

'We'll talk about it some more when you come home. I should like to visit Jane, but I would rather you came with me.'

'Of course. We'll do everything together. From now on, we'll do everything important together.'

'Oh, Nick,' I caught back a sob. 'I do love you.'

'I should have been there with you,' he said, a note of regret in his voice. 'It's the damned job! Look, I'll try and cut things short, get back to London as soon as I can.'

'No, don't do that,' I replied with a shaky laugh. 'I'm all right, Nick. It was the shock . . . Carla's confession and then . . . it was all so sudden. I never thought *she* could have harmed my sister. Not once did I even think it might be her. Everyone else . . . even you for a while . . . but never her. That's what makes it so hurtful. She didn't mean to kill Athena. I believed her when she said it was an accident. She couldn't bear what she'd done. It haunted her. It was all such a waste.'

'Yes, a waste of two lives,' he agreed. 'When something like this happens, it makes you realize how precious time is, Julia, how important loving and sharing is in our lives. Without love the rest is an empty sham. I promise you, we are not going to waste our lives, my darling. I've been thinking. Whatever it takes, I'm going to be with you more in future.'

'Oh, Nick,' I said between a laugh and a sob. 'Forget what I said just now. Come back to me as soon as you can. I need you so much . . . so very much.'

I flew back to Heathrow the next day. My flat seemed empty and I wandered around listlessly, too restless to work or think of the business I had begun with Sandy. For the moment my ambitions had faded into the background. I longed for Nick, and for something that had been missing in my life for a long time. I wasn't sure what exactly – perhaps a sense of belonging, of permanence.

Sleep wasn't easy to come by that night. I lay staring at the ceiling for ages, thinking about Athena and all the wasted years. I missed the sister I had known and loved as a child, and somehow I seemed to have lost her. Everyone seemed to know a different Athena and I could no longer see her face, no longer remember how it really was between us all those years ago.

Where was the sister who had taken me to the seaside – the woman who had never forgotten to send me a card for my birthday even though I hadn't seen her in years? I missed the memories and wanted them back – untarnished.

It was no use, I was never going to sleep! I got up and went into the kitchen to make coffee, taking it back to my sitting room and curling up on the sofa. I thought of trying to work but knew it would be useless. I was in a kind of limbo, but seemed unable to pull myself out of it.

Sandy telephoned me at eleven that Monday morning.

'When are you coming down to Cambridge?' she asked, a note of irritation in her voice. 'We have a lot of sorting out to do, Julia. The shopfitters have almost finished, and the decorators will be here this afternoon. Bernard has delivered the first of our orders. He wants to know what else you need before we go on to the spring lines. You haven't approved the latest samples and—'

'Can't you handle all that?' I interrupted her. 'Please,

Sandy. You're there and you know what we need. I've got rather a lot on my mind just now.'

'That's a bit unfair,' Sandy said. 'I was relying on you to help me out this week.'

'I know but . . . something happened this weekend. It was Carla . . . she killed Athena; it was an accident and—'

'I'm sorry about your sister,' Sandy jumped in before I could finish, clearly not interested in what had been going on at the villa. 'I know this has all been a worry for you, but you're letting it get to you too much. You're not pulling your weight, Julia. I'm doing far more of the designing. Bernard says my stuff is much easier to produce for the ready-to-wear market than yours, especially as you specified hand cutting on everything. You've been giving him a lot of work and your patterns take too much time to produce . . . they're too expensive for the boutique to sell in any quantity and . . .'

'Just what are you saying, Sandy? I know I haven't put in as much time as you, but I've produced some very individual pieces which I think will attract a certain type of client to the boutique. I thought you liked my silk tops, and the mix-and-match range?'

'Yes, I did – I do. Of course, I do,' she said. 'But since then you've been producing less and less practical things. Take a good look at your recent sketches, Julia. You've gone away from what we'd planned. You're designing for a more exclusive market. Most of your dresses are one-offs for a particular client.'

Sandy was right. I had noticed the trend myself.

I paused before asking, 'Are you saying our partnership isn't going to work?'

'Not as it is at the moment. We're too far apart in our thinking. I'm sorry, Julia. I didn't want to say anything – but I had to. We can't go on like this, there's too much at risk.'

'So what do we do?'

'Bernard is prepared to back me with the mail order business. We could split that off from the boutique – and run the shop as a separate thing. We could both design our own lines for the boutique and buy in extra stock, if you like. Or you could take it over yourself, buy my share out. After all, you put most of the money in so it wouldn't cost you much.'

'What you really want is to work full-time with Bernard, isn't it? How long have you been planning this, Sandy?'

'It isn't like that. I just feel we didn't think things through enough at the beginning, that's all.'

'You will have to give me time to mull this over,' I said. 'We had a contract, Sandy, but you obviously want out. I shall have to talk to my lawyers. For the moment, I'll leave you to cope down there. It sounds as if you have it all worked out. I'm sorry you've had to do more than your share, but I think you could have been a little more understanding. If you're pushed, ask Bernard to give you a hand.'

I replaced the receiver with a bang, feeling more upset than angry. Sandy had every right to complain because I hadn't been pulling my weight, but the split went deeper. I sensed that Bernard was very much behind this; he had been toying with the idea of setting up his own label, and with Sandy's flair for picking up popular trends, he could soon build a large business selling both through mail order and to the large chains.

Sandy would be back where she started, except that she would have her name on her designs and a part of the profit. I supposed I would go along with it if that was what she really wanted, but it wasn't what I'd had in mind; it wasn't what I had believed we were aiming for when we started out.

My phone rang several times in the next few minutes. I guessed it was Sandy trying to get back to me, but I'd switched the answering service on to silent and I let it ring. The last thing I needed at the moment was a big row with Sandy, and that's the way things were heading. I had put up most of the money for the business, and I could make things awkward for her if I chose. I wouldn't of course, but her attitude had disturbed me. I was already feeling bruised and battered, and I couldn't think clearly just yet. Coming on top of all the rest, Sandy's desertion was too difficult to handle right now.

I sat down and opened my portfolio, going through the

sketches with a new awareness. Apart from my early ideas, there wasn't very much suitable for the mail order business. Most of my dresses, and the range of separates I'd recently been working on, were exclusive designs, probably too expensive even for the Cambridge boutique.

My clothes were meant for a certain type of woman: women who worked hard and played hard, women who had a considerable income to spend on themselves. Several of my special pieces were suitable to sell as ready-to-wear, but only through exclusive outlets such as I'd envisaged our boutique as being, and the top stores.

Why hadn't I seen the way my work was heading? Or perhaps I had and this was what in my heart I really wanted to do. It had been Sandy who had wanted to join forces at the beginning, and the ideas for the mail order had come from her. Now she wanted to split that part off so that she could go into partnership with Bernard.

I supposed the boutique might still work. I could try selling my own exclusive designs, and I might buy in from other small designers, individuals who thought much as I did. I could employ a manageress to run the business for me – and that would leave me time to concentrate on my own work.

I could even take a few of Sandy's things if she wanted an outlet. Paying her out of the business was no problem, if that was what she wanted. I would telephone her in a day or so and then leave it to the lawyers to sort out.

I laid my sketches aside, still thinking over the new situation as I went into the kitchen to make some lunch. I was staring into the depths of the fridge wondering what to have when my doorbell rang.

Who could that be? I wasn't expecting anyone. The past few weeks had made me apprehensive about unannounced visitors, and my spine tingled as I went to answer the summons. Someone was impatient! Opening the door, I felt a great surge of relief and pleasure as I saw Nick standing there, his arms full of dark red roses.

'Nick . . . Oh, Nick!' I cried as he moved towards me. The roses went down on the hall chair and he swept me into his arms. 'I had no idea it was you. How did you manage to get here so quickly?'

'I cancelled everything and caught the first flight going,' he said, looking down at me. His eyes held a smouldering passion that sent a tremor right down to my toes. 'I felt you needed me here, Julia. Was I right?'

'Yes. Yes, you were,' I said, lifting my face for his kiss. 'I'm so glad you're back, Nick. So very glad . . .' I felt a surge of happiness as his lips brushed softly against mine, and then an urgent desire. I pressed myself against his body, feeling the answering heat in him. 'I need you so much, love you so much. But it must have cost you terribly to drop everything and come back . . .'

'This is where I want to be,' he said. 'These past few days have taught me that much. I'm going to find us a house, near enough to London to commute whenever we need to, but somewhere we can put down roots, a home, Julia – if that's what you want, too?'

'Yes. Yes, it's exactly what I want,' I said, knowing as I slid my arms up about his neck that this, this feeling, this loving between us, was all I really cared about right now.

Sixteen

We spent the rest of the day in bed, making love, talking, planning our future together. In the evening we went out to dinner together, and then on to a fashionable night-club.

'Do you remember that first night in Puerto Banus?' I asked, gazing up into Nick's eyes. 'I was angry with you, and yet there was something special between us even then.'

Nick laughed as he read the expression on my face. 'Do you remember when I picked you up in the park? I'd never done anything like that before in my life. I was sure you would start yelling for the police – or throw pepper in my eyes and call rape.'

'I couldn't believe it was happening,' I said, smiling at the memory. 'You looked like just the type of man I knew I ought to avoid. I was sure it would be mad to get involved with you.'

'And now you have?' He gazed down at me, a gleam of speculation in his eyes. 'This is special, Julia. Despite all the pain, all the mistakes and the anguish of the past weeks, we've got through it. We've found each other.'

'Yes. We have discovered the real you and me.' I reached up to brush my lips against his. 'We have so much to look forward to now, Nick, but I can't help thinking about Christina's daughter. She is only eight years old. I can set up a trust fund to protect her financially, but is that enough?'

'What do you want to do?'

'Could we go down to that school, Nick? I want to see Jane. Just to make sure she's all right, that she's being looked after properly – that she is happy.'

Nick touched my cheek, his eyes warm, caring. 'We'll go

down tomorrow, Julia. I confess I've been thinking about her, too. I should like to know more about the child. I'm curious about Athena's reasons for suddenly deciding she needed more money.'

The school was smaller and more exclusive than I had imagined. It was really a rather attractive country house set in large, landscaped grounds and run privately by Mrs Mary Haddon.

'It was good of you to telephone before you came down, Miss Stevens,' she said as she met us in the drive outside the main door. 'Parents and guardians sometimes arrive without notice and that can be awkward.'

'I'm not sure exactly what I am,' I said. 'My sister told me nothing about Jane, but I believe she had been paying her fees at the school?'

'Yes, for almost two years now. Jane came when she was six years old. She was really too young to be a boarder here, but because of the circumstances we waived the rules. Miss Andrews could be very persuasive, Miss Stevens. She was Jane's legal guardian; it was all done properly by a judge in New York and quite in order. I suppose now Jane is technically an orphan again.'

'My sister left money to me,' I replied. 'It will take some time to arrange, but I intend to set up a trust fund for Jane. It should be enough to see her through school, and hopefully college as well – if that's what she wants, of course. I'm not sure whether to leave her here or move her nearer to where I shall be living.'

Mrs Haddon looked at me oddly. 'You don't know, do you, how talented Jane is? I'm sorry, Miss Stevens, I should have explained at once. We only offer places to children who are particularly gifted in some way. Jane is brilliant. Quite exceptional, in fact. She plays the piano. Not as a normal child of her age would, but with the sureness and knowledge of someone much older. I do not use the word lightly when I say she is a musical genius. It is essential that she be given every advantage at this stage. She must have all the best tutors, special attention on a one to one basis. I am sure you realize how important it is to leave her with us? In time she will go on to a higher education, but even then it will need to be a specialized school. Her vocation is to become a composer and a concert pianist, and I feel she could achieve great success one day.'

'Is that what Jane wants herself?' Nick asked, frowning. 'I am not doubting you have her musical interests at heart, Miss Haddon, but she is only a child. She ought to have time for fun as well as work.'

'She has that facility here, Mr Ryan. Our other students are also gifted, though few of them can be compared with Jane. We allow them all time to be children, I assure you.' She smiled at us both. 'I am so happy Jane has someone who cares for her. I was worried that she would miss out on this aspect of her life. Miss Andrews could not visit often, but she wrote regularly, sent cards and gifts. Jane needs that sort of thing. Now, please come with me. I want you to see something before you actually meet Jane.'

She led us into the house. I was immediately struck by the welcoming atmosphere and the sense of warmth and peace; it was more like a home than a school.

We could hear music coming from a room at the rear of the house. It was light, lively, and yet with a haunting undercurrent that made me stop and catch my breath. I had hardly ever listened to a piece of music I found so moving. It seemed to have been written for a flute, a violin and a piano, each instrument featured in turn, then the tempo became faster as all three came together in a joyful celebration.

'Was that Jane playing the piano?' I asked as the music died away. 'It sounded wonderful . . . happy and full of life and yet sad and thoughtful as well. If that is possible?'

'It is possible,' said Mrs Haddon, giving me an approving look. 'Jane wrote that piece for herself and her friends. She is, as I was telling you earlier, quite remarkable. Come, I know she is looking forward to your visit.'

'Jane wrote that?' I glanced at Nick and then at Mrs Haddon, feeling bewildered. 'I know you said she was clever but that was beautiful.'

'Yes. She will tell you about it herself. Come, let's go in.'

I was uncertain of what a child prodigy would look like,

expecting perhaps a rather plain, serious girl weighed down by a talent she did not quite understand. However, as I looked at the girl sitting at the piano, I realized that I had been very wrong.

Christina's daughter had lovely curly dark hair, which reached to her shoulders. She was pretty as she laughed with her friends, flushed with pleasure from her exertions. As we hesitated, she became aware of us and a certain shyness crept into her expression. She was just an eight-year-old child after all, and she did not know the strangers who had come to see her.

'Hello, Jane,' I said, taking a few steps towards her. 'I'm Julia. Athena's sister. I am sorry I haven't been to visit you before, but I didn't know about you until a few days ago.'

'Hello . . .' She got down from her stool and came to meet me. 'Athena told me a lot about *you*. She said she would bring you down one day but now . . . she can't come any more, can she?' There was a flicker in her eyes and she blinked hard twice.

'No, she can't,' I said, moving closer to her. 'There was an accident, Jane. Athena died. But she left you to me. She wanted me to visit in her place . . . if that's all right with you?'

'Will you take me out sometimes? Athena was going to take me to the sea one day.'

'I should like to do that, if Mrs Haddon thinks it's all right?'

'I don't see why not.' The headmistress smiled at us. 'Why don't you take your visitors into the garden, Jane? We can all have tea in my study later. And then we'll discuss your holidays.'

'I'll show you round,' Jane said, offering her hand to me. She looked uncertainly at Nick, who had not yet spoken. 'Is this your friend, Julia?'

'Mr Ryan is my friend and partner,' I said. 'I call him Nick, and I'm sure you can too.'

'I'm pleased to meet you, Jane.' Nick offered his hand and she shook it politely. 'That was a beautiful piece you and your friends were playing just now. Did you really write it yourself?'

215

Jane smiled, her face glowing. 'I wrote it for Athena,' she said. 'It was my present to her for letting me come here. It costs a lot of money to be here, you know.'

'Yes, we do know,' Nick replied. 'Don't worry about that, Jane. You can stay here if you want – if that's what you would like to do?'

'Yes, please. If you can manage it.' Now she was intent, her small body filled with longing, her face white. 'You see I have to play. I have to let the music out – and all my friends are here.'

'Then you shall stay,' I said, my throat tight with emotion. I understood now why Athena had been determined that someone should secure this child's future. Why she had risked blackmailing an evil man, knowing what might happen to her. 'Of course you can, Jane.' I laid my hand on her arm as she looked up at me. 'Tell me, what did you call that music, the piece you wrote for my sister?'

'I called it "A Song For Athena",' Jane said, 'because it was happy and full of light and laughter. She was like that sometimes. Sometimes she was sad too, but when we were together it was always like the music.'

My eyes met Nick's above her head, and through the mist of tears I could see he understood. Jane in her childlike simplicity had just given me such a precious gift.

Athena *had* been like the music, untamed, joyful, reckless at times and full of light, of the love of life. She *had* known grief and bitterness, but the shadows had fallen away when she was happy – and she had been happy with Jane.

I reached for Jane's right hand and Nick took the other.

'Let's go look at the garden,' I said.

Epilogue

It is two years now since Nick and I married, and today is the first time I have shown a collection in Paris. My very first collection was acclaimed a success in London last spring, and the House of Athena already has several famous clients on its books.

Most of my designs are created at the home in Surrey I share with Nick, but I have a showroom and workrooms in London, and if things continue to go well, I may need to open others in Paris and Milan.

Nick laughs at me because I am constantly hopping on a plane these days. He says I shall soon tire of it, as he did.

He is still far too busy, but most of his work is based in London now, and he often works from his office at our home, so we can see each other more often. We make time to be together – and to visit Jane at her school.

She is here today, sitting out front with Nick, both of them nervous and excited for my sake. Next month she is to play at a very special concert at the Albert Hall. She says she isn't a bit nervous about that, but if she isn't, I am! I want my much loved daughter to be happy, and for that she needs to play, preferably to appreciative audiences. Music is her life, her reason for living.

Nick tells me I worry too much. He is far more laid-back about the whole thing, at least on the surface.

We adopted Jane as soon as they would let us, and the two of them are so close that everyone who sees them together for the first time thinks she is his natural daughter. He finds that gratifying and I just love them both.

Sometimes I think about Athena, about the wasted years when I never knew her. I wish she could be here today, to

217

share in the excitement and the music. How she would have loved it all!

But in a way she *is* here. Jane has recorded her song. We are about to play the recording now. The lights are dimming. Everything is ready. They are waiting for me to go out on stage and introduce the collection, which I have called 'A Song For Athena'.

'Here we go, Athena. Wish me luck!'